Urbino, Unexpectedly

By Maria Chiara Marsciani

MCMassive Publishing, LLC

For information about the author visit:
www.mariachiaramarsciani.com

ISBN 978-0-9913621-1-0
ISBN 978-0-9913621-0-3 (ebook)

Published by MCMassive Publishing, LLC

To Anto,

*thank you for making my life a dream and my dreams
reality*

IV

"Peach blossom with crystal wings, in this unborn spring, among thousands I looked for you, but you weren't there. Now you are here."

-Anonymous-

VI

TABLE OF CONTENTS

VIII

Chapter 1
~ The unexpected ~

Her naked body was completely submerged in the warm water of the pink marble bathtub. Relaxed, calm. Her breathing was regular and slow so as not to disturb the thousands of micro air bubbles that were resting on her pale skin and ready to jump to the surface at the smallest motion. Her hands were floating close to the hips, her fingers softly folded, her fingertips wrinkled, and her toes pointing outward. *I look like a corpse. Maybe one day I'll die like this and someone will find me breathless, naked and wrinkled. How embarrassing.*

It was June. The sun was shining, but not in that bathroom, and not in her heart. She'd turn twenty-three in three months and she was thinking more and more often about death approaching. She felt old. She felt like nothing good was waiting for her. She was in law school, but not interested in law and not all that keen on being a lawyer. She was at her parents' house trying to escape the hot and lonely summer in Milan and her hometown was choking her, as usual. Her parents had always been unable to connect, even briefly, with her deepest needs. Her love life was empty. She was tired of men and wanted nothing to do with them. She wanted to be alone, forever. The only future she could see for herself was a small apartment, a job and a dog to run with on the grass. She felt lost in a world she didn't understand and imprisoned in a life she didn't like, but most of all, she just felt — wrong.

"Clara, are you still in the tub?" Maria yelled cheerfully from the other side of the bathroom door.

"Yes, mom!"

"Come on, honey, get out of there! Go outside and enjoy this gorgeous day. We live five hundred yards from the beach, everybody comes here on vacation from all over Italy and Europe, and you are always home, hiding from the sun. Besides I need to come in to get ready. Do you remember daddy and I are going to the Ponti's country home for the day? They are having the usual early summer party and I need to fix my make-up," her mother exclaimed.

Clara stood up and, without covering herself, opened the door wide.

"Mom, don't tell me you put shoulder-pads on this shirt too," Clara asked smiling while pushing her finger on her mother's shoulder to check.

"Of course I did," her mother answered annoyed, moving one step back.

"But the '80s ended a few years ago."

"And I'm very sorry about it because I love shoulder-pads and I'm not willing to give them up. Don't you see what a nice and narrow waist they give me?" Then, as if she suddenly remembered a very important thing, she added, "Clara, this is my bathroom. You have your own, why don't you use it?"

"It has a shower, mom, and I wanted to take a bath," sighed Clara, used to her mother's moods.

"How long have you been in the water anyway? Look at you; you are all wrinkled up. When you were a child I told you that if you let your skin wrinkle you'd turn into a frog and ..."

"Mom?" Clara interrupted her. "Do you remember I'm going out tonight, too?"

"No, honey. I forgot. Where are you going?" Maria asked while searching for the right shade of red lipstick.

"Paola is picking me up at five. She invited me to go to Urbino with a bunch of other friends and I told her I'd go."

"Oh, sure, I remember now; one of your professors is giving a talk about ... about what, honey?" Maria asked while sitting on the vanity stool perfecting her makeup in front of a magnifying mirror.

"The talk is about the privatization of public companies," Clara answered, bored by the mere thought.

"Of course you have to go. He's one of your professors; it's very important that he sees you and the topic interests you a lot. Go and have fun."

Clara was surprised at her mother's words and raised her eyebrows.

"After the talk we'll have dinner and then go

to a discotheque. I'll be home late. What about …"

But before Clara could finish, her mother answered, "Don't worry about grandma. I'm sure she'll understand if we leave her home alone for one night. It is true that since grandpa died she hasn't been the same, but you need to have fun."

Have fun?!? Thought Clara grinning. *Spending the day listening to a talk, surrounded by people I don't have anything in common with. Does she really think that's my way of having fun?*

Clara entered her bedroom leaving her mother to her makeup session and, standing in front of the mirror, let the warm June air that was coming from the open window dry her skin. It was nice. Looking at her body's reflection, she noticed it still looked immature compared to other girls her age, but she still somehow felt her youth was slipping away. She was tall with long golden brown hair that protected her delicate shoulders. She had big, sad, deep brown eyes that always seemed to be looking for answers and lips that always struggled to smile. Tourists walking under her window laughed aloud; a pigeon landed on the windowsill, and Clara got distracted and stopped looking in the mirror. Her mother was right; it was a beautiful day, warm and sunny, and she should have been outside celebrating life with all her childhood friends. Instead, she was feeling tired and depressed with no purpose in life.

"We are ready," said her mother appearing at her bedroom door. "Go and say goodbye to your father," she ordered, despotic.

Clara hated when her mother treated her as if she were still a little girl, telling her what to do and when and how to do it. As a mother, she always said that it was her job to instruct Clara, but Clara thought that a mother's job was also to try to understand when it was time to quit. Her mother's behavior had always interfered with Clara's relationship with her father, taking all the spontaneity out of it. She would have been happy to yell, "Bye dad, I love you!" from her bedroom door, but instead, she absentmindedly threw on a light dress and calmly went to formally say goodbye.

Her father was waiting in the foyer wearing the clothes his wife prepared for him. Every day Maria laid a different outfit on the bed and he grabbed it and wore it without thinking. That day, for the summer party at their friend's country home, Maria had chosen a khaki cotton suit with a white linen shirt and a blue tie. Once at their friend's house, he could take off his jacket and enjoy the rest of the evening only after receiving permission from his wife; a light nod of the head or a gentle touch on the back. No need for words.

When Roberto saw his daughter, he stood up straight and fixed his jacket sleeves. He smelled of fresh linen.

"How do I look?" he asked proudly, waiting

for his daughter's opinion.

Clara thought he was handsome. She would have loved to hug him tight and find comfort in his arms, but the kind of relationship they had didn't allow her to do it. Instead she faked a smile, raised her eyebrows trying to look cheerful and with a too high-pitched tone said, "You look handsome dad!"

"Your mother put a lot of thought into this outfit. Just between us, I feel like a ghost in this suit, but she says it is perfect for the summer."

"Well, dad, you know mom," said Clara, happy to have some complicity with him.

"I know her, believe me, and if she is happy, life is easier for everybody, right?" he said, winking at her.

"Have fun, dad," said Clara, placing a light kiss on his cheek.

Maria impatiently stormed into the foyer wrapped in an overpowering cloud of perfume. The amount of cologne she wore was always abundant and, depending on the occasion, it was a mix of three or four different bottles because she loved to create her own personalized scent. She did the same with coffee; she couldn't just use one blend at a time, but had to mix different ones to make her own, certain that her unique mixtures were interestingly tasty and wonderfully smelly. Unfortunately, others did not always agree.

"Roberto, what are you still doing here?" she asked, appalled. "It's late. Take the car out of the garage," she ordered. "I'll wait for your honk to come down."

After they both left, her mother's fragrance stayed for a long time and Clara followed the trail she left while going back to her bedroom. She glanced at the clock on the wall. Paola was about to arrive; it was time to get dressed.

Paola had always been her best friend. They met in kindergarten and shared the same classrooms until the end of high school. Their friendship had always been strong and, over the years, it survived issues like jealousy, wrong boyfriends and personal differences. Three years before, when they had to choose which college to attend, they made very different choices that alienated them for the very first time. Paola chose the University of Bologna to study Economics with the prospect of working for her family's business. Clara insisted on going to Milan to enroll in law school. Paola embraced the lifestyle of the local students; she loved to live in the nearby Bologna during the week, and to go home each Friday and keep seeing the same people with whom she grew up. Clara, instead, was still fighting between two realities; she followed the dream of the big city, but when her dream came true, it crumbled when faced with reality.

Clara opened the closet, stared at her hanging clothes and opted for a low-key outfit — washed-silk pants and jacket the color of the sand, sleeveless sky blue cotton shirt, and flats. She knew she was going to be underdressed for the occasion, but she reluctantly accepted the invitation and her bad mood showed through the choice of the outfit. Pants and flats was about all she had to give for that event.

The doorbell rang; it was Paola. Clara grabbed her bag, glanced at the entry mirror one last time and closed the door behind her. Paola was wearing black extremely high-heeled sandals and a teeny, tiny green dress that showed most of her legs and enhanced her dark skin.

"Aren't you elegant for a summer night?" Paola asked sarcastically as soon as she saw Clara climbing down the stairs.

"It's a midday conference, Paola, and I'm sure tonight it'll be chilly. Anyway, I'm fine. It's good to see you," Clara replied, hoping they could change the subject soon.

Paola's Mercedes was comfortable and the stereo was playing Italian pop music.

"You still don't have a car yet, right?" Paola asked incredulously.

"No, I don't. Traffic is terrible in Milan and I wouldn't use it. I decided to save my parents the money," Clara answered calmly.

"Well, as you can see, I decided that my parents owed me a car. After all, my college tuition is not as high as yours. And furthermore, I can't stand to take the train," Paola answered, irritated, as if Clara's decision could undermine her own.

"I like the train," said Clara. "It gives me time to think, to read, and also to observe the changing landscape."

"I didn't know you had become so romantic and meditative," Paola mocked.

"It is very pleasant. Once the outskirts are passed it is possible to admire the cultivated land, the vineyards and the orchards. Each kind of plantation gives the fields a different color and texture depending on the season. Every estate has its own country house. Some of them are beautiful two-floor buildings made out of stone and, with a little luck it is possible to have a glance of the rural life," answered Clara.

"Since when do you enjoy looking at working rednecks?" Paola asked, more and more astonished by her friend's words.

"I can see things that it's impossible to see in a city. It's fun and it reminds me of where we come from."

"Well, I have another idea of having fun and I prefer driving to Bologna, parking my car on the street and not touching it until Friday, when it is time to go back home," Paola replied curtly. Then she changed the subject as she suddenly remembered something extremely urgent to report to Clara. "By the way, guess who I bumped into last Saturday in downtown?"

"Who?" Clara asked, trying not to sound too curious.

"Luca. You know, he is miserable without you. I think you made a big mistake letting him go."

"Paola, it was over way before I decided to leave him. Being together didn't make sense anymore. Do you know how many weekends we spent together in the last six months? Three. And I don't remember him complaining at the time. Does that seem like a successful relationship to you?"

"But now that he has lost you, he understands how precious you were to him," insisted Paola.

"Well, he should have thought about that earlier. Now it's over."

"He is such a good guy, Clara," said Paola, refusing to give up.

"I know, but I can't be with a person just because he is 'such a good guy.' I might as well get a dog, then," Clara replied with a sigh.

"You are too difficult and if you keep acting like this, you'll end up alone," warned Paola.

"How long do you think it'll take to get to Urbino?" asked Clara, timidly trying to distract her friend.

"If the traffic stays the same we should be there right before the talk starts."

~

Urbino was a one-hour drive. It was a small, picturesque citadel in the Marche region of Roman and medieval origins. It rose at the top of a hill, surrounded by thick and sturdy stone walls, which in the past served the purpose of protecting it from invaders, and it dominated the underlying valley. In the fifteenth century, during the Renaissance, Urbino reached its peak thanks to Duke Federico da Montefeltro who established there one of Europe's most illustrious courts. When Clara was younger, she used to visit the little town with her parents. Her mother loved to buy its famous unsalted bread and Clara liked "cresciolina": small pieces of bread dough rolled flat with a rolling pin, fried in hot lard and then sprinkled with sugar. They always went to a tiny family-owned bakery, very different from the ones she used to see in her town that had wide windows displaying the colorful delicacies that came out of the oven through fancy arrangements. This one was a simple bakery that had a poky door up three steep steps and only one small window lacking any kind of embellishment, but just a few simple wicker baskets that plainly showed the best selection of their flavored breads and sugary treats. The husband was the baker baking in the back of the shop and his wife was in the front, serving clients. Neither of them was ever in a rush. The wife served one person at a time, slowly alternating between the baked goods area and the cash register. She never stopped smiling. Clara and her parents, with their favorite breads in a paper bag, always ended the daily excursion stopping at the cafe in Piazza della Repubblica. On warm and sunny days, they all loved to sit at the outdoor tables and, while her parents enjoyed watching people passing by, Clara played next to the fountain that was in the center of the Piazza.

~

Paola and Clara had left the highway, and the street started to narrow and to climb upward. After several elbow turns, they found themselves in front of the fortified walls of Urbino, right at the bottom of the town, and decided to take their chances and enter to look for a parking spot.

Inside the walls, the streets became dense, narrow alleys. After a few failed attempts, Paola gave up and decided to park outside the walls. The lecture was about to start, and in order to be on time they started walking at a fast pace, cutting through alleys filled with cafes, restaurants and souvenir shops.

Sweaty and out of breath, they finally reached the main portal of the Ducal Palace and entered. The talk they were about to hear would take place in one of its rooms.

"We are here for the meeting with professor Lienich," Paola said to the hostess standing right in the center of the entryway.

"May I see your invitations?" the woman asked formally while touching her yellow silk neckerchief.

"Here they are," Paola and Clara answered at the same time, showing the cards.

"This way, please. The meeting is about to start. You are just in time," the hostess added reprovingly.

The room was far from what Clara was

expecting. Besides the carved door lintels, the ceiling medallions and the fireplace mantel, nothing was left of the original decor. It was furnished with cheap modern pieces and it had completely empty white walls. The speakers were standing behind a long conference table covered with a disheartening gray cloth and the audience was sitting on featureless folding chairs. The first few rows were already occupied on both sides, so Paola and Clara exchanged a quick look and silently agreed on where to take a seat.

The crowd became silent. Professor Noti, a short, clumsy man, elegantly dressed and with red cheeks, stood up, cleared his throat and briefly introduced Professor Lienich, explaining how innovative his ideas were and how groundbreaking his theory about the failure of the welfare state was. A loud applause followed the introduction and Professor Lienich, a thin and pompous man with gray hair, gray skin and gray suit, grabbed the microphone. Pleased by his colleague's adulation, he thanked him, thanked the audience, and finally started talking with the usual know-it-all tone of voice that Clara was used to hearing every time she attended one of his classes.

Professor Lienich said his first few words and Clara's mind started to drift away, far, far back in time, when Urbino was at its peak, more than 500 years before. She lost herself in daydreaming. She dreamed that the room transformed to its original beauty, when, thanks to the humanist education of Federico Malatesta, the Ducal Palace was the most glamorous in all Italy. At that time the Palace's rooms were adorned with the finest tapestries, countless statues, rare paintings and musical instruments; the Duke personally chose the furnishing and the visitors were amazed by the tasteful opulence and beauty of the Palace. At court, the daily life was very simple and Clara imagined sober and gracious courtiers being entertained by music and games. She imagined herself in the room dressed according to the fashion of the times — a long dress with a tight corset and puffy sleeves, adorned with lace trimmings, gold chains and precious stones. Her skirt concealed her feet, but it was open in the front showing a very rich petticoat underneath. She imagined being engaged in a polite conversation with other women while nibbling on chestnuts. She imagined that the Duke spent the day hunting while other men played football and that everybody came back to court ready for a sumptuous dinner. During the Renaissance the food had to please both the palate and the eyes and downstairs, in the subterranean level of the Palace, hundreds of servants labored to make the Duke's "simple" life possible. In the kitchen, the cooks were preparing refined and sophisticated foods to please the guests, who, in the meanwhile, assembled in the dining room. Clara could hear the swish of the dames' silky gowns and the gentlemen's capes. Everybody sat at the table around Federico and dinner started with a juicy sirloin beef basted in orange juice and rose water. Women's soft laughter filled the room. The men discussed the afternoon football game and the hunting while salad and egg dishes were served. The feathers adorning a man's hat tickled a woman's neck and she jumped in surprise. Everybody discreetly laughed and dessert came — a rich soup, sweetened with sugar and decorated with pomegranate seeds.

~

A roar of applause brought Clara back to reality. The lecture was over. Clara took a look around and saw that more people had arrived after them, and the room was now full. As she anticipated, most of the women wore short, tight cocktail dresses that left very little to the imagination, accompanied by very high heels. The men were all wearing suits and neckties.

"Stay with me," said Paola. "We have to cross the room to reach the others."

"Hi Clara! Do you remember me?" asked a girl with long black hair.

"Of course I remember you. How are you?" answered Clara with a big smile, having no idea to whom she was talking, but trying to convey her joy in seeing the young woman again.

The room was crammed with people moving in different directions; some were trying to leave, others were trying to catch up with people they knew, and still others were trying to reach Professor Lienich to congratulate him.

It's a madhouse! Thought Clara.

"Clara, this is Stefano," Paola said out of the blue.

And where did he pop up from? Clara wondered, and was about to answer and introduce herself when Paola pulled her through the mass of people.

"Come with me Clara. This way!"

Her eyes roamed around the room; she saw old high school friends and kept following Paola.

A short and robust young man exclaimed surprised, "Clara is that you!?!"

Clara recognized him. "Hi, Giorgio! How are you? You haven't changed a bit!"

"I'll try to take that as a compliment," he replied, laughing.

A blond girl named Elena joined their conversation.

"How are you, Clara. How have you been doing?" she asked.

"Hi, Elena!"

Paola was still holding Clara's hand as not to lose her in the crowd and proudly said, "you see? I told you, everybody would be thrilled to see you!"

"But it's been just a few months since I saw everybody," answered Clara naively.

"Hey, look who's here! Long time no see, Clara!" said another girl with short and asymmetric hair.

"Hi Sofia, how are you?" answered Clara, beginning to enjoy the chaos.

Giorgio kept following them.

Elena gave a few pushes to some strangers and was able to stand next to Clara.

"I heard you dumped Luca and he took it badly, I'm sorry. How are you doing?" she asked Clara, keeping her voice down.

"I'm fine. Thanks for asking, Elena; you are very kind."

The crowd started to push them hard toward the exit. *Not exactly the calm and polite Renaissance people of my dream*, Clara thought, as she and Paola were forced to start walking toward the main staircase. Clara had room only to look straight ahead. Suddenly, she saw a young man coming toward her against the tide. He was tall, had light brown hair, broad shoulders and dark blue eyes that were intensely staring at her. Struggling against the crowd, he stopped in front of her, extended his hand and spoke in a calm and confident voice.

"Hi, my name is Leonardo."

"My name is Clara," she answered.

Clara felt the earth tremble, time stop, and space expand. Suddenly, they were the only ones in the room. His hand was holding hers and an electric shock ran through her spine. She felt confused and pulled her hand back to regain control of her emotions.

You won't have me, she thought in the back of her mind feeling silly to be so defensive. She couldn't understand why she was overreacting to such a simple self-introduction. Surrendering to the pressure of the mass of people that was pushing her, Clara started walking down the staircase. Paola was talking to her; Clara was trying very hard to pay attention to her friend's words and to act like nothing just happened, but she felt the irrational need to have a sign of Leonardo's presence and so she craned her neck and started looking for him. She peeked around, decided to lower her gaze and saw his black, lace-up shoes right on the step behind her. Knowing he was close took her breath away. Her heart started beating fast and, once they reached the courtyard of the Palace, while her friends were planning the rest of the evening, she could think of nothing but the soft grip of his hand and his long fingers grazing her palm while releasing the handshake.

~

The restaurant's entrance was uncomfortable, small and narrow. The door was two steps down from the street level, and everybody had to bend their head to enter. Once entered, on the right were the cash register and a big refrigerator overflowing with ice creams and sorbets; on the left was a solid workbench. A very polite waiter led them to their table in the adjacent room. Clara didn't know how many people to expect, and was surprised when she saw a very long L-shaped table almost full of seated people talking and eating bread while waiting for the others to arrive.

"It's about time you got here! We are ready to order," a corpulent man named Matteo announced jokingly, standing up to greet them.

"Hi Matteo!" said Clara happy to see him.

"Let me hug you," Matteo said, smiling. "I need to see if you are real or just a mirage."

He was very tall and as he hugged her, he lifted her off the ground.

"Come on guys, sit down. People are hungry here!" shouted a voice from the table.

Clara found herself sitting between Matteo and Giorgio and felt at ease. However, she had never met the young man sitting in front of her. Thick glasses covered his eyes, but she could sense that they were protruding, mean eyes, and his lips, which never stopped moving and sputtering, were thin and sharp, like knives. He didn't introduce himself. They ignored each other for the whole evening, but he monopolized the dinner conversation regaling everybody with absurd episodes about his career to show how smart he was. Every story was spiced up with flamboyant erudite quotes and mimed with wide hand gestures.

Clara leaned toward Giorgio and asked him, "Who is this idiot?"

Giorgio couldn't refrain from laughing.

"Clara, you haven't changed a bit! His name is Raul; you don't know him because he joined our group after you left for Milan."

"Sorry, but I just wish he would shut up, Clara sighed.

"Don't be sorry, everybody is thinking the same thing." Giorgio replied.

Leaning toward Giorgio and talking with him without being heard by the others, she noticed that at the end of the table was Leonardo. Her belly shrank and her heart started beating in her throat. Next to him was a blond man and they looked pretty busy talking. *What is he doing here? Does he hang around with this group of people on a regular basis? I wonder if Paola knows him. Probably not, she introduced me to everybody but him. Maybe he is a student in Bologna too.* She tried to calm her thoughts and kept talking with Giorgio. Knowing he was there made it impossible to ignore his presence, and every once in a while she took a peek. Leonardo had removed his jacket and Clara could admire his straight shoulders; he had also taken off his tie, and the unbuttoned shirt's neck allowed her to half see the underneath pale blue t-shirt that intensified his eyes' hue. She felt disoriented observing his hands that graciously moved on top of the table.

After dinner, Elena and Sofia joined Clara and Paola for the ride to the disco. They were all excited about the developing evening.

"Did you see how hot Luciano was tonight?" murmured Elena in a dreamy voice from the back seat.

"What!?!" Paola replied, disgusted. "Don't tell me you like him. I found him as detestable as always."

"He was not detestable. Take back what you just said. He was hot and," started Elena before being cut off.

"And what?" Sofia replied, trying to stop her from saying something stupid.

"Leave her alone," Clara chuckled.

Paola interrupted everybody. "I'd like to point your attention to Francesco, instead."

"Francesco is always the hottest," sighed Sofia, hopelessly.

Clara was hoping one of the girls would comment on Leonardo, but none of them said a word and she didn't dare ask.

It was dark and she couldn't see the surrounding hills, but felt the road winding.

~

The disco was like every other disco Clara had been to — dark, loud and suffocating. She never understood why people liked to spend time there; the loud music made talking impossible, the low ceilings were oppressive, and the blinking lights made everything unreal. Lonely men hoped for an encounter; they wandered around checking the girls on the dance floor, a cocktail in their hand as their only company. *These are places for lost souls*, Clara thought.

As soon as they arrived, Sofia and Paola ran to the dance floor. Unleashed by the rhythm of the music, Elena caught up with a group of friends and Clara joined the line at the bar's counter hoping to alleviate her thirst. She ordered a soda and lingered for a while to watch the bartenders skillfully preparing elaborate cocktails.

"I was looking for you," a voice startled her from behind.

It was Leonardo.

"Hi!" was all Clara could say with a stupid smile on her face.

"Sorry, I didn't mean to startle you. The music is too loud in here, would you like to come outside so we can talk?" Leonardo continued.

Clara felt her knees weakening.

"Great idea," she said, and trying to sound relaxed, she grabbed her soda from the counter and followed him.

Beyond the dance floor there was a patio with the most beautiful view of the Adriatic Sea at night. It wasn't very big, but tastefully furnished with small tables and colorful chairs occupied by people who, like them, wanted to take advantage of the warm air of June to pleasantly chat. One table was reserved for a birthday party and every once in a while the sparkling sound of an opening bottle of Prosecco could be heard followed by happy laughter. In the rear, next to a staircase covered with flowers and plants, were two empty chairs. Clara sat on one and Leonardo sat on the other.

"Do you like dancing?" asked Leonardo, resting his glass on the table.

"I like dancing, but I don't much care for discos," answered Clara, sipping her soda and then placing the glass on the table.

"Nor do I," said Leonardo. "You seem to know everybody very well here, but I have never seen you before."

Clara chuckled. "I was in high school with all of them, but now they study in Bologna and I went to Milan instead. That's why I'm never here. And you? How do you know them?"

"I'm a latecomer," laughed Leonardo. "I met Matteo and Giorgio two years ago at a party and they have been inviting me to join them since then. I can't go every time because I live in Rome, but when I come up to visit my parents and I'm in town, I'm always happy to see them."

"Oh, I see," said Clara, relieved that the mystery was slowly unfolding. "You are right, Matteo and Giorgio are the nicest people."

"What are you studying?" Leonardo asked, interested.

"I'm in law school, but I think it is not the right thing for me," Clara confessed abruptly.

"Don't you like it? Well, I don't blame you," Leonardo agreed.

"It's not who I am," Clara replied.

"So why did you choose law?" asked

Leonardo, intrigued.

Clara grabbed her glass from the table and took a long sip of her soda that was warming up.

"It's neither an easy nor a short answer. Are you sure you want to hear it?"

Leonardo nodded, smiling, and Clara went on.

"In part, I wanted to please my father by **showing him I was able to make a rational, sensible choice**; in part I didn't trust my passions enough. The truth is, I don't know. What I know is that I'm stuck. I live in a city that I don't like and I feel inadequate. Sometimes I wish I was born five hundred years ago or never at all," sighed Clara.

Her words came out in a flood. She was telling a complete stranger thoughts and fears that nobody else knew and that she had a hard time admitting even to herself. What surprised her the most, however, was that she somehow felt safe doing it.

"What you just said is very sad. Why do you wish such a thing?" asked Leonardo in a soft voice, and intensely gazing at her. Clara had the impression of hearing his heartbeat and she answered finding strength in his blue eyes.

"I think that in the past, life was easier. Less expectation, more fatalism," she replied.

Leonardo moved his chair a little closer to Clara and asked her, "Have you ever thought that maybe you simply made a mistake because you are human?"

His words rang in Clara's head and were

painful. In her family, being human was not an option, making mistakes was foolish, and only perfection was allowed. **She took another sip of her sweet soda.**

"Even if it was a mistake, it doesn't matter anymore because I've already started law and I have to finish. I can't throw away three years of my life. Now it's too late," she concluded pessimistically.

"Too late?" Leonardo marveled. "It seems to me that if you *don't* throw away three years you'll end up wasting the rest of your life doing something you despise; it doesn't make any sense."

Clara was speechless. Her heart felt as if it was about to explode and she couldn't think clearly. She had never considered the possibility of quitting and tried to defend her position.

"But I feel guilty; my parents are spending a lot for my tuition."

"I'm sure they'd prefer to see you happy," Leonardo answered candidly.

Clara needed to change the subject.

"What do you do in Rome?" she asked, trying to regain balance and perspective.

"I'm a doctor. I'm in my last year of residency in cardiology."

"Nice. My father is a doctor too, a surgeon. I never understood whether he expected me to follow in his footsteps, but I think he probably thought I wasn't smart enough," she replied.

"I really don't think so. I think that probably

you're the one thinking that, not him."

Leonardo's every word hit her harder. He understood her perfectly and, at the same time, he challenged her. Leonardo placed his glass down and began to unbutton his cuffs. Clara stared at him and saw his long fingers play with the buttons and then roll up the sleeves exposing his forearms. They were a bundle of muscles, tendons and veins. A sweet quiver shook her body, a hard grasp tightened her stomach, and a quick contraction gripped her womb. She knew it was too late to go back.

"Here you are!" Paola interrupted them. "I see you have met our Leonardo," she added, sounding annoyed. "Elena is not feeling well and I'm taking her home. Are you coming?"

Clara took a moment to answer hoping Leonardo would offer to take her home.

"So?" asked Paola, impatiently.

"Yes, of course I'm coming with you," said Clara, disappointed.

Paola moved toward the exit.

"I'm sure we'll meet again, but would you like to give me your phone number?" Leonardo asked politely.

"Yes, but I don't have anything to write it down on," Clara said searching her bag, cursing to be so unprepared.

"Just say it, I'll remember it. If I don't see you I'll call you," he said, adding, "but remember, I never rush."

In the car with the girls, Clara was confused by the unexpected outcome of the evening.

Elena was not sick at all, she just saw her ex boyfriend kissing a young girl in a recessed corner of the disco and got upset. Paola and Sofia were too busy taking care of her wounded feelings to notice that Clara was quieter than usual. Once in her bed, Clara couldn't stop thinking about Leonardo. His deep voice still echoed in her ears. Her heart called his name with every beat. Flashes of him came to her mind — his lower lip a little fuller than the upper one, his tapered fingers around the glass, his narrow and tight hips. Tossing and turning she was hoping sleep would come and take over, but she couldn't stop longing for his hands, his waist, and the plumped veins on his forearms.

~

She knew it was seven in the morning because her father started singing Opera outside her door. He couldn't bear to see her sleeping late. He was an early riser and thought people who slept late were idlers, so, no matter what time Clara returned home the night before, every morning at seven o'clock, he pretended to be so happy he couldn't restrain himself from singing. That morning it was "Nessun dorma[1]" from la Turandot of Giacomo

---

[1] Nobody sleeps.

Puccini.

Very appropriate. She thought. However, that morning there was nobody to wake up because Clara hadn't been asleep. Not even for one brief instant.

Her mother opened the door of her bedroom and entered chirping about last night's party. Clara noticed she was already perfectly dressed, made up with matching lipstick and perfumed.

"You should have seen the decorations on the buffet," she said. "Exquisite! After all, Vittoria is a real lady. Everything was perfect from beginning to end. Oh, you should also have seen the pieces of jewelry that people were wearing, but I didn't look so bad either with the emerald and diamond ring and necklace your father gave me last Christmas," she added.

Her mother was about to describe every little detail of the party, but Clara's head was about to explode. She was tired and in need of telling somebody about what had happened the night before and how she was feeling so, she did something she rarely did.

"Mom, come here and be quiet for a second," she said in a firm but polite voice. "I have something to tell you."

Maria stopped and reached Clara's bed.

"What is it, love? You seem worried," her mother said, sitting on the edge of the mattress.

"Mom, please don't tell anybody, especially dad, but, I met someone last night!" Clara said, straightening up on the mattress.

"That is good news, honey. Why are you so troubled? Tell me what he's like."

Clara started describing Leonardo and told her mother everything. She went into a lot of detail, but she didn't mention what they talked about. Maria saw she was very taken. Her daughter's eyes were tired, but sparkling.

"What does he do?"

Clara was a little disappointed by the question. Her mother was missing the point; what he did was not important. The only thing that counted was that she was completely crazy in love with a stranger. She had wanted to go home with him the same night she met him and she wanted to make love with him all night long.

"What did you say his last name is?" asked her mother. Another meaningless question taking Clara back to reality.

"Buricci, I think, or something like that," answered Clara absentmindedly.

"I want to check the yellow pages and see if I can find out where he lives," said Maria excitedly, and she disappeared into the office like a teenager who just found out a juicy detail about her best friend's crush.

Clara lingered in bed a little bit more and then decided to go to see her grandma. She didn't feel like talking to her father that morning, but in order to go upstairs she had to walk in front of the family room where he usually spent his free time sitting in his armchair facing the door. He was reading the newspaper and raised his green eyes flecked with gold when Clara passed by.

"Hi dad, I'm going to see grandma," she said quickly, hoping to pass unnoticed.

"Hey, hey, come here for a second and tell me about last night. Did you have fun?"

"Yes, it was fun," Clara said, staying by the door. "Tell mom I'm upstairs."

"She'll call you when lunch is ready," he said, hoping to keep her a little longer.

"No, tell her I'm eating with grandma. I want to make up for leaving her alone last night," said Clara, as she smiled a big innocent smile and went on her way.

~

Two flights of stairs separated Clara's apartment from her grandmother's.

Grandma Anna was a very petite old lady with puffy cheeks and a chipper smile. As a mother, she had never been sweet or forgiving; her deep black eyes, always serious and her eyebrows always frowning, saw to it that her rules were always respected. However, as a grandmother, she had always been sweet and cuddly. Clara passed her childhood walking up and down those staircases. In the evening, her mother found her wearing her nightgown and holding her favorite teddy bear.

"Where are you going, honey?" her mother

always asked, pretending she didn't know the answer.

"I go gamma," Clara always answered proudly and with a tone of voice that meant nobody and nothing could have changed her mind.

She loved to spend the night in the big bed getting pampered by grandma, who would rub her back until she fell asleep. On those nights, grandpa Giovanni knew he had to retreat to the guest room.

Clara ran upstairs happy to escape her father's questioning and found grandma silently sitting on the sofa with the TV off. The morning's light made her silvery hair shine as it filtered through the linen curtains that, years before, when her eyesight was still good, she embellished with a crochet border. She had crosswords on her lap and, on the side table, a white saucer with a sliced red apple. She was about to grab a juicy slice when she noticed Clara.

"I was waiting for you," she said, smiling.

"Good morning, grandma," Clara answered, trying to stay calm.

"How did it go last night?" her grandmother queried.

"It was as boring as I anticipated, but something unexpected happened," answered Clara with sparkling eyes and barely able to hold back her enthusiasm.

"What, honey, don't keep an old woman waiting," Anna said, ironically.

"I met someone, grandma, and, I know it sounds absurd, but ... "

"You think you are in love," Anna finished for her.

"Yes! How did you know? I cannot stop thinking about him, about what he said, about his hands."

"I could tell because I know you and I can see you didn't sleep well last night. Your eyes are sparkling, but also very tired," her grandmother answered.

"I'm restless, grandma. I'm happy like I have never been before, but I feel like crying all the time. What can I do?" Clara asked.

Grandma patted the spot on the couch close to her, indicating that Clara should sit.

"First of all, you have to sleep. Remember that sleep is the most important beauty tool and it's essential to see things clearly. Second, don't cry. Never. Crying is a shelter for ugly girls and a disaster for the good-looking ones. You are asking me what you have to do? Nothing. That's what you have to do."

"Nothing? What do you mean?" asked Clara, confused.

"I mean nothing. Nowadays girls think that running after men is a sign of emancipation, but ... do you really want him?" she asked looking straight into Clara's eyes.

"Yes. How many times did you hear me say I'm in love?"

"Very well, then. Does he have your phone number?" her grandmother inquired.

"Yes, sort of; we didn't have anything to write it on and ... " Clara began to explain before her grandmother interrupted.

"If he is really interested, he'll find a way to contact you. In the meanwhile you just have to wait," grandma solemnly finished, finally grabbing the apple slice.

"But Grandma!?!" Clara tried to protest.

"If he wants you he'll call. Trust me. You'll have your chance to know him and to show him who you are. If he doesn't call you, better to lose him now." Her look said clearly that her verdict had been returned and that replies were not allowed. She raised the apple slice to her mouth and bit it.

"Do you want to watch a movie with me?" Anna asked.

"Sure," Clara answered, not really paying attention, still thinking of grandma's last words.

"Have you had anything to eat yet? If you are hungry I have leftovers in the fridge."

Clara had no desire for food and lied.

"Thanks, but I had a very big breakfast just a few minutes ago."

"Last night Cleopatra with Liz Taylor and Richard Burton was on; I missed you," Grandma said, and switched on the TV.

~

Maria was worried Clara would spend another afternoon closed in a room with her grandmother watching old American movies on TV. She didn't really understand the kind of bond they had. She was pleased her daughter wanted to spend time with her grandmother, but she also thought she should have been spending more time with her peers. Determined to take Clara out, Maria put her head into the stairwell and called, "Clara come down for a moment, I need to talk to you!"

No response came from the upper floor, but after a few seconds she heard the sound of fast steps on the stairs.

"I'm going to the beach, do you want to come with me?" she asked Clara when she was in front of her.

Normally Clara would have said no, but considering her emotional state, she thought that it was probably a good idea to get out, lie under the sun, and see people. Her mother was delighted and surprised. It didn't happen very often that she agreed to do something with her.

Clara grabbed the first bikini she found in the drawer. Her mother, on the other hand, gave deep thought and chose a red and white one-piece bathing suit that matched her nail polish and beach robe.

"Do we walk or bike?" her mother asked.

"Let's bike, so maybe later we can go to the harbor and watch the boats that come back with fresh fish," answered Clara.

They arrived at the beach, chained the bikes to the dedicated posts, and walking on the footpath, headed toward the umbrellas. The season had just begun, but the beach umbrellas and the beach beds were already out, the playground for kids was already organized, and the beach attendants were assembling brand new fitness machines next to the picnic area.

"Good morning, Mrs. Maro. Welcome!" the beach attendant and his wife shouted in greeting.

"Good morning, Pino. How are you?" answered Maria, trying to use a familiar tone of voice.

Pino moved close to shake her hand. He was a middle-aged man, muscular, with a few gray hairs on his chest, an outstretched belly and perfectly tanned skin.

"We are glad to have you here with us for another season. Your usual beach umbrella and your cabana are ready," he said.

"Thank you, Pino. Did you see that today I could take my daughter with me? I hope it will bring you luck for the new season," joked Maria.

"Lets hope! We are always in need of good luck," Pino answered good-naturedly.

"What are you assembling over there?" Maria asked with a voice somewhere between surprised and annoyed, adding, "each year you have a new surprise."

"We are creating a fitness area so our clients can also workout at the beach," exclaimed Pino, proud of his idea and looking at his wife who was supervising the job.

The weather was warm, but not yet hot.

Clara's family beach umbrella was in the first row, next to the water, but the wind was chilly and her Mother decided to stay close to the cabanas where there was more protection.

"Pino, would you be so kind as to put two beach beds here next to the cabanas? It is still too cold to stay close to the water," Maria said, hoping to sound polite, but sounding bossy.

It was their first visit to the beach that summer and taking off their clothes was not easy. They were both white as milk, and not having a tan made Clara feel embarrassed.

"I feel naked and the bikini feels more like underwear," she said, taking off her shorts.

For her mother it would be just a matter of time before she'd turn a deep golden brown color. Maria loved when her husband called her "my cookie," but for Clara, tanning was difficult and would require perseverance and diligence … an effort she wasn't willing to make. Lying under the sun, Clara remembered when she was a child and her mother used to take her to the beach every day — that same beach, all summer long. She liked to play under the shadow of the big umbrella, build sandcastles or trace tracks to use with marbles. She played alone or with other kids while her mother lay still under the scorching sun for hours.

"Tell me a little more about this boy," her mother asked, resting under the sun. She was on her back and Clara got the impression she was about to fall asleep.

"I don't know a lot more than what I already told you. I had never seen him before," Clara answered quickly.

She answered hoping her words would induce her mother's sleep. Facedown, with her chin placed on the back of her hands, Clara was looking at the ocean and admiring the waves that were wrinkling the water's surface. A familiar human shape rising from the water awakened her attention.

"It's him!" she shouted, jumping on the beach bed and startling her mother.

"Who? Where?" asked Maria, puzzled, turning toward the ocean.

"Mom, it's him, it's him!" but this time, Clara whispered and sunk deeply into the beach bed hiding behind her mother.

Leonardo was walking toward them with his unmistakable gait wearing a pair of glowing yellow surfer's shorts. Clara was paralyzed. She didn't know what to do.

"Who!?! That one is the one who made you unable to sleep last night!?!" Maria asked, incredulous.

"Yes, why? Is something wrong with him?" Clara asked defensively.

"No, honey. I just, I pictured him, different, that's all."

"Ok, I agree that the shorts are too yellow, but come on, look at him, isn't he gorgeous!?!"

Maria looked at him again and all she could see was a tall and thin young man with a bathing suit that was too bright and too short.

"Look, mom, he is a bundle of muscles; oh my God, he is... " Clara started before her mother quickly interrupted.

"Clara, please. Do not act like a child. If he sees you drooling and hiding behind the towel, what will he think of you?" her mother chided.

"He doesn't have to see me, mom; he can't! I'm unprepared to meet him today, so stay still and cover me," Clara implored.

He stopped by a group of people Clara hadn't noticed before; she knew some of them and she watched him for a while as he talked with them. A lot of girls hung around him, and he was nice to everybody. He smiled, listened, talked, but at the same time looked distracted and distant. Nobody looked like a possible girlfriend, and Clara was relieved.

~

Clara was studying in her bedroom when the phone rang. It was Paola.

"What are you doing?" she asked Clara.

"I'm studying commercial law. I have the exam in late July," Clara answered.

"We are going out for pizza, would you like to come? It'll be no more than five or six people and we won't be late," said Paola.

"Sure! Thanks for asking. Where and when?"

"Eight-thirty. 'La Bussola.' I can pick you up, if you wish," Paola offered.

"Thanks, but I'll take my father's car. I'm sure you'll stay later than I will anyway," said Clara.

Paola didn't say anything about who was going to be there. Clara didn't want to raise Paola's suspicions by asking too many questions, but she was hoping Leonardo would be there even if it wasn't a weekend and he was probably in Rome.

The place was an old pizzeria in the part of town that originally was the fishermen's village. After being forgotten, snubbed, and in decline for many years, it had been recently rediscovered, especially by young people who bought its old houses and renovated them. New pubs, cafes and taverns were opening as well to accommodate the new population's desires, and the contrast between old and new made the neighborhood very interesting and alive. Some of the oldest shops and some of the newest were side by side and the combination was amazingly charming. The same dichotomy could be observed in the people; the old ones simple and shabby, the young ones trendy and elegant. Mimmo's shop, which, before him, had belonged to his father, was legendary among plant lovers. All someone needed to do if a plant was in trouble was to bring him one or two leaves, and he would identify the problem and sell them the remedy. The stench of his fertilizers and medicines could be smelled a block away, but the owners of the new fancy delicacy shops and the cutting-edge boutique didn't mind. The streets were very narrow and full of people walking and riding bikes and scooters. It wasn't easy to find a parking spot, and Clara cursed the moment she decided to leave the bike at home and take the car instead. She was walking to the restaurant and in front of her saw an old man wearing a white undershirt, blue shorts and moccasins with a plastic bag in his hands. She saw him stop in front of a window at the ground level of a house with orange walls. He tapped with energy on the shutters and a young man opened them. The old man handed him the plastic bag and proudly said, "Mario, I hope I'm not disturbing you. This morning I've been out fishing and I thought you and your young wife would like some of the fresh sardines I caught."

The young man smiled and called his wife. Together they thanked the older man, and invited him in for a cup of coffee.

"Thanks, but I have to go. Edna didn't even want me to come at this hour. She said I'd bother you. Maybe another time," the older man said, sad he couldn't accept their offer.

"You never disturb, Manlio. Come anytime, and next time bring Edna with you!" said Mario, cheerfully closing the shutters.

I don't see scenes like this in Milan, thought Clara. For a moment, she appreciated her hometown's genuineness. She saw the restaurant's sign. She entered. The possibility of seeing Leonardo again made her legs weak and she almost tripped on the stairs of the entrance. Paola saw her and waved happily.

"Hi everybody," said Clara, trying to stop her racing heart.

"We have never seen you so often; twice in three days, what is happening?" Giorgio and Matteo kindly teased her in unison.

Clara looked around. Paola, Elena, Sofia, Giorgio and Matteo. Only two chairs were empty, and she hung her purse on one of them hoping Leonardo would soon occupy the other.

"Stop teasing me," she said, smiling. "I haven't been in this place forever. Is it under new management?"

"No! It is always the same legendary Mario," Matteo said enthusiastically.

"Come on, let's order," Paola suggested.

Clara gathered all the courage she had and, with her eyes closed so as not see her friends' faces, she asked, "Aren't we waiting for anybody else? There is still an empty chair."

"Marcello canceled at the last minute, but I don't think you know him," Sofia answered.

"What's up, Clara? You look disappointed," Paola said harshly. "Who were you hoping to find in that chair?"

Embarrassment reddened her face. Luckily the waiter arrived and shifted everybody's attention to the menu and the infinite list of pizzas.

"Did you see what a disastrous day today was for the stock market?" Matteo asked after the orders had been placed.

"Yeah, but it didn't start today. It's been a

while now," Giorgio added, dejectedly.

"The political situation is not helping, either. The investors are afraid," Elena made clear. "Somebody believes that the fact that the North League[2] won in Milan destabilized the markets and it's causing extreme reactions in the sector's operators," she added.

"What do you think of this interpretation of the events, Clara?" Paola asked her. "You live in Milan."

"I think the marketplaces fear more Tangentopoli[3] and all the plots that are coming out from the inquiries than the League obtaining more power," Clara answered, defending her city.

"Today Olivetti lost 2.61%," Matteo interjected.

"Really?" Sofia said, sounding alarmed. "I invested all the money my parents gave me for my graduation in their stocks."

"Don't worry," Giorgio reassured her. "I'm sure it happened only because they are doing the Capital Increase."

"Sofia, if I were you I wouldn't feel so secure," Matteo warned. "I'd sell that stock as soon as possible and recoup as much of your money as you can."

"I wouldn't be in a hurry," Giorgio said

---

[2] Federalist and regionalist political party of the right wing founded in 1991.

[3] Known also as "Bribesville", is a term coined by the media in the 1990s describing the corruption of Italian politics.

optimistically. "Yesterday Olivetti presented in London a new technology for telecommunication. They call it "wireless" and it is a way of transmitting data by ether; it's the future and they have the monopoly," he added.

"This is science fiction!" Paola commented.

"As a matter of fact, if you think about it, now everything is done by cables, but the installation of those cables is very expensive and not everybody can afford it. It'd be great if we could get rid of it," said Giorgio. "Not to mention all the buildings with historic or architectural restrictions that don't allow the invasive interventions necessary to put the cables."

"Giorgio, are you sure Olivetti has the monopoly on this new technology?" Clara asked. "I read that some of the strongest American companies are already providing something similar."

"Maybe, but Olivetti would be the only one for Europe," Giorgio answered.

"I'm sure that as long as they won't clean up the dirty connections between the Government, the Banks and the Political parties … " Elena started.

"But what clarity do you want them to make? They are all embroiled and they'll do anything to prevent the magistrates from doing their job. It's disgusting!" Matteo said.

"Last week they already found the first connections between businessmen, political parties and mafia," added Clara.

"And today the ex-Secretary of Justice was arrested for corruption and violation of the law on the political funding system," Elena continued.

"Right; for us they made up the slogan, 'More market, less Government,' and they want us to think that privatization looks like the solution to all the problems. Didn't you hear the great Professor Lienich last Saturday? But, at the same time, they don't tell us that even if a public company is privatized, it keeps a privileged relationship with the government that will continue to favor it and to give it financing and contracts," Giorgio said.

"Everything needs to be revised. All of Italy needs to be revised," Elena ruled pessimistically.

Clara, slightly bored by the conversation, checked the time.

"Guys, it is time for me to go home. I have a long day of studying ahead, tomorrow," she said, rising.

"Wait a little, come on," Elena said.

"Coffees are coming and then we'll all go," Giorgio insisted.

"Antisocial as usual," Paola commented with gritted teeth.

"If you sit down I'll offer you a cigarette," Matteo said grabbing her hand.

"Ok," Clara said smiling; "but only for the cigarette," she joked.

"Since when did you start smoking?" Sofia asked surprised.

"I don't smoke," Clara said lighting up a cigarette with Matteo's bright green lighter.

"I can see that," said Elena sarcastically.

Clara smiled. "Living in Milan, because of its pollution, is like smoking six cigarettes a day, so why deprive myself of a little cigarette when I'm here with my friends?" she said after enjoying the first inhalation.

"Speaking of privatization," Paola said as if she had to reveal a big secret to the girls, "did you hear that the new private TV station bought the exclusive to air the two most important fashion events of the year?"

"I heard!" Elena exclaimed incredulously. "It looks like they also fought over the location in Portofino and Capri."

"Ridiculous! Don't they have more important things to do?" asked a stunned Paola.

"Apparently, five stylists withdrew and signed with public TV to do a new show, Elena said.

"Really? Who are they?" Sofia asked.

"I think they are Valentino, Ferre', Dolce & Gabbana and Krizia," Paola answered.

~

Clara drove home quietly and climbed the stairs with the energy of a deflated balloon. She felt foolish for thinking Leonardo would have been there. She was ashamed of her feelings and also felt a coward for not doing anything to see him again but just wait and bask in her immature thoughts. Thankfully, everybody was asleep. She wouldn't have had the energy to fake her emotions, not this time. Her parent's bedroom was right across from hers, so she opened her door as quietly as possible and turned the light on only after closing the door behind her. On her pillow there was a note and she could recognize her mother's calligraphy: Leonardo called.

No!!! I mean, YES!!! But no, I wasn't here. Damn! But he called! We met last Saturday and today is Tuesday ... not bad for someone who doesn't like to rush! Thought Clara triumphantly. *What if he doesn't call again? What if he is mad because I was not home waiting for his call? That would be crazy. What if he waits months to call back? I'd be the one to go crazy.*

She couldn't stop thinking about him. With one handshake, one look and a few words, he had torn down her world and left her without defenses. She had trusted him, she had confided in him. She was scared. She needed to find again the immediate synchronicity that united them. For a few, brief moments she tasted what life could be and she didn't want to give up that sublime feeling. With him, she felt like a lioness, powerful and invincible.

~

The next morning, her father's singing voice woke her as usual at seven o'clock and the day slowly started. After she had been studying for more than three hours, she decided to take a break with a cup of tea in the kitchen. The phone rang. The thought that it could be Leonardo paralyzed her.

What if it's not him? I'll be crushed. But what if it's him? Oh, my! Maybe I should take the call because if I don't answer he will get discouraged, but if I answer he could...

And then, the phone stopped ringing.

Now I'll never know... She was regretting having not picked up the phone.

"Clara, didn't you hear the phone ringing?" Maria asked peeping her head inside the kitchen. "It's for you; I think it's the boy from the other night," she added disappearing.

Clara felt her hair straightening up, her heartbeat stopping and her eyes widening. Holding her breath, she ran to the phone in her father's office where she was sure nobody could hear her. Before picking up the handset, she sat in the armchair, took a deep breath and spoke in her most relaxed voice, pretending she didn't know who was calling.

"Hello."

"Hi Clara, it's Leonardo. Am I disturbing you?"

"Hi, Leonardo. Not at all, I was having a cup of tea," she answered calmly. "How are you?"

"I'm fine, thanks. I'm in Rome at the hospital. We are having a break and I'm calling from a pay phone. I don't have a lot of time, but, I'd like to see you again. Are you free next Sunday?" He sounded breathless.

"Sure! At what time would you like to meet?" Clara's voice trembled slightly, and she hoped he hadn't noticed.

"What about four?" asked Leonardo, sounding relieved.

"Four is great," Clara said cheerfully.

"I'll pick you up then. Could you tell me your address?"

"Via Polloni 54."

"Thanks! I have to run now. I'll see you Sunday," Leonardo said with enthusiasm.

"Ok, Sunday. Bye."

"Bye."

Clara hung up and saw the room spinning; a nice feeling between slumber and lucidity, confusion and joy. She waited a few minutes before leaving the armchair and then headed back to her bedroom.

Chapter 2
~ Creaking ~

In front of the open closet, Clara strived to think what to wear. Her mind was somewhere else. *What if I made a blunder? What if he is terribly boring and unpleasant? What if I find out he was just the product of my imagination?*

"For heaven's sake, Clara, try to wear something girly and feminine. Men like a woman in a dress," her mother said, trying to be helpful. "And don't forget the accessories; you are always so plain. I've bought you hundreds of earrings that you never wear. Wasted money, that's what it is."

Her mother was capable of always making her feel inadequate, but at least she brought her back to reality. So Clara finally opted for purple shorts, a colorful shirt, and sneakers.

The doorbell rang at four o'clock sharp. Clara rushed to the door, stopped by the family room threshold to say good-bye to her parents, and darted outside before they could criticize what she was wearing. Their last minute advice would be as pleasant as salt on a wound. Clara heard her mother say something, but she was already running down the stairs. She opened the front door smiling and turned around to close it. Her sun-kissed hair twirled around releasing a green apple scent and when she stopped, she saw Leonardo silently admiring her. He looked captivated by her moves. He was wearing classic suit pants, lace up shoes, and a shirt with rolled sleeves that showed his forearms.

"Hi!" he said, welcoming her and sounding relieved.

"Hi!" answered Clara pleased he was exactly as she remembered.

He had an eye-catching dark green Alfa Romeo.

"Where are we going?" she asked getting into the car.

"It's a surprise."

As soon as Clara fastened her seatbelt she felt at home. She started exploring the inside of the car; it had a lot of buttons to push, pockets to examine, drawers to open and lights to try. Leonardo watched her, astonished and amazed as if it was the first time someone acted like that in his car.

"Are you here for the whole summer?" asked Leonardo.

"No. Actually I should still be in Milan, but the weather is warmer than usual and I decided to come here for a few days. I have an exam at the end of July and then I promised my roommate Francesca I would visit her in Cortina. And you? Any plans for the summer?" asked Clara opening the sun visor and looking in the hidden mirror.

"In August I have to go to Sardinia with my

cousin Andrea. We are both passionate about windsurfing and I know a lot of places where we can have fun," he replied.

"My mom's parents are from Sardinia. Well, now only my grandma is alive and she lives upstairs from us. I love Sardinia," Clara said trying to cover the light embarrassment she could still sense in the air.

"Your father is a surgeon, you said," Leonardo inquired after a moment of silence. "Is your mom a doctor, too?"

"No, my mom is a teacher who decided to stay home. Why?" Clara asked intrigued.

"The other night, when I called and you were not home, your mom answered the phone," he said, smiling.

Clara blushed and shook her head.

"Oh, my, I'm not sure I really want to know. What did she say?" she asked, resigned, with a half smile on her lips.

"Nothing!" Leonardo laughed. "Don't worry. She just told me she knew I was a doctor and that she was in the same business. I simply wondered what she meant by that," Leonardo answered, still smiling.

"I wonder, too," Clara said, embarrassed.

"Your mom sounds like a cheerful person, but from the way you talk, one would think she is trouble," Leonardo said, shifting the engine down.

"Believe me, she is lot of trouble and definitely a character!" Clara concluded laughing.

Well, at least mom gave us a good line to help break the ice, Clara thought, and relaxed a little more. Leonardo had his eyes on the road; she turned toward him and began caressing him with her eyes. His long fingers clutched the steering wheel. Turgid veins marked his forearms. His lips thinned when he smiled showing white and slightly irregular teeth. Desire clenched her stomach. The traffic light in front of them turned red, and Leonardo stopped the car and turned his head toward her. His blue-eyed gaze gave her a chill.

"Do you know Paola well?" Clara asked.

"I can't say we are best friends, but I see her when I go out with Giorgio. Why?" Leonardo became curious.

"I was just wondering why she introduced me to everybody but you."

"I have no idea. She probably didn't know I was there. I came with Luca. We were late and sat down right behind you and Paola. The only thing I could see was your hair and part of your profile. I knew I wanted to know you and, usually, when I want something I don't wait for others to give it to me," he answered.

Clara felt her cheeks turn pink.

"So, is it Luca that was sitting next to you at dinner?" Clara inquired.

"Yes, we hadn't seen each other in a long time and had a lot of catching-up to do."

"Lucky you! I had to listen all dinner-long to that crazy man who sat across from me," said Clara.

"Who? The one who invented the AIDS vaccine and solved world hunger?" Leonardo joked.

"Yes, him!"

"He is a selfish little soul who, in order to live with himself, needs to feel at the center of the universe," said Leonardo.

"I didn't change seats only because I had Giorgio and Matteo nearby. I do admit they saved me!" Clara laughed.

"Do you know Paola well? I have never heard her speaking about you," Leonardo said.

"We grew up together. We attended the same schools in the same classrooms from kindergarten until the end of high school; in other words, we shared everything. Then we went to college and now we are not as close as we used to be. I think we want different things in life," answered Clara with a small sigh.

"What do you want?"

"That is the major difference between Paola and me; she appears to know what she wants. I thought I knew, but I'm not so sure anymore," answered Clara.

An unexpected curve interrupted her words. The street narrowed and began to climb upward. At the end, a small mountain arose, and on its top stood a beautiful fortress. Two round and squat towers supported a fortified wall that fiercely protected one side of the castle while the other sides fell sheer on the cliff.

"Are we going there?" asked Clara, admiring

the fortress.

"Yes. It is San Leo, have you ever been?"

"When I was younger. I don't remember much about it," answered Clara in a dreamy voice.

They parked the car. They slowly walked through the main piazza side-by-side, continuing their conversation without perceiving other people and not noticing the many coffee shops with tables outside. Leonardo asked about her family, and Clara wanted to hear all about his life in Rome.

"I'm an only child," Leonardo said. "My parents wanted me to carry on the family business, but I wanted to be a doctor. It took them a while to digest the news. And you?" he asked.

"I have two half brothers from my father's first marriage. They are older, married, not a source of trouble anymore. I am the remaining thorn in the flesh of my family; my dad is not young anymore and he wants me to finish college, find a job, and remove myself from his financial support. I don't blame him, but I feel like I can't be honest about my doubts and I sink deeper and deeper into my dilemmas," Clara said.

They reached the precipice. The view from the parapet was breathtaking. An endless vista of the Marecchia Valley from the Appennini Mountains, all the way down to the Adriatic Sea. Leaning on the railing that was hanging over the edge of the mountain, for the first time speechless, they looked at the panorama. It was a sequence of round hills covered by lush vegetation and stony, pointed peaks that rose from the valley's bottom. On the top of each one of the peaks was an old citadel or the ruin of a fortress that was a reminder of a turbulent past.

"What a stunning view," Clara said. "Now I understand why everybody tried for centuries to conquer this place; from here you can really dominate the whole valley."

"Did you know that in the seventeenth century San Leo was acquired by the Papal state and became a jail?" Leonardo asked her.

"No. I didn't remember that."

"Among the many criminals hosted here was also the famous Count of Cagliostro," he told her.

"For real? The villain that cheated the aristocrats all over Europe?" she asked, intrigued.

"Yes. He was finally convicted of alchemy and imprisoned for life right here, in the smallest cell of the castle. The only one with no doors, but just a small opening on the ceiling and a tiny window overlooking the valley," Leonardo answered.

"What torture *that* must have been," Clara said

"Do you remember the inside of the castle?" Leonardo asked with renewed energy.

"Not really," answered Clara timidly like a student who hadn't done her homework.

"Let's go in, then!" said Leonardo with a smile.

~

At the end of the castle tour, Leonardo took a look at the time.

"It's seven already," he said sadly.

"Well, I think it is time for me to go home and for you to go to Rome," Clara said, trying to sound cheerful.

"I have to admit," Leonardo interrupted her, "I asked you out on a Sunday at four so, in case the date didn't work out, I had my trip to Rome as an excuse to leave."

Clara giggled and tried to say something.

"No, wait, let me finish. I know you probably want to tell me I'm a jerk, but you need to know that when you opened your front door and I saw you, my heart stopped. Now, that I have spent time with you," he swallowed, "I don't want to leave. I don't want to be anywhere else," Leonardo concluded.

Clara laughed. For a moment, Leonardo thought he had ruined any chance he had with her.

"I understand," Clara said, adding, "I was very nervous, too. Everything happened very fast on Saturday night. It was intense; but today I was afraid you could be totally different. Now I'm not afraid anymore," Clara said, relieved to share these worries with him as well.

Leonardo's lips widened in a smile. "Would you like to have dinner with me, then?" he asked cheerfully and full of hopes.

"Sure. When?"

"Now."

"But you have to drive to Rome even if I'm not as terrible as you feared," Clara answered, surprised.

"That's no problem; I can leave after dinner. I don't have to be at the hospital until tomorrow morning, and even if I leave around eleven, I'll still have plenty of time to rest," he answered.

"Just let me call home and inform my parents I'll be late. Where are we going? Or is it another surprise?" she asked.

They stopped in a coffee shop right in the piazza. While Clara called home, Leonardo checked the yellow pages, found the number of the restaurant he was looking for, and made a reservation from the public phone on the counter. They drove for thirty minutes on a beautiful road immersed in nature that took them to the other side of the valley. The restaurant was a rustic medieval home built with big, exposed stones, and it was furnished with a classic elegant taste that recalled the medieval era. The owner accompanied them to the back of the restaurant and onto a deck sheer on the valley that faced the ocean. The table was waiting for them with a lighted candle, a small vase with a fresh white orchid, and a bottle of iced champagne. The waiter came and explained the menu. It was very refined, but at the same time respected the food traditions of the area. The restaurant's signature dish was a home-made stuffed pasta called "caramelle" because it resembled real candies. The dough was of different colors — red, green, yellow, black — and wrapped the filling of meats and cheeses like a candy. The condiment was a very light butter sauce that enhanced and tied together the flavors.

"Tell me more about Milan," said Leonardo after they ordered. "You said you don't like it. Why?"

Clara took a sip of the fresh sparkling wine before answering.

"At nineteen I loved the idea of living in a big city, and Milan stimulated my curiosity. It was in the North of the country and for me it meant open-mindedness. It was the Italian capital of fashion and of business, a city with the metro, center for the arts and culture with the gorgeous Brera neighborhood, the small avant-garde theaters and other very famous ones like La Scala. Instead, it revealed itself to be a city with iron rules where people seem cheery, carefree and open to new ideas, but in reality they are extremely competitive, prudish and closed-minded. They consider anyone who lives south of the Po River to be a second-class citizen, and they don't miss any opportunity to let you know it. I'm not sensitive, but after a while it's tiring," Clara sighed.

Leonardo was listening, not missing a single

word. "So, it didn't meet your expectations," he queried.

"I thought Milan would set me free, instead I'm more stuck than ever."

"Why did you want to go so far from home?" he asked, interested.

"I always knew I wanted to go away. For me, my town has always been the place to escape from. A place where I felt trapped. I was eight when I had my first thought about leaving there someday," she told him.

"And you still remember it?"

"As if it were today. I was in the car with my mother, our white FIAT 500. She had picked me up from embroidery class. It was autumn, the trees were bare and it was getting dark. I told her about my day and she started to reprimand me about something. I remember looking out of the car window thinking, 'Who cares, I'm leaving this place as soon as I can anyway,'" she said.

"So you did."

"Yes; but I thought that a change of environment would help me to find myself, my true essence, but instead, it didn't. I also chose Milan because, being almost two hundred miles from home, it would give me an excuse to not go home every weekend like the students in Bologna. I wanted to meet new people, try new lifestyles, and start to manage my life, my allowance and my time like an adult. Milan gave me the opportunity to step out of my comfort zone, whereas Bologna would have been like reliving high school all over again, but farther from home. Instead, here I am; I die a little more every day in that city and because of my law studies," she explained.

"What do you think went wrong?" Leonardo asked, even more attentive now.

"I don't know. I left my hometown because I felt like I didn't belong, but when I finally went away, I found out I didn't belong in the new place, either," she answered.

"And what did go wrong in Milan?" asked Leonardo, his attention piqued even further.

Clara took another sip of champagne before answering.

"I didn't belong since the beginning. The first day as a freshman started with mass in the Sant'Ambrogio Church that is right next to the university, and I knew right away something was off. All the other students were wearing business attire; the boys held briefcases and the girls were in white pearl necklaces and gold hoop earrings. I was in white Levi's and motorcycle boots. Then I found out that everybody is extremely business-oriented and so damned competitive. At the end of the day, I used to meet some of my classmates in one of the bars close to the campus. It was supposed to be our time to relax after a day of learning, but the only thing anyone could talk about was how many cups of coffee they drank during the day in order to be more focused and perceptive. Well, I'm coffee intolerant, and all they did was fight with each other to be the one who drinks more and the one who's most productive. But I've stopped thinking the problem is *outside*; right now I'm pretty sure something is wrong with *me*," Clara admitted.

The waiter came holding a wide tray; he served them the "caramelle," filled up their glasses, and left. Leonardo began to speak.

"You know," he started after a brief pause, "I grew up in a small town in the Appennini Mountains, where my parents were born. We used to spend the winter there and move to the coast for the rest of the year, where my family ran a hotel during the summer. So, since I started kindergarten I had two different schools, one in the mountains that I attended until spring and the other on the coast from spring to summer break. It's been very hard. Kids at that age are merciless about who doesn't belong to the group and, anywhere I was, I was an outsider. Nobody ever considered me one of them, 'one of the pack,' and I always felt like I didn't belong; but that gave me strength. Not belonging meant I was free to look inside myself and decide what I wanted," he told her.

Clara stared at Leonardo, amazed.

"You have the ability to look at reality from a different point of view, one that I never considered before, but, for some strange reason, it makes me comfortable. Talking with you is like finally going to the home I have always craved, but never found," she said.

Leonardo smiled.

"I think reality doesn't truly exist, Clara. I

think there are only points of view and when you talk about your own life what can be more important than your own impressions of things?"

"I was raised knowing that there is a very strong and objective reality out there to which I have to adjust at any cost or it'll discard me like useless material. The problem is that I'm miserably failing in this endless attempt to adapt," said Clara saddened.

"Why do you want to adapt? I think this is your first mistake. Of course you can't adjust; a rose is always a rose, even when it pretends to be a daisy," said Leonardo lovingly looking straight into her eyes. "You have to mold your life and choose your own reality."

"Sometimes, I feel so insecure," murmured Clara lowering her eyes.

"Looking at you I don't see an insecure woman, maybe a confused one."

"What do you mean? " Clara asked intrigued.

"For example, last Saturday when I met you, didn't you notice the difference between you and the other women?"

"Unfortunately, yes, I noticed. They were elegant and beautiful. I was shabby and plain," sighed Clara.

"That is not what I saw. I saw a bunch of girls trying very hard to make an impression, too hard in my opinion, and then there you were, with your pants and flats," he told her.

"Well ..." began Clara, chuckling.

"I'm just saying that an insecure person

usually doesn't act like you. You probably don't even realize it."

"Instead, you always seem so self-confident," she told him.

Leonardo moved his hand toward Clara, and his eyes suddenly became deep. Using his index finger, he traced an imaginary line on the tablecloth between the two of them.

"My self-confidence ends here," he said.

~

In front of Clara's house, a streetlamp illuminated them with a suffused pink light. Clara was leaning on the gate, Leonardo only a few steps away.

He sighed. "It's late, I must go or tomorrow I'll be a ghost." He spoke slowly as if trying to stop time.

"Of course you have to go. I don't want you to fall asleep at the steering wheel," she answered, looking at his lips.

"I'll stop for a double espresso before getting on the highway, but, before I go ..." his voice was so soft and calm. He went back to the car, opened the trunk and came back with a small package wrapped in green and yellow paper. Smiling, he got closer. Nervous, he handed it to her. Surprised, with her eyes wide open, she accepted it and opened it. She wanted to get close to him, thank him, but his lips confused her and her own desires embarrassed her.

Later, in her bedroom, she switched on the bedside lamp and set a big sturdy pillow behind her back. Instead of a kiss to remember, she had two books on which to meditate, "The Little Prince" by Antoine de Saint-Exupéry and "Siddhartha" by Hermann Hesse. She felt dazed, suspended in a dream. She began to read and Leonardo's voice permeated the room accompanying each word. The crying started.

~

Another meaningless day was about to begin. Her father was singing "Gelida Manina" from "la Boheme," and Clara was still seated on the bed holding the books in her hands. She gathered all her strength. It was time to set aside the sweet memories, to dry the tears cried during the night, to pretend the void left by his departure wasn't there, and to face the world.

"Good morning, honey! Did you see what a gorgeous day it is?" her father said, happy to see her entering the kitchen. His lighthearted voice contrasted with her mood and sounded like an insult to her emotions.

"Good morning," she answered looking down at the table, searching for a spoon.

"Hello, everybody!" her mother warbled as she entered the kitchen. "How was last night, Clara? You have to tell us everything," she cheerfully added.

"I have to go to work, honey, but I'm sure your mom will be a good listener," said her father kissing her on the cheek "I'll be back for lunch, my dear women!" and with that, he and his good mood disappeared.

Clara's father wasn't nosy and didn't feel the need to be updated on every bit of news. Over the years he made clear what his expectations were, and his attitude toward Clara's life was "I don't want to know everything, I'll just see you at the finish line." It gave Clara a great sense of responsibility, but also great anxiety and fear.

"Now that daddy is gone, tell me everything about last night," her mother said. "Did you find out who his parents are?"

Her mother, on the other hand, was curious and constantly looking for complicity. She always had a lot of questions — the wrong ones as far as Clara was concerned — and she always tried to be part of her life, pushing Clara to open up.

Clara began very cautiously.

"Everything was fine, mom. We went to San Leo and took the tour of the fortress."

"A cultural date. What a nice idea! He understood immediately how he has to treat you," her mother decided.

The conversation had just started and Clara knew exactly where her mother would take it: to the total debasement of feelings, to the disdain of emotions, to the derision of the heart.

"And dinner? I hope he took you to a place

worthy of you," her perfect red mouth said.

"On the hills of Cesena; a marvelous place. He reserved a table on the terrace with a candle and iced champagne," Clara answered, feeding her mother her favorite details, those that defined her reality and that gave solidity to her ideas.

Maria looked her daughter in the eyes.

"Today, you seem more cautious than the other day. Good. I hope that dating this guy will calm you down. I was scared, you know. You were rushing too much," her mother said with a grim voice, getting up from the chair. "You barely knew this guy and you already talked as if he were the man of your life," she chuckled going to the door.

"Well, maybe he is!" Clara answered, surprisingly confident.

~

Clara was in her room sitting at the desk studying when the phone rang. Something in the ringing tone told her it was Leonardo and she rushed to answer it.

"Hello!" she said impatiently grabbing the receiver.

"Hi!" said Leonardo on the other end of the phone "I'm on a break, I don't have a lot of time, but I wanted to tell you I had a great time last night."

His deep voice hit her right in the chest.

"I had a great time, too," Clara answered melting like sugar on fire.

"Do you have any plans for next Saturday?" Leonardo asked.

"Not yet. Why?" Clara asked feeling a bit of trepidation.

"I can leave Rome around one and I can pick you up around five-thirty. Is that ok?"

"Sure!" Clara answered. "Do you have anything particular in mind?"

"Not really."

"So, this time I'll choose where to go," Clare said satisfied.

"OK. Tell me Saturday. I have to go now. Bye."

"Bye" Clara said after he had already hung up.

Six more days to suffer. I'll go upstairs.

At the top of the stairs Clara found grandma's door open, an invitation to enter.

"Grandma, it's me. Where are you? " Clara called entering her grandmother's apartment.

"In the kitchen!" came the reply.

She was seated at the kitchen table, bent over a few papers, holding a pen in her hand.

"If you are busy I can come back later," Clara said.

"No, don't go. I'm done; it's just bills. How did it go last night?" she asked raising her head and showing her sad black eyes.

"It was perfect," Clara said joining grandma at the kitchen table. "Great harmony, just like the day we met."

"Good, good," grandma said folding the papers and slipping them in a leather case. "Did he kiss you?"

"Grandma!" Clara said caught by surprise.

"Did he? Yes or no," grandma smiled.

"No," she admitted feeling ashamed.

"No kiss on the first night is an excellent sign, dear. You probably already mean more to him than you think," grandma commented very pleased.

"To tell you the truth I was disappointed and worried. I was afraid he didn't have a good time, but this morning he called from the hospital and asked me out for next Saturday."

"Now Clara, listen to your old granny; try to stay focused on the present and, if you can, enjoy it, too. You are too young to truly understand what I'm about to say, but remember this; the present is everything you have. The future can give you hopes and motivation; the past is gone and pretty useless. Stay in the present as much as you can." she told Clara.

Clara was silent. Grandma stashed the file with the bills in a drawer; she raised her head and putting her hand on Clara's shoulder said, "Gilda is on today. Do you want to stay and watch it together?"

"Gilda!?! Our favorite! Of course I'll stay."

~

Saturday came and the doorbell rang as promised around five-thirty. Clara rushed down the stairs, took a deep breath, and calmly opened the front door. Leonardo was waiting at the gate holding a fleshy red rose with the longest stem she had ever seen.

"Hi," she said breathless from the excitement.

"A rose to a rose," Leonardo said handing her the flower and smiling.

"Thanks. You make me blush," said Clara shyly.

"You see? You are special also in the little things. It's not easy to find a person who can flush for a rose," he told her.

On the long and thorn-less stem, their hands touched.

"Are you 'The Little Prince' and am I your rose?" asked Clara smiling and turning pinker.

"I really hope I'll be able to take good care of you like the little prince did with his rose," Leonardo said calmly; then he asked curiously, "where are you taking me?"

"It's a surprise. Drive to Cesena and then I'll guide you," Clara answered cheerfully, closing the car door.

"As you wish milady!"

Leonardo exuded a fresh smell of citrus. Clara found him irresistible.

Once on the main street, they got stuck in traffic. The sidewalks were crowed with pedestrians going in every direction; families comprised of several generations wanted to reach the beach to expose grandparents and grandchildren to the safer evening sunrays. Groups of teenagers, who had slept under the burning midday sun, were going back to their hotel rooms to get ready for another wild night. Bikers imprudently crisscrossed between the cars, and scooters impatiently roared by the edge of the sidewalks. Clara saw a group of young boys and girls in front of a gelateria, and one of them caught her eye. Without thinking, as if it were the most natural thing to say, she turned toward Leonardo and said, "did you see what a nice ass that boy has?"

She immediately stopped, petrified, terrified. *What? Why did I just say such a stupid thing? My God, we are on the second date and I make such a squalid comment!?!? Am I crazy?*

She was looking straight at Leonardo. Time froze. She couldn't say how much time went by, but after an indeterminate infinite time, Leonardo looked at her.

"Finally, a person who speaks her mind!" he said sounding relieved.

"I'm sorry," said Clara recovering her speaking ability. "I know it sounded awful, I really didn't mean ..." she began to say before he interrupted her.

"Clara, I know exactly what you meant and I thank you for it; you saw a good looking man and you had the guts to say what you thought," concluded Leonardo feeling reassured.

"I know, but it was so inappropriate. It wasn't very elegant of me."

"It is the unsaid that I fear the most, Clara.

Nothing you say, especially if it is true, will hurt me more than what you think, but don't say."

"You are a very peculiar man, Leo," she said with a smile.

"And you are a very peculiar woman, Clara." He smiled back showing his white teeth.

They reached the end of the main road and the traffic finally thinned.

"I have to thank you for the books. I read both of them the same night and I cried until morning. Uninterruptedly. It was a great relief. You don't know me, but you have the ability to hit right at the core of my subconscious. I don't know how you can do it," she marveled.

"You are right, I don't really know you, but since the moment I first caught sight of you, I had the impression that I recognized you. Tell me, why did you cry reading the books?" he asked then.

"I cried because I'm Siddhartha, Leo. All my life, I have tried to behave, to not be a source of trouble, not to disappoint my parents and to live up to their expectations. I went to Catholic schools, I obeyed the nuns, I believed and accepted everything my family taught me. However, deep down a voice has always told me something different. I tried to ignore it, but the voice is still here and I can't get rid of it. On the contrary it's becoming stronger and stronger," she told him.

"What does it tell you?" asked Leonardo.

"It tells me this life I chose for myself is not

good for me and it wants me to look for something different. Unfortunately, it doesn't tell me what. My father, like Siddhartha's, presented to me his own reality like it was the only one possible for me too. I have tried to accept his opinions and to make his experience mine, but it hasn't worked. **I feel more and more alone in a world whose rules I don't understand.** When it was time to decide on my college, I followed his advice; he came home with newspapers, magazines and statistics about the best job opportunities and the best way to achieve them. He said law was my best choice because it would provide me with a lot of possibilities. I'm trying, but I feel miserable. I repressed my dreams for so long I don't even know what they are anymore. I always thought my town, the house where I grew up, and the life my parents gave me were a starting point for me, not my goal. I tried to compromise between my freedom and my father's desires for me and I probably displeased us both," Clara lamented.

"Don't you think you are too hard on yourself?" Leonardo asked.

"I don't think so. Four years ago, I tried to do something sensible. I deluded myself thinking going against my instinct was not a big deal. The reality of it is I sacrificed myself for my father's peace of mind and now I don't know who I am or what I want anymore."

Leonardo looked troubled. His eyes were serious.

"But if you hadn't had any interferences what would you have done?" he asked.

"I don't know."

"I don't believe that for a moment," Leonardo told her.

"I don't know," she said, and frustration raised her voice slightly. "Have you always done exactly what you wanted?" she asked challenging him.

"Yes," Leonardo said as if it was obvious.

"Well, that is something *I* don't believe for a moment," she said, still not satisfied.

"Of course, sometimes I have to do something I don't really like or want, but only to be able to achieve what I want," he answered.

"For example?" she asked curious.

"For example, I had to take a lot of exams I didn't really care about in order to be a doctor and finally devote myself to what I love to do."

"Why did you want to be a doctor?"

"It happened in a very ordinary way. When I was sixteen I had a motorcycle accident and I was hospitalized for several weeks. During that time, I had the opportunity to get to know other patients like myself, and we became something of a little community. I talked to them and I was very touched by some of their stories. At the same time, I observed the doctors, how they interacted with each other and with us. That was when I knew I wanted to be a physician. I wanted to help people in need and to be even better than the ones who cared for us," he explained.

"When you had to choose, was it a good time to apply to medical school?" Clara asked.

"When I applied to medical school, my parents acted as if I was throwing away the sacrifices of their entire life and all the statistics said there were already too many doctors in Italy. I thought about it and then I decided to follow my wishes anyway," he told her.

"Weren't you scared there would be no job once you graduated?"

"Not really. I decided to put passion before profit or security. I'd enjoy being a doctor even if nobody paid me, and I think this is the only way you can make choices in life. If you choose based only on profit and you don't get it, you really wasted it, but if you do something that you would even enjoy doing for free, everything that comes later is a reward or a gift."

"And weren't you scared of competition?" she queried.

"I think that competition doesn't really exist. I compete every day only against myself. When I do the best I can possibly do, then I win," he explained.

"Wow," Clara said rapt and amazed.

"So? What could you have done?" Leonardo asked again.

"You don't give up, do you?" Clara laughed. "I always wanted to try to create my own life in my own way, but I have also been afraid of rejection and I decided it was easier to be what others wanted me to be. It seemed safe, but somehow I lost myself in the transition."

"Try to think about it now, then," Leonardo implored her.

"It's not easy, I'm not used to thinking about what Clara wants."

~

When they entered the City of Cesena, Clara instructed Leonardo to turn on a wide boulevard, shaded by fragrant flowering linden trees and she showed him the parking lot where to stop.

"Here we are!" said Clara satisfied.

"A parking lot?" laughed Leonardo skeptical.

Clara got out of the car and pointed at a kiosk hidden behind tall scented bushes.

"It's piadina[1] day!" she said hopping around like a little kid.

The kiosk was a portable kitchen that had a white tent with a scalloped hem for a roof. Inside, a mother and two daughters, drenched in sweat, quickly accommodated the requests of the customers who stood in line. In a corner, a machine to stretch the dough was running, and a slicing machine was loaded with a huge prosciutto. In the back, the hot griddle was covered with the flat breads that were cooking and, in the front, on display and inviting, were

---

[1] Flat bread with no yeast typical of the Romagna region.

all the possible kinds of stuffing. Leonardo looked puzzled, but Clara was glowing with satisfaction. They ordered two piadina with prosciutto, arugula and soft cheese and two cans of soda, and went back to eat in the car.

Before swallowing the first big piece of bread Clara asked, "do you like it?"

"A lot!" said Leonardo enthusiastically.

"I don't mean the bread, which I'm sure you've had before, but I mean the way we are eating it."

"It's a lot of fun!" Leonardo answered.

"I'm so relieved. This is a love-it-or-hate-it kind of thing, nothing in between. I decided to take a chance and I'm glad you like it."

"It's not easy to surprise me, but I have to say you keep doing it," he replied.

"How can you really be surprised by something so simple?"

"Precisely because it is so simple! People, especially women, expect me to behave in a way that doesn't allow me to take them to eat stuffed bread in a parking lot," he said laughing, relaxed.

"But that is very sad, don't you think?" she asked him.

"Extremely sad, but it's the truth."

They were both happy. Inside the car, protected from the outside, they created a world that defied the universe's laws. Leonardo was funny, like a breath of fresh air. He was unexpected; he gave a new perspective to her life and she desired him. She wanted to touch him, feel him, breathe him and never let him go.

~

By the time they arrived back at Clara's it was already dark. Leonardo stopped the car in front of the gate.

"What are you doing tomorrow?" asked Leonardo. "We could go to the beach. I know a place where nobody would know us; we could spend the day and stay for dinner." He sounded enthusiastic.

"I can't tomorrow," Clara said feeling sad. "It is Paola's birthday and she organized a whole day of celebration. We are to meet at the beach and then go out for dinner. I'm so sorry; I don't want to go, but it's a tradition and I would hate to offend her."

"Ok, but I must see you before I go to Rome. Can we find a way to meet?" he asked then.

"Well, I should be home around ten thirty. If you don't mind waiting."

"I'll be in front of your house at ten thirty." He smiled.

It was time to say goodnight. This was the time to get closer, to hug and kiss. Their hands and lips hesitated, and a second later Leonardo was in his car waving his hand and Clara was in her bed — awake, longing, aching.

~

The next day Clara was supposed to meet Paola and several other people at the beach, but right after lunch the phone rang.

"I'm coming to your house," Paola said hanging up hastily.

After only a few minutes, she barged into Clara's bedroom.

"Paola! You came at lightning speed," Clara said startled. "I thought we were meeting at the beach. Has something happened?" asked Clara worriedly.

"I don't know," answered Paola bitterly "You tell me if something happened," she added enigmatically.

"What do you mean? You are scaring me"

"No need to be scared, Clara, just honest," Paola retorted.

Paola was standing in front of Clara with her hands on her hips as a sign of defiance and was looking straight into her eyes. Clara could almost touch her anger and impatience.

"So ..." said Clara, confused.

"So, last night somebody saw *someone* giving you a red rose!" exploded Paola.

"Even if that's true, I don't understand why you are so upset," answered Clara.

"I'm upset because you are plotting something big and didn't tell me anything!" Paola screamed outraged.

"I'm not plotting anything, Paola. Who told you?"

"Who told me?" Paola sneered. "Well, maybe Milan made you forget this is a small town and that someone is always watching," Paola said more and more rancorous. "So, who is he?"

Clara didn't want a fight. She couldn't understand Paola's agitation and felt a strange rage growing in her belly. "I simply met a person, he asked me out and gave me a rose," said Clara trying to calm her own anger and to minimize Paola's.

"Why didn't you tell me?" Paola asked still offended.

"There hasn't been either the time or the opportunity. And since when do I have to tell you everything immediately? I don't think you do the same with me," Clara defended herself.

"Ok, but now you tell me who he is. Right now!" Paola demanded.

Clara thought there was no reason to lie and that maybe sharing her feelings with a friend would be a relief.

"Leonardo," Clara said, hoping to end the fight and to find in Paola a friend in whom to finally confide.

"Exactly what I feared, but it's impossible! I can't believe it!" Paola screamed shocked.

Clara was surprised by Paola's incredulity and she became bitter. "Why it is so hard to believe?"

"You don't know him, but Leonardo is one of the most wanted men in town and, from what I understand, also in Rome." Paola's tone was condescending.

"So? I don't see how this has anything to do with me," Clara replied more annoyed.

"Clara, he is used to going out with older women, not students. He has successful entrepreneurs, established lawyers, and classy aristocrats calling him. His last girlfriend in Rome was a young countess who owned several palaces in the capital and large estates all over Italy," Paola said.

The more Paola talked the more Clara was unwilling to believe her. She was stunned.

"Look, I don't know anything about his girlfriends, I just know he asked me out and we had a good time," Clara replied trying to forget the vile feeling of having been deceived.

"Wake up Clara! He had a girl who picked him up in a Ferrari; do you really think he could be seriously interested in *you*?"

Clara's head was spinning; she was confused, she didn't understand what was happening. She felt the hearth caving in under her feet and she didn't know what to say to defend her own stupidity.

"Paola, I don't understand what you are trying to say and I'm not sure I even care."

"I'm saying leave him alone before it's too late; with a person like him you'll end up getting burned."

Paola made Clara promise to keep her informed, hugged her, and left satisfied like a person who had fulfilled her duty. Clara remained alone like a wounded warrior abandoned on the battlefield. *Betrayed!* Screamed a feeble voice in her agonizing heart. The person who always claimed to be her best friend just told her she wasn't worth the attention of a respectable man and the person to whom she confided her deepest thoughts was deceiving her. The wound Paola inflicted was deep and the pain excruciating. Nothing of what she had with Leonardo seemed real anymore. His words sounded empty and meaningless in retrospect; his eyes were the eyes of a traitor, his hands those of a murderer who killed her hopes. She felt stupid, unsophisticated and worthless. In her bedroom, she cried desperately, silently, like there was no tomorrow. She composed herself by breathing deeply in and out and putting icepacks on her eyes. Then, she put on a nice bikini and went to the beach to celebrate her friend's birthday.

~

It turned out to be a very long day. The effort to look happy and carefree wore her out completely. Participating in beach games was close to unbearable. The little chats and gossip were nauseating as she imagined they were talking about her in the same way when she was not around. Dinnertime came; she swallowed every bite without being able to taste its flavor and fighting the physical urge to throw up. After the cake, it was finally time to say goodbye. She hugged everybody, faking until the last smile. She kissed the birthday girl, thanking her for a wonderful and fun day, took her bike, and rode home. She was determined not to see Leonardo. She wanted to be alone with her pain. She had heard too many words already for one day and wanted to hear neither explanations nor more lies. She was just longing for some peace and the opportunity to feel sorry for herself in the silence of solitude. She was comforted in finding out Leonardo had not yet arrived. She was late and maybe he had already come and gone. After putting the bike into the garage, she went to the gate to close it and saw him, standing straight, handsome with his damned sleeves rolled up. Unaware of her torment, he was smiling, happy to see her. Clara looked straight into his eyes and suddenly all her defenses crashed under his gaze.

"What happened? You look like you spent the day crying," Leonardo asked sounding worried.

Clara found his question farcical; she had just spent the whole day with friends who had known her for her entire life and not one of them noticed she had puffy eyes and, here, a complete stranger, who was probably making fun of her, immediately knew something was wrong.

"Is that supposed to be a nice way of telling me I look awful?" she said trying to change the subject.

Leonardo answered seriously. "You know very well what I mean. What happened?"

Clara opened the gate wide to let him in.

"Come in, and hurry, before someone sees

you. We need to talk," she calmly said.

In a corner of the front yard there was a seat swing surrounded by a tall ivy hedge. Clara sat down, and Leonardo sat next to her. She smiled and asked him, her tone serious, "Why do you want to see me?"

"Haven't I been clear enough?" was his reply.

"If I'm asking, probably not. In fact, you definitely haven't been," she said, annoyed. "Paola told me about your girlfriends. She told me how refined and successful they all are. May I ask you what you are doing with me, a troubled student who has no idea what to do with her life, and who will probably waste it? Don't you know you can do better? Or do you need teasing material for your hospital's lunch breaks?" she asked him.

"I thought I told you that I want to see you because I like being with you. I think the problem here is not my conduct, but your friend's jealousy and the low opinion you have of yourself that makes you believe every bad thing they say," Leonardo said as if plunging his finger one more time in her weakest point. Clara didn't have the strength to take more insults and raised her voice.

"So you are saying that what Paola said is not true!"

"No. I'm saying that who I dated in the past doesn't have anything to do with how I feel about you now, and I'm saying that if you could see what I see when I look at you, you would have dismissed in a flash Paola and her obvious need to hurt you," he said.

Clara calmed down and looked intrigued.

"Why? What do you see when you look at me?" she asked after a short pause.

"I see a beautiful young woman, smart and profound. I see two big, sad and intimidating eyes that keep people at a distance, and a heart that is full of passion for life even if it doesn't really understand it completely. I see a strong willed human being who can't see that her own potential is endless, a proud woman who needs to trust herself more, and a swan among ducks," Leonardo told her.

"Ducks!?!" Clara chuckled.

"Compared to you, every other woman disappears. The problem is that you are the only one who doesn't know it. Your so-called friends don't miss a chance to hit you hard and for some reason you believe them."

"Leo, I need to ask you, why haven't you kissed me yet?" she asked keeping her eyes down.

"Because I want it too much and, for the first time in my life, I'm scared of my own feelings," he answered.

Clara raised her gaze, extended her hand, and lightly touched his cheek. She ran her fingers over his forehead and brushed his eyebrows.

"I don't know why, but I can't seem to help but trust you and I'll do it all the way — until the end. I'll trust you completely until you destroy me," Clara said staring at his lips and continuing to caress his face.

"But I don't want to hurt you, Clara. I want to take care of you," he softly said stopping her hand and grabbing her wrist. Their mouths hesitated once more and then surrendered to the inevitable. Their lips touched, and their mouths joined in a tender and passionate kiss. Each completely immersed in the other's mouth, nothing else mattered.

Chapter 3

~ Discovering Rome ~

Each morning, as soon as rounds were over, Leonardo ran to the phone in the nurses' station and called Clara. Just a quick ring to ask how she was doing and tell her he was thinking of her. Each night, before going to bed, he called her again from home; at first it was just to say goodnight, but soon, they started to stay on the phone longer, talking about their day, their feelings and their hopes. Clara connected an extension to the phone that was in her parents' room, dragged it into her room, leaving the cable hanging across the hallway, and hoped nobody would trip over it. Nestled in bed, she hugged the receiver as if it were Leonardo's body and got lost for hours in his deep and caressing voice.

One morning, Leonardo called as usual, but Clara answered in a bad mood.

"Good morning, how are you doing today?" he asked enthusiastically.

"Not well, I'm afraid," Clara answered pensive clasping the receiver. "I'm about to catch the train to Milan. My roommate Francesca called and we are having problems with Ella, the other girl who lives with us. I'm sorry, but I won't be here next

Saturday."

"What happened?" Leonardo asked worried.

"Francesca went back to Milan after spending few weeks at her parents' house and found the apartment a mess. Apparently, Ella has been stockpiling trash on the kitchen's balcony for weeks. Francesca said the smell is terrible and there are flying insects everywhere. She called crying and I really need to go help her," Clara explained.

"I understand."

"I'm very sorry, Leo. I was so looking forward to seeing you, but I cannot leave Francesca alone to deal with this; we'll have to wait one more week to see each other again," Clara concluded bitterly.

~

On the train to Milan, Clara was too busy cursing the day Ella came into her life to notice or appreciate the changing panorama outside the window. Her thoughts drifted backward. At the end of high school, on a sunny day close to the end of summer, her mother took her to Milan on a mission — find a respectable apartment and some virtuous roommates. They went straight from the station to the campus and checked the posting board that was next to the administrative office. It was overflowing with ads placed there by people offering their house or a part of it to students. One ad in particular caught her mother's attention; two girls were looking for two more people to share a two-bedroom apartment. The place was just a few bus stops from the university, so they decided to check it out. It was two o'clock; the scorching sun made the asphalt soft and Maria's heels sunk into the sidewalk leaving a mark with each and every step. The building was in a prestigious neighborhood; it was posh, classy and well kept. It had all the features her mother liked and Clara decided to show enthusiasm. Her mother stopped at the concierge desk and gave the doorman the third degree. Satisfied with the answers she received, she silently entered the elevator, totally focused on trying to use the few minutes she had to understand whether or not the girls were worthy of her daughter. Two well-dressed girls with no makeup opened the door and greeted them smiling.

"Hi, my name is Elisabetta and this is Lisa," they said to Clara after being properly introduced to her mother.

They were both Italian Literature majors; Elisabetta was a sophomore and Lisa a junior. They were kind and polite and explained what they expected from the cohabitation. Clara and her mother took the night to think it over and then, early the next morning, called Elisabetta and signed the contract. Clara shared the bedroom with Francesca, a strong girl from the Alps, with dark hair and muscular legs used to climbing mountains and taming the snow. She had come to Milan only because it was the closest city to Cortina with a university, but she was completely immune to the lure of the big city and truly missed the snowy peaks, the fresh air that smelled of clean, and the endless hikes in the woods. Sometimes, to alleviate her melancholy mood she pretended that Milan's tall buildings were mountains. In the beginning, she and Clara didn't like each other. Francesca was straightforward, frank and informal. Clara was polite, empathic and reserved. Finding a way to be in tune wasn't going to be easy, but it happened. After a few weeks, they both started to relax, to open up, and to appreciate each other's company and mutual advice. However, neither of them ever hit it off with Lisa and Elisabetta. Lisa had turned out to be a ghost; she used the apartment just as a front not to let her family know that she was living with her boyfriend. She showed up only when she needed a change of clothes or when a family member was in town. In that case, she forced everybody to put on a happy face and act like they were all best friends for a few hours. Elisabetta, on the other hand, was a good-looking, chubby girl who was full of herself; an aspiring actress who was trying to build her career more by dating professors than by studying her "craft." She never stopped bragging about her skills and the compliments she received from the faculty members. *Compliments for what?* Francesca and Clara giggled in their bedroom at night. They formed an odd couple, but with their different personalities, backgrounds, behavior and appearance they balanced each other perfectly and, at the end of the first academic year, they decided to move into a new apartment together and recruit a new roommate to help them with the rent and other expenses.

Finding the apartment had been relatively easy; the building was not as elegant as the previous one had been, but the owners were nice, friendly people, and the rent was very reasonable. It was a two-bedroom apartment with a decent kitchen overlooking a covered balcony and a big living room. Francesca chose the master bedroom, Clara instead, preferred the smaller one. All they needed was another girl to occupy the living room, and that was how Ella had come into their lives. The new academic year was about to start and they hadn't yet found anyone, so when Ella's mom called, they gladly gave her the room without asking too many questions. Ella was a tiny and frail girl from Sicily. She had long black hair, huge breasts and full lips. She was a freshman studying economics. She was not very inclined toward her academic studies, but interested in having fun and finding a wealthy man. For her, being away from the small Sicilian town from which she hailed meant freedom — an opportunity for emancipation and a chance to do what she could never have done had she remained closer to her family. Milan was her chance to never go back. Clara was well aware that each one of them had different reasons to be there and she respected that, but now that Leonardo was in her life, she felt like she had more important things to care about than to baby-sit an out-of-control sophomore. She was tired of having to deal with Ella's ungovernable way of life, tolerating her wild parties, with the loud music, the drugs and the weird guys around the house. She was tired of feeling uncomfortable in her own apartment — like the time she found Ella having sex on the kitchen counter with a complete stranger — or suffering the humiliation of coming back home and finding the police at the door to question them like criminals. It was more than enough to put up with the neighbors' nasty comments and calls, remedy the missed chores, her messiness, and having to deal with all the different men she brought home from bars and discos. She and Francesca could have called Ella's parents and tried to put a stop to it, but they were mesmerized by Ella's strong personality. She was the rebel girl who had the guts to do what they could only dream of. Ella entertained them for hours, describing her adventures in every detail, and they listened, fascinated. For Clara, the fascination ended the day Ella showed up, uninvited, at her parents' house during summer break and made a fool out of herself in front of all of Clara's friends. She got heavily drunk, brazenly hit on every male in the room, and showed everybody she wasn't wearing any underwear by spreading her legs on top of a coffee table. Clara realized then that listening to Ella's captivating stories didn't have anything to do with being part of them. What she had witnessed was not what she considered having a lot of fun and had nothing to do with being emancipated; for Clara it appeared to be pure squalor and the total decline of self-respect.

As soon as Clara arrived in Milan, she ran to the apartment. Francesca had just started to clean the balcony with tears rolling down her face.

"Look at this mess! A plague could start here!" she said as soon as she saw Clara.

Clara couldn't believe her eyes: the balcony was full of trash bags up to her waist; the summer's heat made the food ferment, insects were everywhere and the stench was nauseating.

"I'll put down my bag and be with you in a moment," Clara said to Francesca. She stopped, shocked, in front of the living room; Ella and her friends had painted on the wallpaper several sketches of naked people, marijuana leaves, and pot smokers.

"Oh, did I forget to tell you about the living room walls?" Francesca asked sarcastically.

"Where is Ella now?" Clara asked menacing.

"She went to Sicily for the rest of the summer."

"Good for her, but we can't wait for her to come back to fix this mess. We have to do it now," said Clara.

They got rid of all the trash bags and washed, cleaned and disinfected the entire balcony. Then, they moved to the living room, and with a ladder, a bucket full of warm water and some old towels they started ripping the wallpaper off the walls.

"I'm imagining this is Ella's head," laughed Francesca ripping a piece of wallpaper that she had in her hands.

~

By dinner time the apartment was livable again; no more flies, bees and wasps, no more drawings on the walls. Clara and Francesca were exhausted and decided to have Chinese food at the restaurant down the street.

"We deserve it!" said Clara.

The place looked like a garage that had been converted into a restaurant. The front door had an unattractive aluminum frame and was adorned with red lanterns on both sides. The inside was small, tacky with fake flowers decorating the tables. Paintings of colorful dragons and cherry blossoms were hanging on the walls. The owner, the cook, and the waiter were all Chinese and they didn't speak a word of Italian. They were glad to see two returning customers and welcomed Clara and Francesca with plenty of smiles and an abundance of curtsies. In front of the spring rolls, they relaxed and Clara told Francesca everything about Leonardo.

"I can see you are really taken by this Leo. I have never seen you so excited," said Francesca "I have some news too, you know?" she added smiling.

"What?" asked Clara, curiously noticing a sinful expression on Francesca's face. "Have you met somebody?"

"Yes!" she shouted jumping in her chair like she was finally releasing a buried secret. "But I haven't lost my mind like you. Not yet at least. With my previous bad luck I'm trying to stay grounded," answered Francesca.

"What? Like I have been lucky up until now? Tell me everything!"

"His name is Michele and he is very different..." started Francesca.

"But where is he from? Milan?" Clara interrupted her.

"Sorry, no. I met him at home; he is from Belluno."

"Francesca!" said Clara disapprovingly. "You always said you would never consider a boy from your region."

"I know, I know, but as I was saying he is very different from the typical guys from my region. He is nice, he is full of interests and he doesn't get drunk every night."

"Did you tell your parents?"

"Not yet. They think he is just a friend," laughed Francesca. "Do you think we'll be so naïve with our kids, too?"

"I don't know. But a lot of times I wonder whether my parents truly believe everything I tell them or if they just pretend to in order to have an easier life, but go on!" answered Clara.

Over chicken dumplings and some jasmine rice,

Clara forgot about all of her troubles and her fatigue. It was great to talk with Francesca.

Leonardo called before they went to bed.

"How did it go?" he asked in his usual warming voice.

"It was a mess, Leo. We have been working hard all day, digging through smelly garbage and sanitizing everything," Clara told him.

"You must be tired."

"Tired doesn't even start to describe how I feel," she answered, sounding weary.

"Look, I don't want to keep you too long, you need to rest. I just want to tell you I can't go a whole two weeks without seeing you. Tomorrow I'm coming to Milan."

"Really?" Clara jumped on the chair.

"Yes. If I go to the station directly from the hospital, I can catch the two o'clock train and be there at seven," he assured her.

"Can you stay for a few days?" Clara asked hopeful.

"No, I'll have to go back the next day," he answered sadly.

"But, that's crazy!"

"Crazy or not, I'm doing it. Because if I don't, then I'll go crazy for real," he said laughing. "Goodnight Clara, I'll see you tomorrow."

His words had been like a light kiss on her eyelids to wish her sweet dreams.

"Goodnight Leo."

Clara wanted to go to Francesca and tell her Leo was coming and warn her that tomorrow they absolutely needed to paint the living room, but she was too tired. That night she fell asleep without even remembering how she got to bed.

~

The next morning Clara and Francesca bought blue tape, paint brushes and plastic cloth, and painted the living room walls a classic cream color. With some music from the radio for background, the room was done by noon.

"Wow! That was fast. Why don't we do it regularly to make some money on the side?" joked Francesca.

"It's not a bad idea, we should seriously consider it," laughed Clara.

"So, now that everything is ready, are you ready for the big encounter?" Francesca teased Clara.

"I don't know. I look forward to seeing him, but when the time comes I never feel ready."

"You are just too emotional. Take a shower and relax. Tonight I'll stay at Lucia's place so I won't bother you lovebirds," Francesca told her.

"Don't be silly, you have to meet him. I hope you are not getting out of here for me."

"No worries, it was planned a long time ago. It's just happening at the right time and, don't worry, if he is everything you told me, I'm sure I'll have another opportunity to meet him, soon," Francesca said with a wink.

Clara tidied up her room and was in the shower when Francesca put her head inside the bathroom.

"I'm going! See you tomorrow. If you need more room, use my king-size bed!" she said to tease Clara.

"Silly!" laughed Clara tossing the soapy sponge at Francesca who avoided it by quickly closing the door.

~

Clara was ready. Seated on the couch, she tried to distract herself by watching some TV. When Leonardo rang the doorbell she jumped in her seat, her stomach shrank, her heart stopped and her knees trembled. She opened the door and anxiously waited for the elevator to arrive on her floor; it seemed slower than usual. The door opened and she saw Leonardo smiling. He looked surprisingly rested.

"Hi, Clara," he said happily.

"Hi. You arrived; how was the trip?" she asked clumsily.

"Great. I had time to sleep and read," he said getting closer and taking Clara's hands in his. She wanted to kiss him, but modesty prevented her from doing so. He hesitated, too. They both turned and went into the apartment.

"It's my first time in Milan. From what I saw from the cab it is a very nice city," he said to take some of the awkwardness out of the moment.

"Yes," Clara said distracted. "Do you have any luggage?"

"No. I came directly from the hospital. I just have my briefcase," Leonardo answered.

"Follow me, I'll give you a tour of the mansion!" she laughed.

Leonardo looked at Clara while she showed him the rooms and pictured her everyday life with her roommates. It was like discovering one more piece of her and an intense sense of tenderness pervaded him.

Clara stopped in the hallway.

"It's almost time for dinner. If we want to stay close by, there is a Chinese restaurant or a pizzeria; otherwise, we have the city to explore. What would you like to do?"

Leonardo's eyes turned warmer and his smile composed. A shiver ran through Clara's body. He gently took her hands.

"I don't really feel like going out," he said getting closer.

Clara felt her legs wobble; she moved one step back and leaned against the wall. She couldn't break away from his gaze. Leonardo pulled closer. His body gently pressed against hers. She perceived his muscles. She read his thoughts.

"You bewitched me, Clara," he said in a soft whisper on her neck.

Their lips touched, their tongues met. She played with his full and fleshy lips. He unbuttoned her shirt, exposed her lace bra, and caressed her breasts. She sighed in pleasure and arched her back against him. Now he was pushing her against the wall, lifting her arms and kissing her neck. She guided him toward the bed and took off her clothes while he was watching. His hands couldn't stay away from her. They were naked. The contact with his skin was intoxicating. Clara kissed his broad shoulders and his chest; descending on his carved abdomen, she wanted to go down more, but he stopped her, cupped her breasts in his hands and passionately kissed them, inserted the tip of his tongue in her navel and put his head between her legs. She timidly tried to lift him up grabbing him by his shoulders, but immediately surrendered at the delicate strokes of his tongue.

"You are so sweet," he said raising his head.

She was shaking with pleasure, trying to resist, but she soon succumbed to her pleasure.

"I want you so badly," she murmured.

"You make me lose control, Clara, and this frightens me," he said while placing his body on top.

"Lose control inside of me, then," she said softly opening her legs.

He looked in her eyes once more and slowly sunk into her.

She was embracing and soft. He was invasive and strong. They were both lost.

More exploring kisses and wild caresses followed. Totally oblivious of the passing of time, they ignored the morning sun's rays filtering through the shutters and the room getting brighter. Only when the alarm went off in Francesca's bedroom did they regain contact with the outside world and, clasped to each other among the sheets, took a look at the clock sitting on the bedside table.

It was nine am.

"We have been making love for almost fourteen hours straight," said Clara surprised and, pretending to be ashamed, she covered her face with the pillow.

Leonardo uncovered her face and kissed her lips.

"Are you ready for more?"

~

Leonardo silently sat at the kitchen table while Clara moved around the kitchen. She could feel his eyes watching her while she put a pot of water on the stove for pasta, opened a can of tuna and a can of tomatoes, poured everything into a bowl and mixed. Leonardo's scent was still in her nostrils. They ate looking mesmerized into each other's eyes. The pasta was terrible and they both laughed, amused by the catastrophic tuna experiment.

After lunch, Clara decided to accompany him to the train station. On the bus, they held hands. On the metro, they couldn't stop kissing despite people's displeased looks. When his train left, they both cried silent teardrops. Clara took the trip in the opposite direction and went back home. She felt like an addict from whom the drugs have been taken away and she looked like one — pale, tired with black circles around her eyes. Nobody sat next to her. She kept her gaze fixed on the street without really watching. She felt only the overwhelming pain of him leaving. Now that his train was gone, she had no more energy, nothing to hold on to, and she suddenly felt exhausted and sore. The fatigue of the last couple of days took over and she fell asleep on the bus seat.

~

Maria was changing her nail polish in the bathroom. Tired of having red nails she was now longing for deep orange. Her face was already perfectly made up, but she kept looking in the magnifying mirror and checking for any possible imperfection.

"Hi, mom!" said Clara loudly.

"For God's sake, Clara, you made me spill nail polish everywhere! I didn't know you were back from Milan," snapped a startled Maria.

"I came back last night. You and dad were asleep."

"So? Did you have the opportunity to concentrate on your exam or did you spend time only cleaning and painting?"

"Mom, don't worry."

"Anyway, I'm glad you are back," Maria said cleaning up the orange spill with a tissue, adding, "You know what happened yesterday? I met my friend Sofia, the owner of the fur factory. She said they just opened a luxurious showroom in Milan and her son, Nicola, is supervising it. Do you remember him?"

"No, I have no idea who he is," said Clara uninterested.

"But of course you know who he is, honey, you used to play together when you were kids. He is tall with dark hair, very good looking," she hesitated giving Clara time to remember.

"I told you I don't remember him, but go on," Clara said losing patience.

"Well, I told Sofia you live in Milan and I gave her your number. She said Nicola always had a crush on you. I'm sure he'll call you soon."

"Oh, mom, why?" she asked lowering her shoulders.

"Don't start young lady. Mothers are here to help," she said proudly.

Clara knew that trying to reason with her mother when she was "helping" was hopeless, so she decided to give up and went to the kitchen.

She couldn't stop thinking about Leonardo. The night they spent together left her with a sweet and sorrowful feeling. It felt delicious to want him even more, to think about his hands caressing her, his muscles pressing against her, his lips exploring her. She wanted him so much it hurt. It was sorrowful to think that she could almost count on both hands the number of hours that they had spent together before ending up in bed and that the majority of that time had been talking on the phone. She was in love with a stranger. *Everything he told me could be a lie, just an excuse to sleep with me and, now that he has, maybe he is having fun with other girls in Rome*

while I can't eat or sleep or study because of him.
Her fears increased even more when Leonardo called to say he was on call at the hospital and couldn't come up for the weekend. He sounded mortified, but Clara felt the world crumbling under her feet. She tried to stay calm, to focus on her exam, to make rationality prevail and make reason a priority. She went to grandma's to watch a movie, and even called Paola to make plans for the weekend, but it was hopeless. She couldn't find peace. The simple thought of not seeing him gave her an excruciating pain through her chest. Her heartbeat was so strong she could feel it bumping in her ears, day and night.

If I stay here I'll go crazy. I have to do something.

Her plan was risky, but worth it. She told her parents that she couldn't concentrate enough on the upcoming exam and wanted to go back to Milan to study in solitude.

"But you just came back!" protested her father.

"I know, dad, but the exam is in ten days and I really need to focus," she lied looking straight into his eyes.

She threw some clothes in a bag and checked the trains to Rome; then, she called Leonardo.

"I'll be in Termini Station tonight at 7:23 pm," she said to him without allowing any reply.

"I'll pick you up," was all he had time to say.

Her mother took her to the station and Clara jumped on the train to Milan, waving goodbye from the window like a diligent student worried about the upcoming exam. Once in Bologna, she got off and waited for the connecting train to Rome.

The compartment was empty; Clara chose a seat close to the window, sat down, and finally relaxed. She had never been in Rome before; it was way too far and too far south for her and she didn't know what to expect. The little voice in the corner of her heart was still saying she was acting stupid and would be making a fool out of herself, but she was slowly learning to let it talk without giving it too much authority. The flow of her thoughts made the three hours fly and suddenly the conductor announced that they were just ten minutes away from Rome. Clara's heart skipped a beat. She started to gather her things and sat straight on the edge of her seat with her bag on her lap, ready to spring off the train.

Leonardo was waiting. His sleeves were rolled up as usual, and the top button of his shirt was undone. Gazing at each other, they walked quickly among people and hugged. She dropped the bag and put her arms around his neck. With a serene smile, he kissed her and whispered,

"I missed you."

It was all she needed to hear.

~

The oblique evening sun boosted the colors of the city. The sky was a deep blue canvas in which flocks of starlings gracefully danced entertaining any who had the time to look up. The traffic was congested and the drivers anxious to go home at the end of the day. Scooters driven by men wearing suits and women in high heels zipped through the cars trying to avoid the holes in the asphalt. Narrow sidewalks were overcrowded with people and dominated by majestic buildings.

Leonardo's place was on the third floor of an elegant edifice. The doorman welcomed him, calling him "Dotto"[5] and winked at him as a sign of understanding when he noticed Clara. She blushed and was disturbed by the thought that, obviously, she wasn't the first woman to cross that **threshold** with him. She forgot about the annoying feeling in the elevator, when they grabbed each other and kissed for the whole ride up. The apartment was very nice and perfect for a bachelor. It had a big white and green eat-in kitchen, a large living room with a top-of-the-line sound system and a very unusual bedroom in which a big walnut closet covered two of the walls, and the bed was positioned in a corner. Gorgeous pieces of antique furniture were tastefully mixed with contemporary ones and Clara was surprised to notice the apartment was very clean.

"This is where I live," Leonardo said.

"It's a very nice place, I really like it," said Clara looking around approvingly.

Leonardo went into the bedroom and put her bag on the floor.

A deep red rose was lying on the pillow with a

---

[5] Roman slang for "Doctor".

small card attached saying, "Welcome home."

~

They decided to have dinner at a local trattoria behind the Colosseum. It was a teeny, tiny place with just a few tables that, during the summer, took possession of the front sidewalk and used it as its porch. It was walking distance from Leonardo's apartment and Clara enjoyed the light breeze that refreshed the hot summer air.

"It's incredible, this time we made it to the restaurant," joked Leonardo.

They gave a quick, uninterested look at the menu and ordered some food. They never stopped talking; always looking into each other's eyes, with their hands entwined, rubbing each other's knuckles. Clara freed one foot from her sandal and, delicately, massaged his legs under the table, smiling and anticipating pleasure.

"Let's go home," Leonardo said as soon as the check came.

They were alone on the sidewalk. Hand in hand, they began to walk home silently, as everything they had to say for the night had already been told.

"Kiss me," said Clara stopping under a lamppost.

Leonardo pulled her gently into a dark spot, against the wall of a building and kissed her. Slowly, she guided his hand between her legs.

"Your pants are wet," he whispered surprised while tasting her lips.

Clara hugged him.

"It's the effect you have on me," she blushed in the dark.

They rushed home. There was no time to wait for the elevator and they ran up the stairs. The door slammed behind them. His hands were everywhere. His mouth discovered her hidden secrets. Their bodies pressed, quivered, shook.

~

The next morning, the alarm clock rang waking them up.

"I have to run," Leonardo said jumping out of bed. "My shift starts at eight."

Clara was half-asleep and naked. The sound of the shower lulled her and the soft white pillow was a cloud in which to sink. When Leonardo came back in the room, she slightly opened her eyes and admired him while he was getting dressed. He was straightening his necktie in front of the mirror, the fresh scent of his aftershave filling the room. He was handsome in a suit.

"It's so unfair I have to work today," he complained while getting close to Clara to say goodbye.

"You are yummy in a suit," Clara said tasting his lips as he bent to kiss her.

"Clara, don't do that, you know I really have to

go or I'll be late," he begged her.

"I know, I know," she reassured him. " I'll see you when you come back."

"I should be here by six tonight. This is your home, do anything you like. Explore Rome if you want. You can find maps of the city in my desk."

"Don't worry about me. I'll be fine" she waved and turned over in the comfy bed.

The white sheet slid exposing her back before he left the room.

Clara heard the door opening and then immediately closing. *He is gone.* She closed her eyes for another nap.

"Clara, you are a very naughty girl," Leonardo said suddenly reappearing in the room, dropping his jacket on the floor.

Clara smiled.

He unzipped his pants and took her hard and deeply as if by pushing hard he could become part of her. It was quick. Intense. Then he collapsed on her breasts. Small drops of sweat beaded his forehead and Clara held him as if he were a little baby who just did something forbidden and needed reassuring.

~

In bed, alone, Clara could still feel his body on top of her and smell the scent of his aftershave on her chest. Trying to decide whether to get up or not, her thoughts went back to the night before and she basked in sweet memories. Birds were chirping right outside the window and two people were talking on the street. She couldn't hear what they were saying, but they sounded playful. A sudden desire to open the shutters and see the city grew in her.

Another ten minutes and I'll take a shower.

Suddenly, the phone rang. Her daydreaming was too good to be disturbed by a ring-tone and she covered her ears with the pillow. The answering machine went off and Leonardo's sexy voice began reciting the outgoing announcement. Clara was pleased to hear his voice again and rolled in the sheets.

The beep sounded and the totally unexpected happened; her mother's voice rumbled into the room, uninvited and menacing.

"I know you are there. Pick up the phone. Now!"

"Hi, mom," said Clara in a thin voice. She felt the size of an insect and wished to fly away.

"Clara, have you lost your mind?" Maria asked outraged.

"Mom, how did you know I was here?"

"How do I know!?! Well, young lady, you didn't call last night and you also forgot to warn your roommate of your sneaky little plan. But the question is not how I know, the question is what the hell occurred to you to go to Rome?!?"

"Mom."

"No, no, don't 'mommy' me. Is that what we taught you? Is this the way to behave? By now, he probably thinks you are a tramp, and you know why? Because you are acting like one! I put you on a train thinking you are going to Milan and, instead, you go in the opposite direction? And you have an exam to take! I'm disappointed, very disappointed, Clara," said her mother in the most condescending tone she could muster.

She was unstoppable, relentless and, probably right. What could Clara have possibly said in her defense? She felt stupid and naive. She wanted to sink into the center of the earth and never reemerge again. She felt like a little worm crawling in the dirt — useless and unworthy. Trying to feel better, she promised her mother that she would concentrate on the exam, reassuring her that everything would be fine and that she would take the first train to Milan. Her mother promised not to tell her father anything — "for now."

"I'm not keeping my mouth shut for *you*, but for your father's own good; he'd be crushed to know about your stupid behavior," her mother added before hanging up.

Clara was frozen. She couldn't hear the birds chirping anymore, the outside sounds were muted and she could hear only her brain buzzing. She felt alone in her compromising behavior. Overlapping thoughts expressed their disappointment, displeasure and disenchantment.

Under the shower, the cold water helped her clear her mind of the background noise. Every time she was with Leonardo everything was great; together they had common rules and common eyes through which to look at the world. Together, they created a new reality in which she was happy and comfortable. But as soon as he wasn't there, other people's points of view took over and she returned to being a lost girl with big sad eyes who felt wrong in the world. Opening the windows and looking at the sun helped her regain control of her emotions. The big mistake was already made and she couldn't leave without saying goodbye to Leonardo, so, she decided to go out, take a look at the city and enjoy the day. Clara started walking on the streets of Rome and, suddenly, felt free. A group of old people was chatting under the shade of a big tree on the sidewalk, while others were seated on a wooden bench playing a card game on a little folding table they obviously brought from home. She crossed the street and noticed the contrast between the gray sidewalk and colorful window displays of all different kinds of shops. Almost every corner had a coffee shop crowded with people acting as if they had known each other for a long time. Clara entered one for a glass of water; the bartender immediately knew she was not a familiar face and started talking to her, asking her questions and telling jokes. Clara stopped at a newsstand and bought the paper, and an irresistible vanilla aroma came from a bakery right around the corner where people were waiting in line to buy pastries for Sunday lunch with family. She was tempted to buy some huge cream puffs, but resisted and kept walking. A local farmers market attracted people to a beautiful little square; the stands had colorful umbrellas and Clara browsed through them with curiosity. Her attention was drawn to a lot of different vegetables she had never seen before. The vendors invited her to taste and buy their products and, noticing she was confused, they happily suggested recipes on how to cook them. Then, she took the bus and headed toward Piazza Venezia, the big square where Mussolini used to appear from the balcony of one of the buildings and declare his orations to the multitudes. Close to lunchtime, she stopped in a small grocery store that was displaying focaccia with all sorts of mouthwatering toppings. She bought two big pieces and ate them sitting on the Fountain of the Four Rivers in Piazza Navona, watching the tourists and cooling down from the heat accumulated during the walk. The city's colors were astonishing; Clara had never seen so many intense hues all together. The sky was a deep blue with soft white clouds, the buildings were red and the bright yellow sun lit up everything. It was pure poetry.

~

When Leonardo came home she was sitting on the sofa watching the news.

"Hey," he kissed her sitting next to her.

"Hi! How was your day?" she asked turning the TV off.

"Are you all right?" he sounded worried.

"I'm fine; I think I'm still disoriented by my walk. This city is fantastic!" said Clara looking into his eyes.

"Did you have fun?" Leonardo asked slightly apprehensive.

"I found a treasure. It never crossed my mind Rome could be so wonderful."

"I was worried you wouldn't like it," Leonardo sighed in relief.

"Until today my world was black and white, but wandering the streets of Rome I saw colors for the first time. It was amazing! Life is amazing!"

"I'm glad you liked it because I have plans for the next few days. I have a lot of places to show you," he told her.

Clara interrupted him before he could go further.

"My mother called. She knows I'm here and I promised her I'd go to Milan as soon as possible," she said mortified.

"What did she say? Was she angry?"

"Angry doesn't cover it. She was frantic, agitated, out of her mind and truly disappointed in me," Clara said with a sigh.

"But you are twenty-three; you are an adult and," he started.

"I'm twenty-two and I'm still a student. I depend on my parents. They are spending money for my education; I'm a few days away from an important exam, and what do I do? I go to a stranger's house to spend the night," said Clara, obviously disappointed in herself.

"A stranger, wow; is that you or your mother talking now?"

"It's my mother and the side of her that's inside of me. She said you are a stranger and I'm a whore, " Clara said bitterly.

"What!?!"

"Well, *she* said tramp, but we know what she meant, right? Every time I'm with you I feel I am where I was always meant to be. You and I look at life with the same eyes, we laugh at the same things, we understand each other without talking. But when I'm not with you, I find myself forced back into my black and white world. A world in which I don't understand the rules, but in which I'm forced to play anyway," she explained.

"It's the same for me, Clara, but I trust what we have. I believe in us."

"I still fluctuate," she said.

"Because you don't believe enough in yourself and maybe you don't believe enough in us," he said, hurt.

"I don't know. What I know is that my parents know how to hit me in my weakest point. It's always been like that. Every time I make a step forward they say one word and everything I conquered crumbles."

"But you need to grow up, to detach yourself from their moods. You are not responsible for their happiness," Leonardo assured her.

"It's easy to say, but since I was a kid, I have always thought my job was to protect them from frustrations. In my mind they are the weakest and I have to care for them."

"I have always found that my unhappiness doesn't do any good to anyone, but, if I'm happy, everyone around me is as well, even if they don't know why," Leonardo explained.

"I have a lot to learn from you, then. I remember

that when I was ten years old, right before I started middle school, I was sitting at the dinner table and my father started a long lecture about me growing up and having to follow my own nature. At the end of the speech, he made clear that I was free to do anything I wanted, but if my nature did not meet with his approval, he would close the door behind me and never open it again. I never understood his need to tell me such terrible thing at such a young age," Clara lamented.

"It was fear, Clara. Fear of losing you."

"You think so?"

"I'm sure of it. What else?" he queried.

"Well, I have always thought he couldn't have loved me for who I really was," she answered.

A tear ran down Clara's cheek and Leonardo tenderly embraced her in the silence of the room.

"Don't worry, Clara. Everything will be fine," he said as he held her close.

Chapter 4
~ Cortina ~

Clara's exam turned out to be a success. The professor congratulated her and approved her thesis, telling her he'd be happy to be her advisor. Her father was proud of her commitment and her mother forgot everything about the "Rome episode."

"Grandma, I can't stay with you tonight. I'm sorry. It's Leonardo's birthday and we are going out for dinner," Clara told her grandmother.

"Don't be sorry, dear. I'm happy for you and for him." Her lips were smiling, but her eyes conveyed a very different emotion.

When Clara came back from Milan she found that grandma had aged. She was bent over and more introverted than ever before. As a consequence of that, Clara made a real effort to spend more time with her even though during the weekends Leonardo totally monopolized her attention.

For his birthday, they had decided to spend the day in Numana, a little place on the coast just a few kilometers south, where the beaches were small, the sand coarse, the water crystal blue and where nobody knew them. They got used to the secrecy of their relationship and decided to keep it that way for a little longer.

That day Clara was happy, she hummed in her bedroom and felt very attractive. Her mother noticed.

"You look glowing today. What plans do you have?" her mother asked arranging the pillow on Clara's bed and trying to avoid looking into her daughter's eyes.

"We'll stay at the beach and then have dinner. I don't know anything more. I'm just happy to see him," Clara answered enthusiastically.

"I see; so things are going well between the two of you?" Maria asked lightly disappointed.

"Yes, mom." Clara cut it short **sensing her mother's feelings**.

"Outstanding!" Maria replied with too much emphasis. "I'm very glad you two are having fun together," and with that, she hastily left Clara's bedroom.

Lately her mother was acting strangely. She was cold and distant. Clara would have liked to ask her why, but decided to leave her alone and possibly avoid any kind of conversation that could turn out to be unpleasant. *If she has something to tell me, she'll tell me.*

For that special day at the beach, Clara decided to wear a vivid orange flared dress that barely covered her legs and that made her skin look even whiter. She felt confident, considering that orange was Leonardo's favorite color and that he loved her pale complexion.

The beach was fantastic. It had big umbrellas, beach beds and a small café that made it very functional, but at the same time, it was in a secluded bay and not crowded at all. They arrived when the sun was still scorching, lay down on the same beach bed under the shadow of a big umbrella and spent the first few hours clasped to each other, passionately kissing. Suddenly, in the afternoon, the wind changed direction, beginning to blow from the sea. Initially, the water's surface started to lightly ripple, but soon, the tiny undulations turned into high waves that crashed loudly on the shore.

Leonardo suggested having a swim and they both challenged the turbulent water like little kids usually do; they jumped the water's surges holding hands, hollering, enjoying being swept away by the foamy current and laughing with no inhibitions when they re-surfaced from the bottom.

Wet and chilled, Clara's bikini was sticking to her body like a second skin and Leonardo couldn't take his eyes off her.

Taking advantage of a longer pause between two waves, he got close to Clara and hugged her.

"I want you," he said sliding one finger under her bikini's bottom.

"Careful! People are watching," she joked kissing his lips and plunging into the sea.

The long swim gave them quite an appetite, so, once they were dry, they decided to go to the restaurant. It was a romantic little place on the beach just a few coves away. In order to reach it, they had to climb down an extremely steep and unstable stair made of wooden logs. The sun was about to set and it was inflaming everything in pink and orange; the water was calm, now, and the golden sand was still warm. Clara felt like she was on another planet. The table Leonardo reserved was right on the sand, in a private corner sheltered by a few hibiscus plants. They felt as if they were in their own little nest.

"Leo, it's really beautiful," she said. "I don't want to know how many other girls' hearts you won taking them here," she said looking at him sideways, but smiling.

"I came with some friends a few years ago and, I agree, it's better if I don't tell you how many women I won in this place," he said with a smile that meant she'd asked for it. Clara laughed.

"What would you like to eat?" he asked immediately after.

"You choose; it's *your* birthday! You know I like everything."

The owner approached them. He was a short, corpulent man, very tanned and with deep creases that marked his face. He looked like an old fisherman. He introduced himself and suggested the fresh catch of the day. Leonardo ordered a bottle of Prosecco, Catalana's lobster[6] and a mixed seafood grill.

"Clara, I have been thinking and," he started after the owner left, caressing her hand. "I want to cancel the vacation in Sardinia with my cousin."

"No. Leo, don't do it, please," she replied speaking from the bottom of her heart. "It's an engagement you had way before we met and I'm sure he is really counting on it. It wouldn't be

---

[6] Lobster with mixed fresh vegetables.

fair."

"But being distant is not fair either. I really don't think I can stay away from you for so long knowing you are here," Leonardo protested.

"I won't be here. I'll be in Cortina at Francesca's house and I sincerely think it will do us good to be apart for a while," she insisted.

"What are you saying, Clara? We are separated most of the time! Seeing each other from Saturday evening to Sunday night is not enough for me, I'm going crazy!" he said pulling back his hand.

"I know. It's hard for me also, but, trust me, we can use this further separation as a chance to understand more about us," she said gently taking his hand back into hers.

"Are you having doubts about us?" he asked, serious.

"No. I'm not having any doubts, but I truly think we should use this as an opportunity," she said smiling and timidly laying a foot on his leg under the table.

"Ok, then. You always win. It'll be hell, but I'll follow your wishes. But on the condition that you let me drive you to Francesca's and that, before I do, you officially introduce me to your parents."

"It's a deal!" she said satisfied. " You are right. It's time you meet them."

The food started arriving. They barely nibbled on it. Clara was completely captivated by Leonardo's eyes and voice while Leonardo couldn't turn away from her mouth and her smile.

"I have something to tell you, too," Clara said trying to remove any trace of embarrassment from her voice.

"I'm ready, I think. Shoot."

"I've decided to quit law school," she said quickly to get it rapidly off her chest.

"Good!" said Leonardo with a bright light in his eyes.

"Shouldn't you try to talk me out of it?" she said pretending to be disappointed. "Shouldn't you tell me that quitting four exams from the end is a waste? Isn't this the time to tell me it'd be wiser to finish what I started before engaging in a new adventure?"

Leonardo smiled.

"Apparently you already know all these things, why should I tell you again? I'm much more interested in knowing how being four exams from the end, makes you feel."

"Trapped and scared," said Clara without hesitation.

"I think quitting is a great idea. Most people wait until they are around forty to admit or discover that they are doing something they hate and, at that point they wasted far more than three years in the wrong college and far more opportunities. What would you like to do?" he asked Clara.

"Psychology, but I honestly don't know what I will do with it, not yet, at least."

"Try not to think of the route from A to B like a straight line or you'll be disappointed. Most of the time when we start a path it turns, bends and goes back a little. I think you are tired of walking and are ready to start running." He stopped and squeezed her hand tightly. "Clara ... I love you," he said emotionally for the first time.

She gasped and smiled.

Leonardo continued. "I have been crazy in love with you since the moment I saw your profile in Urbino, sitting behind you."

Clara blushed and clutched his hand. "I love you too. I have loved you since you came to introduce yourself with your confident attitude and ..."

"And what?" he asked giggling.

"And if you'd asked, I'd have made love to you that same night."

~

It became dark, the sky was black, the sand cold, and the horizon was illuminated only from a few lanterns hanging from the fishing boats' bows. Clara and Leonardo were still sitting at the table, but both dinner and the day were over, and knowing that it would soon be time to say goodbye was painful. He would have to take her home and leave for Rome. No more time to say I love you, to hug and kiss.

"Here is the check," said the waiter handing a crumpled piece of paper to Leonardo. "Please, take your time and thank you for joining us tonight," he added before disappearing.

"Excuse me for a moment," said Clara standing up and laying her napkin on the table.

"I'll meet you in the front, then," he smiled.

Leonardo silently watched her walking away. The little orange dress allowed him only a glimpse of her hips moving under it, but just imagining them gave him palpitations. When Clara opened the restroom door, Leonardo was standing in front of her with one hand on the doorframe and gently pushed her back inside.

"I need you," he said closing the door behind him.

His lips were already on her breasts and his fingers untied the strings of her bikini letting it drop to the floor. Clara took off his t-shirt and brushed his abs. Leonardo lifted her and Clara's legs wrapped him.

"I never have enough of you," he whispered sinking deeply into her.

"Push hard; you won't hurt me," said Clara brushing her tongue on his teeth.

Leonardo could hear Clara's soft moaning becoming intense while he wore her out with his kisses. They remained in a silent embrace that concealed the excruciating scream caused by the pain of having to say goodbye.

~

Maria heard a door bang hard and saw Clara on the kitchen doorstep.

"I've lost so much weight, nothing fits me anymore!" Clara said nervously on the verge of crying.

Her mother looked at her, unsure of what she meant.

"I'm not following, dear," she said turning off the burner and sitting on a chair.

"Leonardo is taking me to a charity ball at Villa Carlotta and I don't have anything to wear."

"You mean *the* annual charity ball at Villa Carlotta!?!" Maria asked with a spark in her eyes.

"Whatever. I've just lost so many pounds I disappear inside my own clothes," said Clara upset that her mother was more excited about the party than worried about her daughter losing excessive weight.

"Forget about your old clothes, darling!" her mother said glaring and getting up from the chair.

"For an event like *that* you need a new outfit and today we are going to spend some of your daddy's money!"

It was extremely rare for the two of them to go out together. Clara never liked to go shopping, but this was an opportunity her mother wouldn't have missed easily and, that same day, when the stores reopened after lunch break, she took her daughter to the most fancy boutique in town, determined to make her the queen of the ball. Clara couldn't remember the last time she saw her mother so happy. The unexplainable bad mood she was in completely disappeared in a split second. Maria was bursting with joy and Clara felt like she was taking her own teenage daughter out for shopping with unlimited funds.

~

Maria entered the boutique like a tornado, and immediately started browsing through the clothes. Two salesgirls observed them for a while from behind the counter with an austere look, but they both changed their attitude when Maria started bragging about Clara's invitation to Villa Carlotta. Succumbing to her mother's enthusiasm, the two girls let down their guard. They congratulated Clara, said they could only wish to be there themselves, and started showing off the most fabulous dresses they had.

"These are the new arrivals," the older girl said eagerly.

"Can you guarantee nobody will have the same outfit that night?" asked Maria sounding like a professional personal shopper.

Clara felt like a puppet in a show that wasn't hers. The two girls began bringing out clothes, emptying the back storage room, and taking them directly to her mother and ignoring Clara completely. Knowing little about the behavior of women in boutiques, she was surprised to witness the performance that was taking place in front of her. Snickers, comments on fabrics, appreciations of craftsmanship, praises for the new arrivals and the recitation of the perfect dressing etiquette. *How long can they discuss the shape of a skirt or the color of a belt?* Clara started feeling nervous.

"Mom?" she said trying to catch her attention, but her mother was too excited to hear.

After a few more timid attempts, Clara could no longer hold back her irritation.

"Given that I am the one who has to wear the

outfit, what do you all think if I start trying on something that I like?" she yelled attracting everybody's attention.

Silence filled the room. The salesgirls and Maria looked at each other surprised and suddenly remembered Clara's presence.

"Of course, honey," said Maria. "Why don't we start with this one?"

The parade started and, Clara had to admit, trying on all those clothes to see how they looked on her was fun. Bright, dark, sparkling, ridiculously short, too long, puffy, flowery, romantic, and trashy, she tried them all. The hassle was the fighting with her mother about what she looked good in. The two girls revealed themselves to be good salespersons; they understood the situation and also Clara's personality. Without inviting the wrath of Maria, they started to show more outfits that complied with Clara's character and she found what she liked. It was, of course, very different from what her mother had anticipated, but with the masterly ability of the salesgirls, Clara succeeded in getting her way.

"My gosh, Clara, with all the beautiful colors we saw, you had to choose an all black ensemble?" complained Maria while at the cash register.

"Black enhances your daughter's beautiful ivory skin," the older girl intervened skillfully.

"And black is not only always a classic, but it is also, without exception, extremely classy," added the younger girl.

"Yeah, sure. Extremely classy and extremely

boring," mocked Maria before giving up.

Mission accomplished. Clara was very pleased.

As soon as they were home, Clara ran upstairs to show the new purchase to grandma.

She found her sitting in the living room wearing her glasses as she fought with a thread that didn't want to go into the eye of a needle.

"Grandma, you should have come with us. You would have had a lot of fun watching mom and me fight over every single item," Clara said gaily.

"I can imagine the scene, my dear. I'm relieved to know you got your way. I really like what you chose," laughed grandma. "Do you want to stay with me tonight?"

"Sure."

"What about some bread, butter and sugar?" Anna joyfully suggested.

"Great idea," Clara answered.

It was her grandma's favorite snack. When Clara was a child, after her homework was finished, she loved to sneak upstairs and grandma always gave her a thick slice of bread spread with an even thicker layer of butter and sprinkled with sugar. Maybe it would help her to gain back some of the pounds she had lost.

~

The night of the party at Villa Carlotta came quickly. It was the first time Clara and Leonardo showed up together at a public event. It was time to let everybody know about their relationship and stop the hiding and deception. Clara was extremely nervous and, in her beautiful dress, she tried to look strong and relaxed squeezing Leonardo's hand.

The setting was absolutely fantastic. It was an old villa on the hills of Romagna surrounded by acres and acres of land. The legend said that five centuries before, Villa Carlotta had been destroyed by an earthquake sent by God during what was known as the "Ball of the Virgins," a ball organized for the purpose of introducing to society the girls who had just come of age, but that instead, it had turned into an orgy. For centuries it had been forgotten, until an old countess from Tuscany had decided to buy it, restore it, and return it to its original magnificence. The front garden was of a spectacular simplicity. A road lined with European beeches accompanied visitors from the front gate to the villa where it widened becoming a grassy square with two big fountains. Leonardo and Clara left the car to the valet and headed for the villa walking along flowerbeds of roses and lavender, magnolia trees and oleanders. On the grass, in the center of the garden, a runway covered in white silk had been set up on which spindly models would march, after dinner, to present to the public the new fashion trends for the next fall and winter seasons.

Clara and Leonardo were holding hands giving each other strength.

The first people they encountered were

Leonardo's acquaintances.

"You see? Nothing is going to happen, just take it easy and enjoy the event," said Leonardo putting one hand on her shoulder.

Walking toward one of the fountains they saw Giorgio.

"Hi, guys! How are you?" he greeted them warmly. "Wait a minute, are you *together*?" he asked incredulous.

Leonardo nodded in the affirmative. Clara smiled blushing.

"Well, I guess I missed something big between the day in Urbino and today, right?" Giorgio joked.

A brief exchange of witty remarks ensued, and then they parted company hoping to be seated at the same table for dinner.

"You are right, it's not so bad after all," said Clara satisfied also about their second encounter.

They decided to take a look at the inside of the villa; it was dazzling. The walls that survived the earthquake still had the original frescos, whereas precious canvases embellished those that had been recently built. In the main room, an orchestra was playing on a raised stage waiting for the guests to start dancing while, in two smaller rooms, there were tables for the buffets and still more to accommodate all the guests during dinner. Clara recognized some old friends from high school that were standing in front of a marble table topped with a golden mirror. Some of them were speaking while the rest were laughing very loudly, each holding a glass of wine in one hand and a cigarette in the other.

"Let's see if we can pass these people without being noticed," said Clara clutching Leonardo's hand.

But a girl with frizzy hair and cracked lips saw them and yelled Clara's name, waving her arms to make sure to be noticed.

"Hi Clara! How are you doing? You look thinner and thinner every time I meet you. Luckily I don't see you often or you would have disappeared by now," the girl said scanning Clara from head to toe.

"Sabrina," reproached a tall young man with curly hair, putting himself close to Clara. "This is not the way to greet an old friend you haven't seen in a long time."

"Hi, Antonio. How are you?" said Clara indifferently recognizing him.

"I'm well, thanks. Don't listen to her, Clara. You look gorgeous. You have always been beautiful. Tonight your skin looks softer than usual and, I know your skin very well," he added getting closer to her face. Clara took a step backward.

The girl next to him, probably his girlfriend, brusquely turned around with her eyes wide open to check what was happening and leaned against Antonio grabbing his arm.

Leonardo, instead, grabbed Clara by the waist and pulled her closer; both of them had established ownership.

"Who is that buffoon?" asked Leonardo annoyed when they left. "And what does he know about your skin?"

"Are you jealous?" asked Clara giggling. "Don't worry, he is just a jerk who has been trying to get into my panties since high school and never succeeded," Clara said hugging her beau tightly.

The orchestra was still playing, but nobody was dancing yet.

"There is Paola," said Clara alarmed. "I'm so nervous. I'd do anything to avoid her."

"Lets put an end to this torture, Clara," said Leonardo firmly. "It's becoming a ridiculous situation, and you have no reason to be afraid of her."

"You are right," replied Clara encouraged. "Sooner or later I have to face her, so let's do it now so we can concentrate on something else."

They got closer to Paola and the group of people she was with. Clara tried to maintain a calm attitude, opening her lips in a big smile and cheerfully greeting everyone.

Paola was pretending she hadn't seen her, but when Clara said hi she was forced to greet them.

"Hi, Leo!" she said with enthusiasm, then she lost her smile "Clara, I didn't expect to find you here. You are so pale, don't you ever go out during the day?"

Leonardo jumped in before Clara could say anything.

"Clara doesn't need to be tanned to be beautiful," he proudly replied.

"Oh my God! Someone must be seriously in love here," snapped back Paola with a mocking voice.

Clara found herself at a loss for something to say, unable to understand why Paola was being so hostile and malevolent. During their long friendship, they had lots of fights, but this time Clara knew it was different; Paola's bitterness seemed deep-rooted. The conversation was interrupted by the sound of bells encouraging the guests to sit down at the assigned tables, and Clara sighed with relief when she realized that Paola was seated at a different one.

The buffet was fantastic. Each corner of the room had been dedicated to a different kind of food. The corner with the appetizers and the one with the desserts were the two most colorful and decorated with sculptures carved out of fruit; they displayed delicious and inviting little bites of food stylishly laid on trays in patterns. The tables with the first and second courses were adorned with statues made of ice. The recipes were all traditional, but slightly modernized to indulge younger palates. The different kinds of pasta dishes were all handmade, and the seafood table was an explosion of opulence with an unlimited stock of lobsters and oysters. The whole presentation was stunning and innovative. Clara and Leonardo were having a pleasant dinner with the nice people seated at their table.

"I'm ready for the second round," exclaimed Giorgio getting up. "Who wants more? Clara, can I bring you anything?" he added gallantly.

"Thanks, why don't you bring something you like for the whole table, I'm sure we'll eat it!" she answered.

"Clara," broke in a young man called Gianni. "This means that you actually eat!" and trying to be funny, he added, "How can you eat so much and be so thin? I bet you spend all day sitting on the toilet!"

A quick pause of silence and then the whole table erupted with laughter. It took a moment for Clara to realize she was tired of all that farce, tired of everybody feeling entitled to tell her the first thing that came to their minds and tired of always responding with a smile hoping they would stop. Leonardo was about to say something, but she put a hand on his thigh to stop him. Within a fraction of a second, she turned, looked at Gianni and said, "Are you saying that the fact that you are fat, means you are full of shit?"

Everybody gasped, not expecting Clara to say anything of that sort.

"You deserved it, Gianni!" said Giorgio laughing and everybody followed him in bending over with laughter.

Clara joined the burst of laughter trying not to give too much value to her last words. She didn't feel relieved like she had hoped. Giving vent to her rage didn't make her proud of herself the way she thought it might.

~

The day after the party, Maria entered Clara's

bedroom waking her up before her father could start his morning lyrical performance; Maria was too curious to know all the details of the party. Clara decided to make her happy and really made a sincere effort to spend time describing all the possible details that she usually considered useless, but that her mother loved — the decoration of the villa, other people's outfits, jewelry, hairdos, food, and especially the comments other people made on Clara's dress. Her mother didn't ask anything about Leonardo. Clara didn't know if she didn't remember that the previous night was important because it was the first time she was showing herself in Leonardo's company or if she simply didn't want to acknowledge that her daughter was really serious about Leonardo. Clara was determined to ask her, but decided to give up. In a few hours Leonardo would meet her parents and, besides being very curious to see what was about to happen, she didn't want her mother to be in a bad mood.

Leonardo showed up after lunch perfectly on time. Clara's father decided to receive him in the family room to make the meeting an informal gathering, and when Leonardo entered the room he was reading the newspaper.

"Dad, this is Leonardo," Clara solemnly proclaimed hardly breathing.

Roberto got up, smiled, and the two men shook hands. The sheer curtain was closed to keep the early afternoon sun from reverberating in the room and preventing her father from reading; it diffused the light making the flowers on the pillows' fabric stand out. Clara sat on the couch and let Leonardo sit close to her father.

"It's an honor to meet you, doctor," said Leonardo with a big relaxed smile. "I'm a great admirer of your work. You have always been an inspiration to me and, one day, I hope to be a doctor of your stature."

"Well, thank you," answered the somewhat embarrassed Roberto surprised by Leonardo's confidence and talkativeness.

"Can we offer you anything? Maria!!!" he called with a thundering voice. "Where is your mother, Clara?"

Clara didn't know where her mother was, but soon enough the sound of heels banging across the floor and clanging metal preceded her arrival. Her mother emerged from the door wearing a caftan with big yellow and green flowers, gold bangles around her wrists and a necklace with stones as big as golf balls that made it difficult for her to hold her neck straight. She had backcombed her hair and it looked like an artichoke had landed on top of her head. Her makeup was flawless, but too black around the eyes and too red on the lips. The amount of perfume was dazing and Clara was grateful it was still summer and the windows were open.

"Hi, dear Leonardo, it's a pleasure to finally meet you," Maria said extending her hand and sounding like a dramatic actress in the old black and white movies.

Leonardo immediately sensed the character and tried to please her right away.

"The pleasure is all mine. Finally I know where Clara's beauty comes from," he said shaking her hand and slightly bowing while she giggled.

Clara didn't know he could be such a charmer. It was fun watching them.

Roberto cleared his throat and regained Leonardo's attention. The two of them started talking about medicine and plans for Leonardo's future. They looked and sounded in tune and at ease with each other. Maria felt left out of the conversation and was not interested in what they were saying, so she tried to get back in and fulfill her own curiosity.

"So Leonardo, do you have any siblings?" she asked out of the blue interrupting Roberto's sentence.

"No, I'm an only child," Leonardo answered very politely.

"Where do you live in Rome?" she continued the questioning.

"I bought an apartment in the district of San Giovanni. It's close to my hospital," he said candidly.

"I see. I have friends in the Parioli neighborhood, but, of course, that one is the most elegant in Rome," she kept going using a nasal voice that she probably considered aristocratic.

"And, what do your parents do? I'm sure I don't know them."

She had reached the point, the main question had been finally expressed, but Clara felt like the conversation was about to derail and that her mother needed to be stopped.

"I think Leonardo wants a cup of coffee, mom. Why don't you come with me into the kitchen and help me? I'm sure he'll appreciate one of your unique homemade blends," she said pulling her mother by one of her wide sleeves.

When Leonardo left, Maria didn't say a word. She silently went into her bedroom to undress like a seasoned actress goes to her dressing room after the last applause. Roberto instead, called Clara back into the family room. He was still sitting in the armchair; the sun had moved and the room wasn't as bright as before. Now the flowers on the pillows were blurry.

"Clara, come here for a moment, honey," he said in a heavy voice. "The person you invited home today is not a boy, Clara, he is a man; a very fine one, but a man. You do understand this, right?"

"Yes, dad," said Clara staring at him.

"He is starting a medical career in Rome and, if he wants to keep practicing medicine at a high level, he will stay in Rome."

"Ok."

"What I mean, what I want to say is, just try to take it easy, at least for a while. Go slow, don't rush things," Roberto advised his daughter.

"Ok, dad. Don't worry," said Clara reassuring him, then, she went to her bedroom, leaving her father to his newspaper.

I think it is just a little too late, dad.

~

Clara's suitcase was in the trunk of Leonardo's

car. She waved goodbye to her parents from the front seat and they left. Leonardo was quiet and Clara broke the silence.

"I can't believe that when we see each other again it'll almost be September."

"I don't know what I'll do to pass the time with my cousin," he said sounding desperate.

"You'll surf in the deep blue sea of Sardinia. Poor you!" Clara tried to lift his spirits.

"And you'll have your friend," Leonardo answered thoughtful.

The atmosphere was heavy. They were both sad. Nobody was really forcing them to be apart and they felt like victims of their own will.

"I miss you already," Clara said reaching for him from her seat and caressing his cheek.

Leonardo, keeping one hand on the steering wheel, moved the other onto Clara's thigh. She felt a shiver running through her spine that awoke her senses.

"Leo, I have been trying to control myself since we left, please, don't provoke me," she begged.

"But I don't want you to control yourself," he smiled looking at her.

Clara leaned over to him, kissed him on the cheek and then rested her head on his shoulder.

"I don't think I can handle all this time without you," he said checking the rearview mirror. Then, he raised the hand he had on Clara's thigh further up and started to titillate her.

Clara gave him another kiss on the cheek then reached the corner of his mouth and inserted the tip of her tongue between his lips. He smiled amused. She let her hand delicately slide between his legs.

"Do you think you can keep driving?" she whispered in his ear.

"I'm sure," he whispered back.

She unzipped his jeans and bent over.

~

Cortina d'Ampezzo was a little town nestled in a verdant valley in the heart of the Dolomites. The beauty of the surrounding mountains made it an elite destination for the European upper class since the 18th century. On those mountains, Clara had learned how to ski. Her mother insisted on buying an apartment in that enchanted place and her husband, exhausted by her persistence, surrendered to her wishes. So they got in the habit of spending part of year in Cortina, usually leaving right after Christmas and staying until the end of February. Her father went back and forth, Clara and her mother stayed the all time, while Aldo and Flavio, Clara's older brothers, who were in college at that time, joined them for the weekends bringing with them hordes of friends that made Maria crazy. The little downtown was home to elegant hotels and spas. The main street, Corso Italia, split Cortina in half and hosted the most prestigious names in fashion, small artisan shops, refined jewelers and antique shops. In front of the church, a charming little square was a place for locals and tourists to meet. Just outside the intricate streets of the little downtown, the roads narrowed and clambered up the hills becoming steeper and steeper leading to beautiful little villas. Clara loved the mountain lifestyle and devoted her time to the practice of winter sports; she had private skiing lessons in the morning and private ice-skating classes in the afternoon. The evenings were usually reserved for homework and TV. She also enjoyed strolling back and forth on Corso Italia with her mother elegantly dressed and showing off her wide collection of fur coats and matching fur hats. The time for the stroll was before dinner. At that hour, everybody emerged from their hotel rooms or from their houses smelling fresh after a shower and dressed in fashionable clothes. She loved to stop at the tearoom at the back of the church for a slice of pie or a hot chocolate with whipped cream. She liked to go check the fanciest deli stores for the new arrivals —porcini mushrooms preserved in oil, and venison sausages were her favorites. The place she loved the most, however, was "La Cooperativa," a three-story shopping center founded in 1893. On the cold winter nights it was always very crowed, but it had a toy store with the most unusual toys, and for Clara, going there was an adventure in which she discovered something new each time.

Soon after Clara became a teenager, the apartment was sold, but now, thanks to her unexpected friendship with Francesca, she was back in Cortina, thinking about her past and dreaming about her future.

~

Francesca's house was a beautiful white villa surrounded by spruces and larches with wide dark wood balconies lightened by blooming red geraniums. When they arrived, Francesca was waiting for them on the porch. The two friends hugged and Clara introduced her to Leonardo.

"I told you I would have another opportunity to meet him," Francesca said cheerfully. "I'm so happy you are here, Clara. We'll have fun!"

Francesca's parents invited Leonardo to stay for dinner and he happily accepted. Francesca's little sister, Lucia, quietly stared at Leonardo the whole time from her seat on the other side of the table.

Francesca's parents were very nice people — kind, warm and wise. Since it was very late, they invited Leonardo to stay the night in order to postpone the five-hour drive until the next day.

"Thanks, you are very kind to offer, but my cousin and I have the ferry from Civitavecchia tomorrow at two," he told them.

"I envy your energy young man," said Francesca's dad shaking Leonardo's hand.

Outside, under the porch, it was a cold summer night. Clara and Leonardo couldn't break away from each other's arms.

"I really have to go now," he told Clara.

"I know," she replied.

"I'll miss you."

"Me too," was all she could muster.

"I love you."

"I love you too. Now go or you'll be too tired to drive," Clara warned.

"Ok, I'll go now."

"I love you," she reminded him.

"I love you, too," he whispered.

"Kiss me."

~

As soon as Clara was alone she realized that Leonardo was right; it wasn't going to be easy being apart. The vacation was already turning out to be very different from what she had anticipated.

Francesca had applied for an internship in a preschool and had been accepted so, she left every morning before everybody else woke up and returned no earlier than three in the afternoon. Francesca's parents went to work and took Lucia to a neighbor's house where she could play with two girls of her same age. Therefore Clara started the days completely alone, in a house that wasn't hers and with her only goal in mind to find a way to make time go faster. The first thing she tried to do was linger in bed longer hoping that the unconscious sleeping state could calm both her anxiety to leave and her circular thoughts about Leonardo, but it was a failure. She couldn't fall back to sleep and the result was her being even more anxious. What should have been a relish under the blankets was instead a nervous tossing and turning trying to ignore the shattering beats of her heart. So she preferred to wait until everybody was out, get up and face the days. Francesca's mom always left everything Clara needed for breakfast on the table and always made sure that her favorite cake was available. It was a typical cake from that region, made with buckwheat flour and red currant filling that for Clara was a real delicacy.

After breakfast Clara situated herself on the soft couch in the living room that faced the garden and patiently read the newspaper both to keep up with the daily news and to give the sun time to warm up. Francesca and her family were used to the crisp and dry August morning air, but Clara was a beach town girl used to a hot and humid summer, and before being able to go outside she needed the air to thaw. So she waited for the late morning to arrive and then went for long walks along the trails in the woods or on the sidewalks going toward the little downtown. She brought along a sandwich and a bottle of water from home and had lunch alone with her thoughts.

The afternoons were easier. Francesca was back and there was always something to do — errands to run, Lucia to pick up, shopping, and sometimes cooking. After dinner they always went out. Michele picked them up and then they joined some of their friends for a beer or a dessert. Michele was a thin boy with bushy black hair that touched his shoulders. He was very nice and totally in love with Francesca.

"Tonight we'll meet Mario and Valentina in a new place that opened up just a few weeks ago, but is becoming very famous for its sweet pizzas," Michele said when the girls got into his car one evening.

"Sweet pizza!?!" asked Francesca puzzled.

"Have you ever tried it Clara?" asked Michele.

"No. Actually I didn't even know it existed," Clara answered amazed.

"It's a novelty. It is exactly the same dough as regular pizza and it is baked in the wood oven, but it has all kinds of sweet toppings," Michele explained.

"Sounds yummy," said Clara looking at Francesca. "I'm very curious to taste it."

The restaurant was a normal pizzeria with modest prices, full of young and loud people. The tables were assembled in a half circle around the wood-burning oven and they had red and white gingham tablecloths. A large counter in the back had a wide selection of wines and draft beers.

"We have a reservation under the name of Furlan," said Michele to the young girl who was seated next to the cash register.

"It is the table down there. The rest of your party is already here," she said pointing and smiling and extending her arm. On her wrist there was a tattoo of a big blue snowflake.

"What are you getting?" Francesca asked while perusing the sweet pizza menu.

"I don't know, everything is so attractive," answered Clara.

Mario and Valentina were both high-school friends of Francesca; he had hair color of wheat and eyes black like tar; she had hair dark like coal and blue eyes that seemed to be made of glass. They had been together since high school, never agreed on anything and were very nice. Clara listened to the conversation that was taking place at the table.

"Have you heard that Marco became a Reiki master?" Mario asked.

"So that's why we don't see him anymore," Valentina said sounding slightly annoyed.

"I still don't know what this Reiki is," said Francesca.

"It is a spiritual practice from Japan that is used as an alternative form of therapy," Michele said looking at her gently.

"That's what I've heard, but I don't think it can really work," Mario said sharply after sipping his cold and foamy beer.

Clara felt alone. The racket in the room slowed down her thoughts, but couldn't soothe the emptiness she felt from Leonardo's absence.

The waiter arrived with their sweet pizzas and everybody was speechless. In place of the tomato sauce there was a thick layer of custard topped with berries, pine nuts and powdered sugar. The comments had just calmed down and Clara was about to bite her first slice when she was interrupted.

"Clara! Is it really you!" she heard a voice without knowing from where it was coming. "Do you remember me? It's Nicola. Our moms are friends and we played together when we were kids; I can't believe I'm running into you here, of all places."

Clara had a brief moment of confusion then she remembered him and smiled. She recalled the dinners with their families, the games with his German Shepherd, and she linked him to the fur factory of which her mother told her a few weeks before.

"It's even more amazing to meet you here after so long knowing I'd have called you after the summer," he said happily "I just moved to Milan to supervise our new showroom and my mom asked your mom for your phone number. I'd really like if you could give me a guided tour of the city. What do you think?"

Francesca kept her eyes on Clara with a little naughty smile on her lips. She didn't want to miss a bit of their conversation.

Nicola didn't give Clara the time to answer to his question and kept talking nervously "Did you taste how good the sweet pizzas are?"

Clara lowered her gaze and saw her yummy pizza getting cold.

"What are you doing later?" pressed Nicola again without waiting for an answer "My friends and I are going to the bar at the Hotel Cristallo."

This time Clara was ready to answer "I'm going straight home. I'm with them and we are all very tired tonight," she answered, looking around at her tablemates.

Michele intervened with the enthusiasm of a little boy who hasn't understood what is really going on. "But tomorrow we will go to a billiard room. There is a very nice place that only the locals know, why don't you and your friends come with us? I can leave you my office phone number so we can make arrangements."

Clara's eyes zapped Francesca and frowned as if to ask her what was in Michele's mind. Francesca answered widening her eyes and raising her shoulders as if to say she had no idea.

"Great!" Nicola said "Thanks! I'll see you all tomorrow."

"What occurred to you to invite him? What were you thinking?" Francesca scolded him as soon as Nicola had returned to his own table. "We don't even know him."

Michele was stunned "Why are you mad at me? I did it for Clara; they seemed to be old friends, and then, I liked him," he said to justify himself.

"Didn't you see Clara's face while he was talking? You men are just on another planet," Francesca criticized.

"Please don't fight because of me," Clara said. "It is not the end of the world if they come with us tomorrow night. I don't know the others, but Michele is right; Nicola is a good guy and he is nice. It's just awkward because he always liked me, but I never liked him, and our mothers hope that we'll end up together."

"Hmm, I wonder if," Francesca stopped talking. Her eyes became sharp and she looked absorbed by an idea.

"What?" Clara curiously asked "What are you wondering? You look like someone who just solved a mystery," she continued smiling.

"Well, knowing you mom and her aversion for Leo, I wonder if she has anything to do with Nicola's fortuitous presence here in Cortina."

"Aha! I didn't think of that before, but I wouldn't be the least bit surprised."

~

The next morning, Clara listened for a few minutes to the total silence of the house and then went down to the kitchen. Next to her daily slice of buckwheat cake, she found a note from Francesca's mother. Leonardo called and left his hotel's telephone number. At the bottom of the note, she kindly asked Clara not make a long distance call from the house. It said nothing more, no time or day when to call. Clara forgot about breakfast, the cake, and the air that was still too cold. She ran to her room, got dressed quickly in the pair of jeans and the t-shirt that she found on the back of the chair, gathered all the coins she could find in the pockets of her other outfits and in her backpack, put them in her pocket and walked to downtown looking for a public phone. While she was walking she didn't notice the crisp air that made her face cold, her calves burning from the steep street, and the heavy breath that suffocated her from her quick and steady pace, but could only hear her heartbeat calling Leonardo's name. She saw the telephone booth in front of her and two people outside waiting to use it. She began diligently waiting her turn pretending to be calm, smiling to the other people ahead of her and checking her watch at each heartbeat. Her turn finally came, and she inserted the coins with shaking hands. A voice peppered with fake kindness answered and put her on hold. Now the phone was ringing in Leonardo's room and Clara was anticipating his voice.

"I'm sorry, but nobody is answering. They probably left already," said the same voice, but this time with a cold and detached tone.

"Thanks," Clara said and hung up. The disappointment was overwhelming and she couldn't hold back the tears. A young boy who was behind her saw her red and wet eyes.

"What happened? Did your cat die?" he mocked her.

Clara didn't hear him; in that moment in her mind there was no room for the outside world. Discouragement had invaded her and the tears were a simple and primitive way to express the crowded thoughts and feelings that were pervading her.

When Francesca came home that afternoon, Clara confided her emotions in an attempt to be free of a lot of tension.

"But please, don't think that I'm not happy to be here with you," she said, fearing Francesca might misinterpret her pain.

"I know, I know. Don't worry about my feelings, I'd be in exactly your same condition," Francesca answered hugging her. "I'm sure tonight you'll forget all about your heartaches with cocky Nicola around," she joked hoping to cheer Clara.

"Geez, I completely forgot," laughed Clara wiping her tears.

~

The place was an old log cabin with eight pool tables and a well-supplied bar. In the big garden in the back there were tables with benches, hammocks and swings. Michele and Francesca were recognized by the crowd and warmly greeted, while Clara, as a new face, was suspiciously inspected. They started a game in which Francesca and Clara alternated as Michele's rival. Nicola arrived soon after with two friends and, at their appearance, they received the same skeptical look reserved for all the strangers.

Michele called them. "Nicola, tell your friends to start a game. I'll destroy these two rookies in no time and then we can play together," he said winking at Francesca.

"I wouldn't be so sure. We can still destroy you," she answered matter-of-factly.

Every time that it was Clara's turn to hit the ball, Nicola stepped close to her to give her advice on how to position her hands, how to correctly bend on the table, and on what trajectory was best. Clara saw Michele and Francesca laughing at her back and she was almost laughing too. Even

Nicola's friends looked at them every once in a while and giggled.

"Francesca, I can't go on like this," Clara said when she had her friend at her fingertips "Let's leave these two here, get ourselves a couple of beers and go outside to drink them in peace."

"Are you kidding?!?" Francesca said smiling. "I'm having too much fun watching you and Nicola flirting. Didn't you notice how he washed and perfumed for you?"

"You'll pay for this," Clara said laughing and going back to the pool table.

The game ended and Clara could finally take Francesca outside leaving Michele and Nicola at the pool table. But every excuse was good for Nicola to come to them and tell them something.

"Clara, maybe your wishes are coming true," Francesca said interrupting Clara who was speaking. "Nicola's friends just put down the billiard cues and are talking with Nicola. I think they are leaving."

"Lets hope. Keep looking."

Michele and Nicola got close.

"Ladies, we decided to join you for a beer," Michele said barely holding back a big smile.

"My friends left," said Nicola. "But Michele was kind enough to offer to give me a lift when you go home," he concluded sitting down on the bench next to Clara.

Clara gave a withering look to Michele who answered with a facial expression that feigned innocence.

~

The next morning, Clara woke up ready to run to the phone booth in downtown. The house was silent; she went down to the kitchen already dressed and with her pockets full of coins. She wanted to go out as soon as possible and decided to eat only the cake in order to have the energy to deal with the distance she had to walk. She heard the noise of a car outside, but didn't give it too much attention; she wanted to hurry to straighten up the kitchen and race to the phone to call Leonardo. However, when she opened the front door, she found Nicola waiting for her in the front of the house.

"Hi!" he exclaimed as soon as he saw her. "Last night when Michele and I took you home I wasn't sure I understood where the house was, but this morning it was very easy to find."

Nicola's look gave Clara the creeps. She suddenly felt trapped with no way out. The house was isolated and out of sight from the neighbors; she was alone and Nicola was getting closer. She just wanted to get out of there as soon as possible so she turned toward the front door and pretended to say goodbye to Francesca's mom.

"Yes, don't worry!" she yelled. "I'll be back soon with your supplies."

Nicola was getting closer and closer. "What's up, Clara? You look scared. Are you afraid of me?"

"Don't be silly, Nicola. It is only that I can't stay; I have some errands to run for Francesca's mom who is waiting for me to return."

"Where are you going? I can give you a ride."

"To the Cooperativa," said Clara happy to get out of that isolated corner of Nicola's "paradise."

"Get in," he said to Clara pointing at his car.

Nicola continued to talk. "You'll think I'm crazy, but the fact that I moved to Milan, and that is the city where you live, and now meeting you here; I think that they are both signs of fate, Clara. A fate that is slowly bringing us together."

"Nicola, life is full of coincidences; anyway I already told you that I'd be happy to give you a tour of Milan, you don't need to convince me. I'm sure you'll be happy there."

Downtown was much easier to reach by car and seemed much closer than when she had to run, uphill, on a very narrow sidewalk. Clara, shrunken in her seat, was glad to see they had arrived.

"Clara, don't pretend you don't know what I'm saying; you know I've liked you since we were kids," Nicola said looking at her and almost running over a man who was crossing the street.

"Look in front of you, Nicola!" Clara warned him. "Listen, I'm sorry, but I'm in a relationship right now, and I'm deeply in love."

"But I won't give up on you," he said without losing hope as he stopped the car in a spot reserved for the Cooperativa's clients. "I have waited so long that I can wait a little longer. Even the biggest love stories end, you know?"

"I don't think this one will end," she warned.

"Clara, please," Nicola begged her with innocent puppy dog eyes. "Give me a chance. Just one. I don't think I'm asking too much. Fate brought me here while you are on vacation alone. Where is this great love of yours? Why did he leave you alone?"

"Nicola, you don't know anything about me. Please, you can't judge things you don't know anything about."

He seized her hand. Clara tried to take it back and Nicola squeezed it hard. He closed the car doors and the noise startled Clara. His eyes were inflamed.

"But I'm here now!" he screamed all of a sudden. "Take me, Clara! Lets make love and I promise I'll make you come like nobody ever did before," he said taking her hand to his mouth and sucking her pinkie.

Clara pulled her hand back violently and wrested herself free of his grip.

"What are you doing?!?" she shouted. "I probably made a mistake allowing you to drive me, but I just told you I'm in love with another man and you make such a scene? If you don't care about yourself, at least try to respect *my* feelings. And also, where is all this love for me coming from? We've known each other since we were kids; you know where I live and only now, suddenly, you can't live without me. Go tell somebody else your tale of woe and open this fucking car immediately!" She got out furious, angrily slammed the car door, and disappeared inside the Cooperativa. She hastily climbed the three steps to the entrance, sneaked in the first store she found open, leaned her back on the wall and collapsed onto her knees. She looked at her

156

pinkie and burst into laughter.

It took her a long time to get ahold of herself, but she resumed her usual composed attitude and was able to conquer her turn for the phone. The familiar receptionist from the concierge answered with her buttery voice and put her on hold. The phone rang like the day before.

"Hello!" answered a soft and deep sleepy voice.

"Leo, it's me!" Clara exclaimed with an enthusiasm she almost forgot she had.

"Clara, How are you? I miss you so much," he said waking up.

"I miss you too and I'm counting the days until this torture ends."

"This is much harder than I expected," he said whispering into the receiver so as not to be heard by his sleeping cousin.

"Leo, I love you immensely," said Clara with her mouth close to the receiver as if her voice could reach Leonardo sooner.

"You are the love of my life Clara. I'll be back the same day as you; I'll take my cousin home so I have an excuse to come to see you before I go back to Rome. If I can, I'll call you, but if I can't just wait for me, ok?"

He had just enough time to finish his sentence and the line broke off. Clara had no more coins.

Listening to his voice reassured her. He still loved her and missed her, but the call had been too short and left her with a bitter nostalgic aftertaste.

~

"No, no, please. My belly aches, I can't stop laughing!" Francesca said when Clara told her about her adventure with Nicola "Retell about the scene of him sucking your pinkie again!" she kept bursting into laughter from Clara's tales.

"At that point I lost my patience and I said everything that came to my mind." Clara was laughing, too, holding her belly to restrain the tremors.

"Oh, Clara, you should have told it when Michele was here."

"Why do you laugh so hard?" Lucia asked popping her head into Francesca's bedroom.

"Nothing. Go back to your room," Francesca told her little sister.

"I want to laugh too," Lucia replied.

"It's stuff for grown ups. Go to your bedroom."

~

On the train, Clara found a seat next to the window; she rested her forehead on it and never stopped looking outside. She saw the steep mountains getting away and the vast and fertile Po Valley with its wheat fields that had been harvested not long before getting closer. She felt like those fields that were only waiting to regain life. *Go train, move faster*, Clara implored longing for that sense of emptiness to disappear. When she arrived home, her parents were in the living room. Her father was in his chair reading the newspaper and brightened up when he saw her entering; her mother was on the sofa holding a gossip magazine. Clara knew it was impossible to postpone their questions about Cortina, Francesca and the beautiful vacation.

"Hi, I'm back," she said entering the living room and sitting down next to her mother. It was the moment of truth. The dreaded moment of the vacation report. The moment when her parents were eager to listen to her amusing tales about her vacation and when her mind unfailingly went blank. On the couch, with her parents' eyes fixed on her and longing to participate in her life, she felt like when she was little and they picked her up from summer camp. Seated in the car's back seat, she could feel their impatience to know everything and suddenly she had nothing to say.

"How did it go?" her father timidly asked widening his big green eyes.

Clara shrank into the sofa. *One thing, please. I just need one thing to tell them. Please, please come to me funny episode.*

Luckily Maria was full of endless questions that filled up Clara's silences.

So, what Clara perceived as an interrogation was soon over; her parents were satisfied with her scanty narration of the events and she went upstairs to hug grandma. She was in bed and Clara sat at her side. All of a sudden the things to tell were many.

"Are you ok, grandma?" asked Clara running

her fingers through her soft silvery hair spread on the ocher pillow.

Anna closed her eyes "Just a little tired. And you?"

"I missed you, grandma."

"Was it really so boring you missed grandma?" said Anna exposing her chipped tooth.

"Not exactly. It's just that I missed Leo very much and time didn't flow fast enough. At least, when he is in Rome, I can hear his voice, but these past weeks have been of total stillness and the energy and the optimism that he instills in me, has dissipated. When I'm not with him my stupid fears and insecurities return."

"You'll learn how to be your new self even when he is not around, but it will take time. Be patient, my dear, time is our best friend. Is he coming back today?" asked her grandma slowly getting up.

"Yes, tonight!"

"You have been brave to ask for this separation, Clara. I'm proud of you," her grandmother replied going toward the kitchen.

"Thanks," answered Clara embarrassed. "What can we do? Is there a movie to watch?"

"Of course. Are you staying?"

Summer was ending, the days were shorter and, after dinner, it was already dark.

Maria called from the staircase "Clara, we are going to bed!"

"Ok, mom. I'll come down when the movie ends. Good night!" called Clara without moving from her grandma's couch.

It was ten. Grandma and the movie were not enough to hold off her anxiety. *Where is he?* Clara thought pulling impatiently at her cuticles. Her heart was making her chest explode and she didn't know what to do to restrain it anymore. She checked her watch; the second hand had vanished, the minute hand had stopped, and time was refusing to go by.

"I can feel your heartbeat from here," grandma said taking Clara's hand. "Remember to breathe, at least every once in a while."

Finally, grandma's doorbell rang and Clara's heart stopped.

"It's him! I'll see you tomorrow," said Clara swiftly kissing grandma good night and vanishing without hesitation.

Leonardo ran up the outdoor stairs and stopped at the entry door. Clara rushed down holding her breath, and from the last step, jumped into Leonardo's arms and kissed him. His soft tongue searched her mouth and his scent melted her weak defenses. Wrapped in a tight embrace, she felt his contracting muscles and her primitive instincts — those that the separation had sent into slumber — awake.

"Now I can start breathing again. Don't leave me ever again," Clara whispered grabbing his forearms.

"I won't," he reassured her while his lips went slowly down her neck.

"I missed you so much," she whispered.

His delicate fingers slipped in her summer dress,

found her breasts and gradually glided over her hips. He grabbed them gently. Clara heard the rhythm of her breath getting heavy when his lips rested on her breast.

"I couldn't stop thinking about you," Leonardo said sitting down on the steps.

But now Clara didn't want any more words. She kindly shushed him with a kiss that suggested what she wanted from him. Slowly she sat on him. Leonardo grabbed her hips and gave a strong thrust of his back. She repressed a muffled scream. She held him by his shoulders, stroked his back and grabbed his arms. They turned and he pressed her against the stairs plunging deep between her legs. She lost control and moved harder under his strokes ignoring the edges of the steps bumping into her backbone.

"Marry me, Clara," he whispered before falling in her arms.

Everybody was asleep. The staircase was dark and they were lying down on the uncomfortable stairs, holding each other tightly and both completely exhausted.

"Did you hear what I said?" he asked timidly, raising his head.

"Yes," she answered.

"Well?"

"Well, I don't know if you just said it out of the impetuosity of passion so, I'm trying to give you a way out," she laughed nervously.

"Clara, I'm serious. You said to take this time apart to think about us and I did. I found out what I already knew. I'm miserable without you. I have never felt like this about anybody. It's impossible to imagine my life without you at my side. I don't know how long I can go on seeing you only one day a week. I'm sorry, it probably didn't come out the right way and at the right time, but ..."

"Oh, no, no trust me, it came out perfectly and at exactly the right time," she interrupted him brushing his hair.

"So? Do you want to marry me?" he impatiently asked again.

Clara kissed him passionately.

"My life started the moment you came into it; you brought me colors, you understand me, you give me strength, hope and, most of all you make me laugh. Yes, I want to marry you."

Chapter 5
~ San Leo ~

It was September. While the days were still warm, the nights started to be chilly. Classes in Milan had not yet resumed, so Clara was still at her parents' house. She was spending the days watching movies with grandma and the nights lying in bed hugging the receiver, pretending it was Leonardo's body and settling for his voice instead. She anxiously looked forward to their affectionate nightly conversations.

The time had come to decide whether to enroll in law school for the next year or quit now. Leonardo suggested that she keep everything as normal as possible and to wait for them to be married to start her new path in Rome, as his wife, in another university. It would definitely have been easier for her parents to swallow the news one bit at a time; first the wedding, then everything else.

"Just take it easy for a few months," Leonardo said during one of the interminable phone calls at the end of the day. "I'm sure once we tell our parents about the wedding, you'll be busy with the preparations, and then, next year, you can think about making a change."

"Ok. I think it's a good plan," agreed Clara. "But how are we going to survive until the wedding? I miss you more every day," she murmured into the receiver.

"I miss you too, but at least now, we know when this misery will end."

"Right; so, for now, we just act like nothing is going to happen, ok?"

"Ok, boss," he laughed.

Clara thought it would be very romantic to get married on the same day they had met.

"We met on Saturday," she murmured while browsing the calendar that was on her mother's desk and holding the receiver between chin and shoulder. "So next year it should be ... Sunday! Leo, it's perfect! It's Sunday!" she erupted with joy.

"When do you think it is best to tell our parents?" he asked amused by her exhilaration.

"I think it is better to wait at least until January. If we tell them sooner, they'll think we are crazy," she said laughing.

"They'll think that anyway, but it's up to you. Anything that makes you feel comfortable is fine with me."

"Do you love me?"

"Immensely."

"Do you miss me?"

"Terribly," he told her truthfully.

"Do you want me?"

"I can't stop thinking of you. And you? Do you love me?"

Whispering and repeating their feelings over and over made them feel close; unfortunately, however, it couldn't make the wedding come any faster. Even though it was a topic of all their conversations, it was still nine months away; an eternity.

~

One night Leonardo called and he was particularly joyful.

"I have something planned for Saturday night, Clara. Please, dream!" he said enthusiastically.

"What do you have in mind? Tell me, please, I'm too curious!" she said almost stomping her feet on the floor.

"It's your birthday and I have a surprise for you. That's all I can and will say."

"Oh, I love surprises! Tell me, tell me," she begged him.

"No, my dear Clara. I won't say a word. Just dream. I want you to be happy!"

Since that conversation, Clara had no rest. Her curiosity didn't allow her to think of anything else. Upstairs, with grandma, she tried to figure out the mystery.

"'Dream, Clara' he said. What could it be, grandma?" she asked before a cup of tea and a slice of bread with butter and sugar.

"I don't know, honey, but I like his passion. This boy is full of positive energy, I like him a lot, and I haven't even met him!"

"But I'm losing sleep over this!" Clara softly protested.

"Let's see," grandma said trying to be helpful.

"Could it be a fancy dinner?"

"I don't think so, we've had plenty of those; he said it'll be something different," she answered **rejecting the idea.**

"But if the place were really special ...maybe," Grandma tried to insist.

"No, I don't think so. It must be something else."

"A surprise party, then!"

"I really hope not! He knows I'd hate a surprise party. Oh no, grandma, what if it *is* a party?" now Clara was beginning to worry.

"Why don't we try to think about something else?" suggested grandma. "I'm sure it'll do you good."

"A movie, grandma. I need a movie," Clara said putting her mug in the sink.

"Let's look at what are they airing today!"

~

Clara impatiently waited for Saturday night. She was very excited. After dinner, she made up an excuse and waited for Leonardo seated on her bed with her coat on and her handbag in her hands. When Leonardo rang the doorbell she appeared for a quick moment in front of the living room where her parents were watching TV and rushed down the stairs.

"Have fun!" yelled her father, but she didn't answer. She was already outside and he heard the front gate closing. "Well, happy birthday," her father whispered to himself.

Maria quietly smirked.

Clara was finally in Leonardo's car.

"Hi," she sighed.

"Hi. How are you?" he answered.

"How am I !?! You kept me awake all week with this 'dream, my dear Clara' thing; I'm exhausted!" she joked smacking a big kiss on his lips.

"I'm sorry, I hope it'll be worth it," he said a little nervous.

"So, where are we going? You can tell me now."

"Actually, not yet," said Leonardo and, before starting the engine, he took a scarf out of his pocket and put it around Clara's eyes.

"Be a little more patient," he advised.

"Now that we are together, I have all the patience you could want," she laughed satisfied.

~

Clara couldn't tell how long they drove; being blindfolded took away her perception of time, but she felt the curves of the road and knew they were going up into the hills. After a few sharp turns, Leonardo stopped the car and carefully removed the scarf from her eyes. They were on top of the San Leo hill, right next to the fortress. The square was empty and Leonardo was able to park the car right in front of the railing on which they had leaned to confide their first secrets.

"We are in San Leo!" exclaimed Clara surprised.

"Yes. This is exactly where we came for our

first date and, if I had the guts, I would have done this that same day," said Leonardo holding her hand.

The sun was asleep. Millions of stars lighted up the black sky. The valley was dark, studded only by discreet rosy beacons that illuminated the castles on top of the surrounding hills.

"At night it's gorgeous, Leo! Thank you, this is great!" said Clara hugging him.

"But the surprise is not complete, yet," Leonardo added swallowing hard.

"No? What else?" asked Clara, moving toward him.

Leonardo took a small red box out of his pocket and opened it in front of her amazed eyes.

The light of the stars made the contents of the box sparkle.

"Leo, what is it? I mean, I know what is it, but, why?" she mumbled embarrassed and incredulous.

"Happy birthday, Clara! I love you more than anything," he said putting the ring on her trembling finger.

"It's beautiful; I don't know what to say"

"Don't say anything, words are overrated," his long fingers took her chin and he kissed her full on the mouth.

Silently, they reclined in the car's front seats and made love while a magnificent moon was watching.

~

The next morning, Clara went straight to her mother to show her the ring. She couldn't really anticipate the kind of reaction she would get; Maria was always unpredictable. She found her in bed and Clara sat on the mattress' edge next to her.

"Look what Leonardo gave me for my birthday," Clara said thrilled showing her finger and waiting for a reaction.

Maria's eyelashes fluttered incredulous.

"What a strange birthday present. Luckily we are in Italy and a ring doesn't mean you are getting married anytime soon!" she said with forced happiness.

Once more, her mother had chosen to turn her back on reality, but this time Clara didn't care and smiled back.

"Tell me everything about last night," her mother said sitting straight on the bed. She sounded curious and resigned.

Clara started to tell, emphasizing the feelings she and Leonardo had for each other.

Maria listened very carefully, then something changed and the resignation turned to irritation.

"However, Clara," her mother abruptly stopped her. "I keep asserting that you two are rushing things. Did you hear your father? You are too young to become so attached to someone; you have to think about your degree and your career before everything else. Plus we don't know anything about this guy. Only that he is now beginning his path in medicine and that he lives on the other side of Italy. I think this Leonardo is distracting you too much from your goals." she said angrily as she kicked off the bed. "Let's go to show this birthday present to grandma," she said grabbing Clara's hand.

"Mom!" Maria yelled once at top of the stairs "Where are you?"

"I'm in the living room as always, where else could I be? What is all this noise about?"

"Look what Leonardo gave Clara last night!" Maria said pulling Clara's hand seeming to forget it was attached to her arm.

"A ring!!!" Grandma exclaimed brightening. "Honey, I told you his intentions were serious!" Anna added satisfied.

"What are you saying, mom?" asked Maria shocked "What are you two talking about when you are here alone? I thought you were watching boring old movies," Maria said growing annoyed.

"Why are you so frantic, Maria?" asked grandma in a calm voice.

"Because I was telling Clara that she doesn't have to think for a moment that this means marriage. She is too young, right?"

"Oh, I see, you are looking for backup! Well, I'm sorry to disappoint you, dear, but I don't find anything wrong with two young people falling in love and wanting to start a life together and ..."

"Mom, it's not the thirties anymore; now women think about having an education and a job before getting married," Maria tried to prompt her.

"Yes, but it is also true that nowadays women don't marry the man their mom wants, either," grandma said serene.

"But we have never seen this one before, he jumped out of the blue. We don't know anything about his family," Maria answered indignant.

"Listen, I'm probably selfish like most elderly people are, but I have been waiting to see Clara in a wedding dress since the day she was born and if she hurries, maybe, I can still make it," she concluded sharply winking at Clara.

Maria was furious.

"You two spend too much time together and I have no intention of staying here while you drive me crazy," said Maria, as she turned nervously on her heels and went down the stairs as quick as lightning.

"You are evil, grandma," said Clara smiling as soon as her mother disappeared.

"I know honey, but making your mother angry is too much fun for me," she chuckled. "Now, sit down and tell me everything about last night," she added in a soft voice.

Chapter 6
~Roommates & Colleagues~

Going back to her life in Milan was not easy. In front of her apartment door with two heavy bags on her shoulders Clara heard the neighbor who lived on the same landing opening the door slightly and putting her head in the aperture.

"Is it you again? Are you all coming back today?" she said disappointed and closed the door. Being too busy fighting with the door that didn't want to open, Clara didn't pay attention to her. *What is it blocking the door?* She put down her big bags and started pushing harder being able to open it just a few more inches. A loud ding announced the elevator had arrived and Francesca stepped out of it.

"Are you just arriving now or have you been inside already?" Clara asked annoyed.

"I'm coming from the station. Why?" Francesca asked dropping her suitcase on the floor.

"Because this damn door doesn't want to open, and the doorbell is broken; I just arrived and already I want to go home!" Clara yelled losing her patience and kicking the stubborn door.

Francesca got closer to the door opening. "Leave it to me. I think I know what happened," she said to Clara and putting her lips inside the small opening she started to call Ella by yelling her name.

"Why didn't I think of it sooner? When something is wrong who else could be responsible?" Clara laughed.

Ella had dumped her suitcases in the first place she found, which blocked the door, and now she was taking a shower and couldn't hear her roommates trying to enter.

"If this is the beginning, I don't want to know how the rest of the year will be," Francesca said while sitting on the stairs close to Clara.

Clara leaned her back against one of her bags and looked Francesca straight into her eyes, and, unable to contain her happiness, she told her dear friend about the wedding.

"Oh my Gosh, Clara! I'm so happy for you! Let me hug you," Francesca said squeezing her hard.

"Do you want to be my bridesmaid?" Clara asked even though she still couldn't believe it was going to happen.

"But of course. It's an honor! Tell me everything. When? How? Where? And your graduation? Where are you two going to live?" Francesca rapidly fired off questions for Clara.

Francesca showed a lot of enthusiasm and gave Clara great support, by which she was deeply moved.

Ella took her time getting out of the bathroom, and with one towel wrapped around her body and her long hair dripping everywhere, she came to the door.

"Welcome! How was your summer?" she said after opening the door and padding into her bedroom wetting the floor along the way.

"Do I kill her now or do I wait until later?" murmured Clara.

Francesca laughed "And she is not even apologizing for keeping us on the staircase for almost half an hour," she commented flabbergasted.

"Ella, what do you have in those suitcases? Did you bring all of Sicily?" Clara tried to joke to alleviate their bad mood.

They waited for the evening to come and in the kitchen they talked to Ella. The sensation Clara felt from Ella's reaction was a combination of extreme anger and profound tenderness. They were reprimanding her for the trash, the insects, the loud parties, the graffiti on the living room walls and all she seemed able to do was look at them lost with her small black eyes wide open as if they were speaking of someone else.

"You are totally right," Ella said with wet eyes, "but I didn't do it on purpose. I didn't think ..."

"This is the problem with you Ella, you never think before acting. You never think about consequences," Francesca scolded.

"This is not the first time we've warned you. You have to show us more commitment because it is not possible to go on like this. For now no more parties, more accuracy in the house chores, and more respect for we, who, like it or not, live with you," Clara said.

Ella promised to do her best. Life started again. Classes resumed, and Clara led her usual student life — going to classes and seeing her classmates, but she didn't really make time to study. Conversations with Leonardo were difficult; they called each other in the evenings, but Clara's apartment had only one phone attached to the wall in the entryway that forced her to talk sitting on a stool in precarious balance while Francesca and Ella passed through, talked, eavesdropped, and giggled.

The weeks were marked by lonely weekends passed holding the receiver in the entryway and insane weekends spent for the most part on the train to be able to see each other for just a few hours without ever emerging from the bedroom.

One day Leonardo called joyous.

"Clara, I have been invited to a party here in Rome next weekend, and you absolutely *must* accompany me!"

"Are you sure that's a good idea?" she asked uncertain.

"Of course I am! Everybody I have known since I was a freshman will be there. It's a huge opportunity for you to meet everybody at once. It's the perfect excuse to have you here sooner and everybody is looking forward to meeting you"

He sounded so passionate.

"Yeah, right, and I'm sure they'll love me," joked Clara and they both laughed. The thought that they'd see each other soon put them both in a good mood.

By then, Clara knew the train schedule to Rome very well and the six-hour trip seemed to go by faster every time. She kept a bag with clean clothes always ready in her bedroom so she didn't have to think about what to bring at the last minute. Rome was more and more beautiful every time she went and its fall weather made it even more pleasant. Fall in Rome was very unusual for Clara. It was a warm and sunny season that made the colors even more vibrant than in the summer. The doorman in Leonardo's building revealed himself to be a very friendly man. When Clara arrived, they would wink at each other, and sometimes Clara stopped by the doorman's lodge to have a little talk with him. She found out his name was Romeo; he had a wife, three sons and four grandchildren. Born and raised in Rome, he loved his city, his job and his grandkids, whom he saw every single Sunday for lunch. That day, when Romeo saw Clara opening the front door he greeted her with a big smile and raised his hand to touch his hat as a sign of respect.

"Ciao, signori'![7] Welcome back! Sooner than usual this time," he greeted her joyously.

"Hi Romeo. How are things going?" asked Clara in return.

"The doctor is not home yet," he sounded sorry.

"Thanks, I'll wait for him."

Every time she arrived, even when Leonardo couldn't pick her up from the station, she found a fresh red rose laying on her pillow and a love note next to it. Clara deeply inhaled the sweet scent of the rose's heart and read the note. "Peach blossom with crystal wings, in this unborn spring, among

---

[7] "Miss" in roman slang.

thousands I looked for you, but you weren't there. Now you are here."

~

The party was in the center of Rome, next to the Pantheon.

"I'm looking forward to seeing your impressions of the people you'll meet tonight," Leonardo told Clara.

"I'm a little nervous," she said with butterflies in her stomach.

"I know; I read you well, but don't worry. It's just a way for you to put faces and names together," he said, trying to reassure her.

"You always tell me not to worry, but I grew up with my parents telling me the exact opposite. It was always 'worry, worry Clara, how come you are not worried enough?'"

Leonardo hugged her tightly.

"Everything will be fine."

From the outside, the building was nothing special; on the contrary, dirty spots from pollution and graffiti on the walls made it look like any building in any city. But inside, it was astonishing and different from anything Clara had ever seen. The opulence of the furnishings was extreme — every single piece was an original antique. Busts made of marble immortalized ancient leaders and human-sized golden statues held candelabras that lighted up the dark corners of the rooms.

Handmade tapestries, illustrating hunting scenes, covered the walls, and heavy velvet drapery softened the loud buzz made by the cheerful guests' voices. The men were in gray pants and blue jackets, almost like a uniform. Their shirts had tall, stiff collars and the neckties had knots that Clara found excessively large. The women were short and were wearing ridiculously high heels. They had long, dark hair that most of them kept untied, big breasts that they were not afraid to show, and short dresses with no sleeves. They looked alive. They were very different from the stuffy Milanese Clara was used to, with their hair dyed blond to look northern, low heels and covered shoulders so as to not look like sluts, and most of all, etiquette-conscious. Leonardo and Clara entered the room holding hands and when people became aware of their presence, Clara squeezed his hand harder.

"This is Clara, my fiancée," he proudly said every time he introduced her to someone new, and Clara was caught by surprise each time.

He had never referred to her in those terms before and she had never thought of herself as one. It was nice, reassuring. She liked it. She felt like an adult, secure and still holding his hand, her grip became softer. She stopped holding on to him and became his companion.

"Come here Nino," Leonardo said to a short man with thin hair and a bent back. "I want to introduce you to Clara, my fiancée. Clara this is Nino, my mentor. It is his job, more than anyone else's, to put up with me every day."

"Good evening," said Clara smiling made strong by her recently acquired confidence. "Leo talks a lot about you."

"Good evening," answered Nino lowering his gaze and keeping his hand flaccid when Clara shook it. He gave a hint of a smile and left.

"Is he always like that?" asked Clara.

"He is peculiar. He has his moments, but he is not a bad man; he is just introverted and socially awkward," Leonardo explained.

Around the dinner table everybody was chatty and the people close to Clara were very nice and seemed eager to know her better. After the waiters collected the second course plates, all the guests were summoned into the adjacent room to attend a special presentation of the desserts. Everybody was standing at the side of the big room decorated in yellow and joyfully waiting for the dessert show to start, all of them trying to guess what kind of presentation was about to take place. Leonardo was speaking with a colleague about cardiac therapies and Clara was listening. Nino approached her and called her aside.

"I need to talk to you," he began, squinting his small eyes behind thick glasses. He was looking at her without being able to find the right words to go on.

"I'm listening," said Clara smiling and trying to encourage him.

"Listen," he finally said. "Leonardo is our flagship. He worked hard to be where he is now and more hard work is about to come if he wants to stay in Rome. Now, I understand his enthusiasm for you, but I would hate to see this 'fiancée' thing get out of hand. I don't know your plans, but his job comes first, it must come first, so, back off, find your corner, and get comfortable in it."

Clara stood with a petrified smile on her lips. She was not expecting anything of that sort. She was speechless. Nino was not looking for answers and, satisfied about his speech, he left her to join a group of colleagues.

So much for the hospitality of the people of Rome.

She agreed to go to the party to have a sense of Leonardo's environment, and she was beginning to have a pretty clear idea about it.

Standing alone she looked for Leonardo and found him close to a bronze vase that held a huge indoor palm. He was talking to a beautiful girl, tall, with blue eyes, long hair and curvy with welcoming hips. Her attitude suggested intimacy; with one hand she touched her hair and with the other one she held Leonardo's arm.

Clara predicted trouble.

"You are back! Where have you been?" Leonardo said relieved and pulling Clara close to his side.

"You must be *the fiancée*," said the girl with a mocking voice.

"I'm Clara and, you are?" asked Clara annoyed.

"I'm Deborah," the young woman said raising her nose and waving her hair. "Didn't, 'lover boy' here, tell you that he and I almost lived together?" she added sure to incur a mortal blow.

"He talked about a lot of 'ex' girlfriends, but no, I don't recall any Deborah," Clara said smiling and hugging Leonardo tightly. "I think the key word you just said is, 'almost.'"

Deborah grinned, collected herself, and tried to inflict another blow.

"I'd be careful. What happened to me could happen to you. Leonardo likes them hot and you look more like a cold northern," she said with disdain.

Clara reacted believing in what she had with Leonardo.

"It's very nice of you, but don't worry about me. In Milan, everybody says I'm a passionate southern. I learned a long time ago not to care about what people think based on prejudices. I assure you I know how to take care of Leonardo," she concluded with a heart that was exploding and hands that were sweating.

Deborah left angry, and Clara took a deep breath.

"I think we've had enough. Let's go!" said Leonardo.

"But we'll miss the grand show of desserts," said Clara sarcastically.

"Who cares?!?"

They sneaked out without saying goodbye to anyone. They ran down the stairs before anybody could notice they were missing and, as soon as they were outside and felt secure, they began laughing like naughty little children amused by their own transgression.

"You were right, Leo, everybody loved me!"

said Clara out of breath.

"Wow! I have never seen two women so combative," said Leonardo.

"And I guess you were gratified by it," Clara said caustic.

Leonardo stopped. They were in front of a gelateria, and for a moment Clara thought he wanted to buy her an ice cream.

"Clara, I just want to tell you that what Deborah said is not true. I mean, we had been together for a while, but one day, in front of a jewelry shop, she started showing me the rings she liked and told me she wanted to move in with me. I broke up with her that same night."

Clara looked into his eyes and saw his fear. Frightened that she could lose faith in him, in them.

"Leo, I believe you. I told you, I'll believe in you until you destroy me. And for now, I'm not very interested in your past, just in your future," she brushed his cheeks with her fingertips and kissed him.

"I love you, Clara. You are the only one for me. There has never been never anybody like you."

"I love you too," she answered in return.

"By the way, what did Nino want from you?" Leonardo asked suspiciously.

"Nothing. He just wanted to better introduce himself," Clara said cutting it short.

"That sounds like Nino," Leonardo said satisfied by her answer. "Let's go home," he said tranquil. They ran to the car never stopping for a breath and never stopping laughing.

~

In bed, naked and clinging to each other, they left the world outside the door.

Leonardo held her like she could run away at any moment, and his hands brushed her soft arms.

"I was so looking forward to leaving that get-together" he said moving his strokes to her belly "I'm glad you met them, but I just wanted to come home and be with you," he said kissing her on the neck.

"I like to go out because then I just want to go home and be alone with you," Clara said.

His kisses dulled her mind and awoke her senses. She kissed the hint of the horizontal wrinkles he had on his forehead and he closed his eyes. She kissed his eyelids, then the tip of his nose and his lips. Moved down his neck to his shoulders and then his chest.

"Clara, you make me crazy," he whispered with his eyes closed.

"Leo?" she said as if to warn him. "I have been listening all night to people who claim to know you deeply and to know what is best for you."

"Nobody knows me better than you," Leonardo said searching for her mouth.

Clara moved back and looked at him intensely.

"Now, however, my dear Leo, it's time you understand to whom you really belong."

"Do I have to worry?" he smiled.

"Not at all, my love; but I'm about to do something I have never done before. Maybe you have, and I don't really want to know, but tonight I want you more than ever and I need to have you this way. Just stay still," she told him.

He understood and held still so as not to hurt her.

Now he was hers.

~

Fall in Milan was gray, foggy and dull. After classes or during the tedious weekends in the city, Clara liked to go to Piazza Duomo to observe the crowd. She took the metro to enjoy the strong sensation that gave her every time — seeing the duomo stand out magnificently against the sky as she emerged in the piazza from the metro's underground stairs. She often had to hold back tears of emotion when she saw the duomo's outline in front of her eyes as its roofline dissolved into openwork pinnacles. She stopped at the newsstand, bought magazines, sat in a café in the Galleria Vittorio Emanuele II, ordered a sandwich, and read. The first time she had seen the Galleria she was with her mother and was intimidated by its monumentality and awestruck by its beauty. She was a young girl looking for an apartment in the city, ready to start a new life, and had been dreaming of Milan. Now, instead, she was used to its mosaics on the floor and the arched roof; she didn't want Milan to be her home anymore and was immune to its charm. She used to love to listen to a band of young men that played under the colonnade. They were from Chile, and looked like kids with their round faces, genuine features and dark skin. They wore colorful ponchos, played unique instruments and their music brought the desolation of the Andes to Milan. They were melodies of merry melancholy that recalled landscapes of snowy peaks, soft grassy hills and crystal lakes. Most people passed by pretending indifference fearing those street musicians from far away that dedicated their unusual notes in exchange for an offering. Clara instead stopped to listen and let their music take her and calm her. She waited for time to go by. She counted the weeks, days and hours left until she could finally tell her parents about the wedding. The feeling that nothing was moving forward was driving her crazy. For Clara the city was stuck in fog and monotony. The days were identical one after the other and she was frozen in waiting.

Francesca was busy taking exams trying to graduate as soon as possible and make up for lost time. She missed her mountains and now that Michele and a preschool were waiting for her back home, she too was eager to put an end to the Milan chapter of her life. She had never intended to stay there forever, but she didn't see a valid reason to go back home either. Now she had more than one.

Ella, on the other hand, was determined to never

to go back to the old provincial life in her small Sicilian town. She studied during the day and had fun at night. Late at night, when the city was dampened, the three of them sat around the kitchen table for a while and talked.

"You are both leaving me soon," Ella said incredulous.

"Actually I have at least one more year," Francesca answered laughing; "So don't think you are getting rid of me any time soon."

Ella laughed. "But Clara is leaving now. What will the two of us do?"

"I'll keep the apartment until June," Clara said.

"Come on, take comfort in a glass of grappa[8] I took from Cortina," Francesca said.

"I'm sure you'll survive very well even without us, Ella," Clara continued.

"Are you sure you want to get married so young?" Ella asked perplexed pouring the grappa in her glass.

"I happened to meet the right person now. What should I do, turn him down only because I'm still young?" Clara answered.

"Thinking of it, you are right" Ella concluded. "As soon as I find a man with tons of money I'll do the same. But he needs to have a lot of it!"

"You want him with money and from Milan, am I right?" Francesca asked.

"Money is absolutely the priority, but the city is not important as long as it is in the north of Italy. Every time I go back home and look at my mom I

---

[8] An Italian brandy distilled from the pomace of grapes used in winemaking.

know exactly what I don't want to be. Anything else is fine."

"You are very harsh," Clara commented.

"Maybe, but you don't know how it is to listen to your own father and brothers treating her like a maid, seeing her slogging, knowing what everybody in town expects from her just because she is a woman; it's sickening."

"Ok then, let's make a toast," Francesca suggested.

"Yes! To Clara's wedding, to your graduation that will take you to your Michele, and to my millionaire!"

They raised their glasses and drank all in one sip.

"Girls," Ella said putting her glass on the table. "I forgot to tell you that Gustavo is coming — my boyfriend."

"Isn't it time that you break up with him?" Clara asked.

"I don't know. It makes me feel good knowing he is there waiting for me and I don't want to make him suffer."

"If he knew the stuff that you do…" Francesca started to say.

"Sometimes I have the feeling that he is the only good part of me left. He still believes in an Ella that doesn't exist anymore and maybe never existed," Ella said absorbed in her thoughts.

"When does he arrive?" said Clara interrupting Ella's thoughts.

"Tomorrow, I think; he left today by car,"

"By car? Poor him!"

"But he is taking a friend, so they can take turns at the steering wheel."

"And may I ask where they will sleep?" Francesca asked imagining the answer and getting upset.

~

The next morning Clara's alarm clock went off at the usual time. She switched it off and tried to ignore the fact that it had rung, but then decided to get up and went to the kitchen. Francesca was already there and was preparing her breakfast.

"Good morning; why aren't you in class today?" Clara asked Francesca, surprised to find her there.

"Didn't you hear the racket Ella, Gustavo and his friend made last night?" Francesca asked.

"No. Why? Are they already here?"

"They must have driven like crazy. The doorbell rang at three and they laughed, talked and moved furniture around until five. I fell asleep at six, and then I couldn't wake up until now."

"Now, everything is silent," Clara said.

"I think they finally crashed."

"Do you think we should be quiet so as not to wake them?"

"They didn't worry about us. How could you not hear the hullabaloo?" Francesca asked amazed.

"The only excuses I have are that I was very tired and that my room is not next to the living room like yours."

"Better for you," Francesca told her.

Clara took a cup, poured some milk in it and added some cereal; then she put a small pot on the stove for the tea.

"Tomorrow I'll go home for the weekend. Leonardo is taking me to meet his parents."

"Wow! I still think it is a dream when you talk about it," Francesca said.

"I understand. I feel the same sometimes," Clara giggled.

Francesca had sad eyes; she stared at her melon slices and seemed distant. Clara got close to her.

"Francesca, is everything all right?"

Francesca reacted as if she had just awoken from a light sleep.

"Yes, of course. I'm just tired because I didn't get enough sleep."

"Francesca…"

"Alright. Honestly, I'm very happy for you, but I'm also sorry you are leaving. I'm looking forward to finishing myself, but I'm sad we are growing up and this is ending. What a bore; you see, I don't even know what I have. I told you, I just didn't get enough sleep and I'm confused."

"What matters is that we met. Our friendship won't end," Clara said smiling.

"You are right and we can't stop time anyway," Francesca agreed.

Clara smacked a big kiss on Francesca's cheek.

"I love you! Come on; watch my water while I go to the bathroom for a moment."

Clara left the kitchen and realized she didn't have to go anywhere; she just wanted to prevent the tears that surfaced in her eyes from going down. She wanted to distract herself and run some fresh water on her face. She opened the bathroom door and found Ella completely naked inside the empty tub riding a young boy. There was a moment of embarrassment and instead of closing the door Clara spoke.

"I'm sorry," she told them.

"No, we are sorry," the lustful couple answered in unison.

"I thought you were asleep," Clara continued. "Nice to meet you Gustavo," she said ready to close the door and go away.

"Actually," the boy said still keeping his hands on Ella's breasts, "Gustavo is sleeping. I'm his friend."

"You know what Ella?"

"What?" Ella asked ready to be scolded.

"I'll miss you," Clara said quietly closing the door and going back to the kitchen, smiling.

~

Leonardo's parents invited Clara over for Sunday lunch in the apartment they had on the coast. At last something was changing. Not as fast as she'd hoped, but it was better than being in Milan just sitting at her desk counting the hours pretending to study.

Leonardo always talked about his parents in sweet terms, like two people with whom he was getting along and who instilled serenity. Clara knew only that they were older than her parents, that they spent their life between the home on the coast and the one in the Appennini Mountains, and that they were willing to do anything to make Leonardo happy. She was ready to meet two old-fashioned people, who lived in an out-of-date apartment full of odds and ends that reminded them the past, very attached to tradition and very protective of their son. She decided to wear a classic pair of navy blue pants and a large sweater that wrapped her, providing security. The building was a middle-sized corner edifice, with white walls and wide balconies painted in turquoise.

"I have been passing by here for years," Clara said amused by the coincidence.

Leonardo's father, Bruno, opened the door; he was a tall and thin man who resembled Leonardo except for his still thick black hair. As soon as he saw them a welcoming smile appeared on his lips and never left them until the end of the afternoon. He hugged Clara and kissed her on both cheeks, then impatiently called his wife.

"Laura, they are here!" he said raising the tone of his voice.

"Here I am," she said emerging from the kitchen.

Laura was a short and chubby woman with wavy brown hair who released energy and enthusiasm. Under the apron, she was very elegant, but not flashy. She was sober and had a very modern necklace in white gold and onyx that showed her will to keep up with the times.

"Welcome," she said taking Clara's hand and

pulling her close to hug her.

Clara was taken by surprise by their kindness and reacted by stiffening slightly.

"Leonardo, while we finish preparing, sit down and get Clara comfortable in the living room," she said sweetly, but determined. "And you, Bruno, come in the kitchen with me, I need your help," she added with a more severe tone of voice looking at her husband.

"Pronto," he said springing into action and smiling. "At your command!"

The apartment strongly contrasted with their age; the living room had furniture varnished in white, an enormous Persian rug on top of which rested an extremely modern blue couch, two Frau armchairs and one coffee table made of crystal and stainless steel. Also the dining room was modern and essential; a glass table, stainless steel chairs with cushions of the same blue as the couch in the living room, and a futuristic chandelier. The only antique objects were the paintings, all of which represented hunting scenes and landscapes. Laura was very proud of her cooking abilities and what she had prepared was not a lunch, but a banquet. Melon and prosciutto were on the table when they sat down. Soon, wild boar sausages and a homemade cheese that Clara had never tasted appeared. Rich lasagna and tagliatelle with porcini mushrooms were the first courses; lamb with spinach and roasted chicken with potatoes the second. Soon thereafter the flan and the apple pie arrived. Clara, who didn't want to disappoint Laura's expectations, ate everything with no inhibitions. Leonardo was watching very entertained.

"Slow down or you'll explode," he murmured into her ear.

"It's almost over, one last effort," Clara answered.

Laura appeared holding a bowl of fruit salad, whipped cream and sorbet.

"I wasn't expecting this. I think I'll die now," Clara said worried holding Leonardo's leg under the table.

During lunch Laura had been pretty silent, while Bruno had been very talkative attracting some disappointed looks from his wife. Clara felt at ease. She felt treated like the daughter they never had.

When the binge was over, they moved to the living room for the espresso. Clara asked for a hot tea. Leonardo sat next to her and held her hand. Laura finally relaxed not having to think about the kitchen anymore and Bruno started telling stories about Leonardo as a child.

"One day in August, when Leo was three, he decided to dress himself and came down to the kitchen wearing wool pants and a thick turtle neck sweater; poor Leo, he was sweating and didn't know why! We laughed and he looked so confused. He reminded me of Pinocchio!"

Laura tried to stop her husband from saying things that could embarrass Leonardo, but her son seemed fine and Bruno kept going.

Clara was having a lot of fun trying to imagine the man she was madly in love with running around naked because he didn't want to change his diaper or crying in front of the teacher because he hadn't done his homework.

After a while, Laura, who had been pretty quiet until then, spoke.

"I have always told Leo not to bring any girl home because I didn't want to get attached to her in case they broke up."

Clara nodded smiling not sure where she was heading.

"The night Leo met you, when he came home I was still awake and I immediately knew something had happened; he had a new glow in his eyes. Indeed he looked at me and said, 'Mom, I just met the woman I'll marry.' I laughed, of course, but in my heart I knew he was serious. I hope you can love him as much as he loves you. That is all I wish."

Clara felt a chill of embarrassment going through her spine. She wanted to get up, hug Laura, and tell her that, yes, she could rest assured because she loved him very much. She also wanted to thank her for their kindness, their welcoming heart, and their warmth. But, a combination of her personality, her upbringing and her genes prevented her from saying anything; she could only smile and hope they understood. Something in Laura's gaze told her that she did.

"Why don't you guys take a nap?" Laura said standing up as if it were time to put an end to the chitchat. "Enough with the past. Bruno likes to remember old stuff, but I prefer the future. Daddy and I have to clean up the kitchen and tonight you both have big trips to make to different destinations. Resting a little will do you good."

It was a soporific and misty Sunday — one of those days when the sun never seems to rise. A bored voice was commenting on a soccer game on TV. A dog was barking and the tiny water droplets suspended in the air muffled its yelping. Clara felt content.

Leonardo took her to his childhood bedroom. He had left it more than eleven years before and since then the room had been updated, but a few toys remained. Some wooden cars were sitting next to a collection of super-hero comics, but what caught Clara's eye was a big brown plush dog almost falling off the shelf.

"How sweet! Did you sleep with it when you were a child?" she asked in a facetious voice.

"Don't you try to make fun of me, missy," Leonardo answered straightening the dog up. "I was a child once and, yes, this was my dog," he continued getting closer to Clara and putting a hand on her waist.

"I don't want to make fun of you. I just love imagining you as a child. Your parents are adorable people and this is the first time I've seen where you come from."

"You have been very sweet with my mom. Thanks. I was worried that you were going to explode from eating all that food. Are you ok?"

"I have to say that when I saw the fruit salad I almost got sick," she laughed. "But now I'm fine. The hot tea and the chitchat helped a lot. Listen, did you already tell your parents about the wedding?"

"No, why?" Leonardo Asked.

"I was just thinking of what your mom said about you having met the woman you'd marry."

"I didn't say anything, but they know me well, Clara."

"Did you really say that, when you came home the night we met?"

"Yes. Don't you believe it?"

"It's not that. It's that I don't know if I should feel offended or pleased," Clara said hesitating.

"Your choice. But I told you that when I want something I go for it without asking for permission."

"Well, in this case, you have to ask me first. Don't you think?" Clara said somewhat resentfully.

"And, in fact, I think I did, didn't I?" Leonardo answered not understanding Clara's anger and fearing she was just looking for an excuse to have a fight.

"To tell you the truth, I'm more gratified than upset. Since the beginning, you have been very different from everybody else I'd met before. Usually people are afraid to approach me, but you went straight forward."

"In the defense of those others, Clara, you look dour and like you don't want to be disturbed."

"So, why didn't you have any hesitation?"

"Because I just knew I wanted to approach you. As you know, a little egoism can take you a long way," he said laying his hands on Clara's hips and kissing her. His mouth tasted of coffee.

"You look great in these pants," he said caressing her. "Did I ever tell you your hips make my head spin?"

"Yes, but," she chuckled while he kissed her.

"And did I ever tell you your butt cheeks are the roundest and sexiest?" he added brushing them lightly.

"Yes, that too," she whispered noticing her heart had started to beat faster.

"I was watching you when you were in the kitchen with my mom and," he lifted her sweater and caressed her breast.

Clara jumped.

"Leo, your parents are here!" she said alarmed.

"No, they are on the other side of the apartment."

He kept on kissing her and caressing her.

"You know what I mean, silly."

"And I seem to recall it has never been a problem before," he said pouting a little bit.

"I know, but."

His kisses were sweet and there was nothing to say to resist him any longer. His hands were already all over her and she dropped what was left of her defenses to love him and have him.

Chapter 7

~ Getting stronger ~

The whole month of December was spent in anticipation of the Christmas celebrations and of the time to announce the engagement to their families. Even Milan was more cheerful. Like each year, the month began with the commemoration of Saint Ambrogio, the patron saint of the city to whom the Milanese were very devoted. For the occasion, the external perimeter of the Sforzesco Castle was colored with lively stands that displayed all sorts of handcrafted objects, culinary products and oddities. Further along, streets and squares were decorated with white and red lights that cheered them up after the sunset and a grandiose Christmas tree was lighted up in Piazza Duomo.

Clara was on the train home and, while waiting for it to leave the station, she looked outside the window thinking of how moved she was the first time she had seen that crowded place. Getting off the train full of expectations and hopes, she was struck by its original combination of liberty and art deco that created an astonishing visual impact, made it an absolutely unique place and gave her the feeling of having arrived in an important city.

In her eyes, all the people around her were important and in a hurry because they were busy and she found the energy released by all of them extremely energizing. Now, seated as usual next to the window, she was just hoping for the train to leave. It was the first time in years that Clara was happy to go home to her parents. Her mother was a great decorator and each Christmas she devoted a lot of time embellishing the house with her festive creations. She always started in the fall picking branches, pinecones and flowers from the garden. She properly dried them out and then she had fun painting them with spray glitter. Each year, she selected a different color theme and for that year she had chosen a palette of gold and burgundy; a classic match, yet more elegant than the usual and ordinary red. The Christmas tree was always set up in the foyer so it had a lot of room around it for the gifts that started to arrive very early both from distant relatives and her father's patients. When Clara was a child, she had fun helping her mother decorate the tree and assisting her in the creation of an original centerpiece for the Christmas Eve table. At that time her family was not numerous and they could all comfortably sit around the dining room table; they gathered at her house to spend Christmas Eve together, to open the gifts after midnight and to spend Christmas day together, also. It was a moment of great joy for Clara who, as the youngest child in the family, awaited the attention of her big brothers and her uncles. Now, the family had gotten bigger, her brothers were married and had to share the holidays with their spouse's families, they had young children who made difficult to sit all together at the same table, and the uncles got lazy and didn't want to travel anymore during the cold season. That was also the first Christmas without grandpa. Clara was sad and she saw the same melancholy clouded over the eyes of her grandma and her mother, who, however, decided to celebrate Christmas Eve as usual. The three of them withdrew into the kitchen and prepared the traditional recipes, chatting and singing along with a small portable radio. Clara's father, who could hear their voices from the living room, was heartened in his armchair hiding behind the newspaper and anticipating Christmas delicacies. Clara helped grandma in preparing the filling for the tortellini and closing them. Together they were a perfect assembly line; grandma prepared and spread the dough, Maria cut it into squares and arranged the filling, and Clara closed them making sure they resembled little belly buttons with a small hole in the center so the broth could go in and properly warm them.

Leonardo had been invited to join them for Christmas Eve and Clara would spend Christmas Day with Leonardo's family who gathered each year on the Appennini. The table that Clara's mother designed was very elegant; a burgundy tablecloth showed through golden lace laid on top of it like a cloud of voile, white porcelain plates with gold pattern on the edge, silverware perfectly aligned according to the precept of the etiquette,

Bohemian crystal glasses that sparkled under the chandelier's lights dangling on the table, and two solid silver candleholders that completed the centerpiece created by Maria.

Clara's mother also required that everybody dress in a decorous way reflecting the Christmas spirit. For her husband she chose a dark suit with a burgundy tie and handkerchief, while she wore a golden fitted dress and several long pearl necklaces. Grandma opted for a blue dress with white collar that made Maria turn up her nose, and Clara chose a gray and burgundy ensemble of which her mother actually approved.

"Welcome to our humble home!" Maria greeted Leonardo with a fake smile.

"Here we go. I hope she can relax and leave you alone," Clara whispered in Leonardo's ear.

"Don't worry about me, I'll handle her. Enjoy the evening," he reassured her.

At the table, Clara looked at the place where grandpa usually sat; Christmas for him was always an opportunity to divulge old tales about his youth in his beloved Sardinia. They were always the same old stories that everybody in the family knew all too well and didn't wish to hear again, but grandma found in Leonardo not only the possibility to remember them once more, but also a keen listener. Indeed, Leonardo not only listened, but also nodded, smiled, and participated.

"You are a very nice man, my dear," Grandma said patting the back of his hand.

"Leonardo!" said Maria suddenly, a little

irritated and jumping up from her chair. "Would you be so kind as to help me in the kitchen? My husband is hopeless, my mother is tired, and Clara has done enough for today."

"Of course, let me take these plates for you," he said winking at Clara.

"What are you plotting, Maria?" asked Roberto having fun.

"I have a surprise for dessert and I want Leonardo to help me. Come on, follow me," she directed Leonardo.

They disappeared into the kitchen. Roberto and grandma, satisfied with Maria's excuse, started talking about the unusual snowstorm that hit the center of Italy. Clara, however, was not totally certain that her mother had spoken the truth, and, suspicious and curious, couldn't stay still any longer; she needed to check out what was going on in the other room, made up an excuse, and left. Her father and her grandma were so absorbed in their conversation that they barely noticed she was gone. The kitchen door was open and Clara could hear everything Maria and Leonardo were saying.

"I'm worried about that girl," her mother was saying in a harsh voice.

"May I ask why?" Leonardo asked sounding puzzled.

"She is immature and doesn't know what she wants. She has always been insecure; she still is and you are distracting her from what should be her goals. Do you know that she hasn't taken any exams since last summer? You have a lot of influence on her and you must help me," Maria concluded, determined.

Clara's heart stopped and a sharp pain went through her chest; her lungs seemed unable to expand and she felt out of breath. *This is pure betrayal! She called me "that girl" like I was a stranger and she is trying to convince Leonardo to take her side.*

"Help you? How?" Leonardo asked.

"You must tell her to concentrate on her exams and her career. She doesn't listen to me, but she'll listen to you. You are distracting her from her priorities; you must tell her you are busy and keep your distance from her. At least for a while."

Leonardo interrupted her and Clara understood he was trying very hard to stay calm.

"Mrs. Maro, it's not my intention to be rude, but I don't think you understand what is really going on here. First of all, Clara is neither immature nor insecure."

"Really?" said Maria angrily. "And just what do you call a person who acts the way she is?"

"I call it a person who is growing up and making big steps forward," Leonardo answered immediately, firm in his point of view. "I'm in love with her and my duty is not to tell her what to do, but help her to find her own way. Second, I don't take orders and I don't like to be used. In the future, I'd like you to consider Clara and me as being one person, and if you have something to tell her, do it yourself."

Maria sniggered arrogantly. "You think this heroic behavior is honorable and I'm sure you feel very proud of what you just said, but the truth is that you are hurting her and I'm not sure this is how Clara needs to be loved."

"It's not me who should be proud, but it is you who should be ashamed. And, as far as how Clara needs to be loved, I'd let her choose. However, I'm sure that being manipulated by the people who are supposed to help her is not a good method," answered a confident Leonardo.

The conversation was obviously over. Leonardo went back into the dining room and joined the chitchat about the snowstorm. Clara hid in the bathroom; after listening to what Leonardo said she could breathe a bit easier, but the wound her mother had inflicted was deep and she felt it in her stomach like a bleeding laceration.

"Where are you Clara!?! The surprise is ready!!!" her mother called joyfully like nothing had happened.

"Bitch," Clara murmured opening the bathroom door and heading toward the dining room.

The lights were off, then suddenly, a twirling of sparkling flames came from the kitchen and Maria appeared holding a cake shaped like a three-dimensional upright Christmas tree, on top of which she had placed lighted silver sticks that produced sparks. Everybody applauded and cheered at the surprise, and Clara's father made a toast to Maria and her ability to organize such a pleasant family night.

~

Leonardo's village was a little hamlet on the Appennini Mountains where each member of his family owned a house and where each year they celebrated Christmas. Everybody arrived the night before and complained about Leonardo's absence. During the drive, Clara took the opportunity to tell Leo about how she had heard his conversation with her mother and what kind of effect that had on her.

"I feel betrayed by the person that should protect me the most," she screamed almost crying.

"Try not to take it too hard. In her own way she is trying to protect you and in her mind I'm the villain," Leonardo said trying to calm her down.

"She called me 'that girl,' and are you defending her?" Clara said offended.

"No, but …"

"She is acting like a desperate person who is afraid of losing power over another," Clara said interrupting him.

"Exactly!" Leonardo exclaimed relieved. "Her behavior is not absence of love for you."

"Maybe, but it is love based on control," Clara sighed.

~

They arrived right before lunch. The hamlet was totally covered in snow that made it silent and similar to a nativity scene. The road cut the hill right down the middle and the houses of all the uncles, aunts and cousins were on both sides. Most of the relatives used these houses just for the Holidays, so only a few of them lived there year round. It was their tradition to gather in aunt Isabella's house because it had a marvelous basement that resembled a tavern and was able to contain all of them — a room with stone walls, a wide French door, an impressive fireplace and a big gourmet kitchen. The French door faced a hamlet whose tower stood out at the top of a snowy rock and for Clara evoked tales of ancient princesses and valorous knights.

Leonardo said he had a large family, but Clara found an unexpected crowd. All together, they were almost thirty people; no little kids yet. Leonardo and his cousins were the last generation and none of them had taken boyfriends or girlfriends to the Christmas reunion, so far. Clara was the first outsider to cross that door and she was treated like one. After the introductions and the obligatory greetings nobody paid any attention to her. Waiting for lunch to be served, the men had gathered in front of the fireplace, smoking pipes and cigars, making small talk, complaining about their jobs and the economy's trend. The women, on the other hand, were busy in the kitchen trying to figure out a way to feed everyone before somebody started to protest. Every once in a while Laura, Leonardo's mother, checked to see if Clara was alright, but she had no time to entertain her, and Bruno, Leo's father, approached her several times, but was always called back by the uncles who insisted on his presence. Clara tried to help the women in the kitchen, but was told to sit down and relax, so she decided to quietly sit down close to Leonardo and learn about his family by observing their behavior. The cousins had grouped in the sitting area in front of the French door and interacted mainly through teasing each other. Francesco was the timid one, Mario and Giulia were the polite ones, Giuseppe and Giovanna the bored ones, Rachele and Remo the angry ones. Rachele was the one who showed more interest in connecting with Leonardo, asking him a lot of questions about his job in Rome and telling him about her life as a student interested in doing research, but always making sure to ignore Clara. *Is it truly possible that she never looks toward me, not even as a mistake?* The dinner table was big and wooden and simply decorated with a red tablecloth, pinecones, small candles and little handmade cards that indicated where guests should sit. When Leonardo noticed Clara's name was among the group of the aunts and not the group of young cousins, he complained and switched Clara's card.

"What are you doing?" Rachele screamed disrupting the joyous atmosphere.

"I'm moving Clara next to me," Leonardo innocently said. "I'm sure it's a mistake that she is sitting with the aunts."

"I personally chose the table arrangement and I assure you there is no mistake," Rachele continued screaming louder than before.

"But it doesn't make any sense," Leonardo replied determined to have Clara close to him. Rachele's blue eyes became inflamed by rage and losing control she began to scream at Clara. "We have traditions in our family and you are not part of them! Only with time and only if you behave, will we include you!"

The family elders pretended not to hear; Mario, the youngest of all the cousins, took Rachele by her sleeve and took her in another room before she could add more resentful words, and Leonardo, furious, wanted to follow them.

"Leave her alone, Leo," said Clara, stopping him.

"This is unbelievable, Clara, my family should know better," he replied outraged.

"I know, but I don't think you can reason with a person when she is in the middle of a nervous breakdown. Leave it alone, please," she implored.

"Ok. But you are sitting next to me," Leonardo concluded not adding any other kind of reasoning.

~

After lunch, the men once again sat in front of the fireplace where they decided to enjoy some cake and brandy by the warmth of the flames. The cousins stayed at the table and kept teasing each other while the women finished up in the kitchen. Rachele, who looked like she had recovered and who had been quiet for most of the lunch, went to Leonardo and, from the back of his chair, threw her arms around his neck and lay her head on his shoulder.

"Leo, it's time for music. Play something for us like you always do," she requested.

Clara didn't know Leonardo played an instrument. In a corner of the room, under everybody's winter coats, hats and scarves, there was a piano. Leonardo pretended to protest a little and then sat at the piano and started playing. *He is good. How many other things do I not know about him? Maybe Rachele is right; I don't belong here.* Clara felt like an intruder. She looked around in need of some air and met Laura's warm gaze. She had a reassuring smile like she had guessed Clara's thoughts. Suddenly, Clara remembered how safe she felt the day she met Leonardo's parents and how they had immediately embraced her. She knew she had the right to be there.

The music stopped and the time came for bingo. Leonardo, Clara and his parents sat close and that was the best part of the day. When midnight struck, all the cousins got up because the "great family tradition" was for the young ones to retire into a separate room to play poker and smoke cigars until dawn. Everybody, especially Rachele, was waiting for Leonardo to excuse himself from Clara and join them, leaving her alone. Leonardo instead, refused to go.

"I'm sorry guys, but we are tired and I have to take Clara home," Leonardo said rising from his seat.

"What?! No, we won't allow you to spoil our

Christmas tradition," said Giuseppe.

"I'm not ruining anything, there are too many to play poker anyway," Leonardo persisted.

"I think that love has made you weak," interrupted Remo. "And that is exactly why I don't want women around when I want to have fun."

"What's up Leo? Clara can't be without you for even a few hours?" Mario mocked him.

"What foolishness," replied Leonardo annoyed.

"Are you afraid of making her angry, then?" asked Giuseppe teasing him again.

"Guys, this has nothing to do with me or with Clara. It is just that you don't want to acknowledge the fact that things change, time passes, and acting like it doesn't is not enough to stop it," Leonardo said.

Aunt Isabella, the lady of the house, felt the need to intervene before someone said something further that they might regret.

"Come on, guys, stop acting like little kids and let them go," she sounded determined.

Then she hugged Clara and said, "Don't worry it's not personal, they are just jealous of their big cousin. Thank you for joining us and I hope to see you soon."

"Goodnight everybody. Thank you, aunt Isabella," said Leonardo waving.

His parents restrained themselves from any comment that would have certainly caused a family feud and decided to stay a little longer now that the spirits had warmed up and everybody was ready for the usual talk about politics.

Leonardo and Clara went to his parents' home, a big stone house right next door.

"What a night!" he sighed.

"Actually, between last night at my house and today, I don't know which one was more stressful. I only know that I've had enough of relatives for a long time," Clara sighed smiling.

"I apologize for my relatives' behavior, Clara. I didn't anticipate anything like this."

"No worries, after all, I'm the first one to invade their space and every family has a crazy one — or two. You have to be thankful that *my* relatives were not around this year or we'd be laughing even harder!" she said hugging him tightly. "This place is beautiful, you know? Is this where you spent the winters growing up?"

"Yes and I loved it, and I hated moving down to the coast," Leonardo said squeezing her.

"I can understand."

"Look, it's late, it's dark and it's icy; why don't you call home and tell them that we will sleep here? I'll take you down tomorrow," suggested Leonardo.

"Great idea, but what will your parents say?" Clara asked worried.

"I'm sure they'll be happy we decided not to drive in this weather."

Clara collapsed on the bed while Leonardo closed the curtains locking out the old-time hamlets, their towers lighted in pink, their princesses and knights. Only the desperate whistle of the wind that howled bumping against the corners of the house could still find its way in.

"We have seen too many people lately, Leo; I need more time alone with you," she said rubbing her eyes.

"I agree. I miss you so much."

"I feel like everybody is trying to interfere with us and our feelings. Why is everybody so upset about our relationship?" Clara asked fixing her face on the pillow.

"I think they don't understand what's happening; they are worried or simply jealous," was his reply.

Leonardo didn't hear an answer; he turned his head and saw Clara was sound asleep. Moving carefully, he went close and stared at her; her breath was peaceful, her hair still smelled like shampoo, the contrast with her white skin made her eyelashes look longer, and the corners of her mouth were lifted in a sweet smile. He took a blanket from the closet, lie down next to her, put the blanket on top of them both, and fell asleep holding her.

~

The delicate touch of Leonardo's hands brought Clara slowly back to reality.

"Good morning," she said opening her eyes.

"Good morning," he answered.

"I love your hands on me," Clara said closing her eyes again.

"I was thinking that today, before I take you

home, we could stop at the church and book it." Leonardo said serenely caressing her.

"I think it is a great idea, but for now keep cuddling me," she smiled half asleep.

"I just realized I have never asked you what kind of ceremony you'd like," he said.

"It'll probably sound strange, but, unlike most girls, I have never dreamt about my wedding day. Actually, I thought I'd never get married. If it were up to me, I'd elope now, in a small and cold church covered with snow; just us, the priest and the sexton as witness," Clara said while brushing Leonardo's feet with her toes.

"But?" he asked curious brushing her feet back.

"But I realize our parents probably deserve better. My father has been fantasizing about taking me to the altar since the day I was born, and my mother, well, you know, she loves events. And you? Any preference?"

"Not at all. Everything is in your hands. Are we going for a classic church wedding, then? With reception afterward and pictures with friends and family?"

"I think so. Do you mind?"

"I told you, I have no preferences, but I want you to know what you are getting into. It'll be more your mother's wedding than ours. Is that ok?"

"As long as you are there and, at the end of the day, we are husband and wife, I'm fine," Clara said pressing her body against Leonardo's.

"I'm having the final test for my residency at the beginning of June. From now on I'll be pretty busy. I'm not even sure I can come up every weekend, but if we want to get married the same day we met, I can make it just in time," he told her.

"Don't worry, I'll keep you posted on the planning and the developments and you just have to show up on the right day at the right time," she laughed.

"Ok, then. Done," he concluded, and Clara saw a shadow of concern in his eyes.

"Are you ok, Leo? There is still time, you know? We don't have to do it if you are not sure," she said sitting on the bed and looking straight into his eyes to detect any possible lie or hesitation.

"Don't be silly! I asked you to marry me, nobody forced me."

"I know, but promise me you'll tell me if you have last minute doubts. Sometimes I have some," she confessed.

"Really!?! You see, I envy your ability to be in touch with your feelings and to be able to express them so easily," he grabbed her warm hands. "Every day I learn something new from you," he told her.

"Well, last night for example, I didn't know you could play the piano and, while I was listening, I realized there are probably millions of other things I don't know about you. I was scared," she said and Leonardo held her hand tightly.

"I want to marry you, Clara. I assure you, you already know everything important there is to know about me. For everything else, we have the rest of our lives to find out. It'll be fun, I promise," he said lovingly.

~

They had chosen to get married in San Fortunato, a small church built in 1418 by Carlo Malatesta, which sat at the end of a steep road surrounded by the green hills of Covignano. It was at one time the abbey of the "white monks," Benedictine Olivetani, labeled such because of their white dress symbolizing their devotion to the virgin. It was a serene place, detached from the mundane life of the seashore that was taking place just a few miles away and that allowed meditation and peace. During the centuries, it had undergone a lot of renovations, but the Renaissance style remained intact. The facade was still the original one and, at late in the day, the slanting sun's rays turned its stones to the most delicate shade of pink. Years before, Clara's youngest brother Aldo got married in that same place. From her child's eyes, it had been a sad day, the day her brother had chosen to marry another woman and not to wait for her. Now, thirteen years later, she was proud that his happy marriage had given her three wonderful nephews, one beautiful niece and a fantastic sister-in-law. Clara remembered how beautiful Aldo's bride looked at the end of the ceremony on that cold December day, dressed in white, holding Clara's brother's arm under the rain of rice. In front of the church, there was a large paved churchyard, and on one side a colonnade made it possible to find relief in the hot summer days.

"You'll wait for me here with all the guests," Clara said while walking on the irregular stones of the pavement.

"I'll be very nervous," Leonardo answered getting close to the stairs that climbed toward the main portal.

"Just remember to raise your gaze and look at this breathtaking view. I'm sure that the ocean and the hills will calm you. Now everything is covered in snow, but in June it will be a triumph of colors," she reminded him.

They crossed the portal together. The inside was simple. Along the nave, four statues of the monks remained as witnesses of their long ago presence, uncomfortable benches accompanied the eyes to the altar behind which there was the painting "The Adoration of the Magi," Giorgio Vasari's masterpiece that the eclectic artist made on the premises to thank the monks for their hospitality. The only ostentation in the church was the rich golden frame that encircled the painting in which a complex choreography of people and animals composed itself around the Madonna, baby Jesus and the three Magi. The divine scene was pervaded by a choral atmosphere of celebration; baby Jesus, joyous and curious, tried to touch the Magi, while the

Madonna looked like she was protecting him from the crowd flocked to greet him foreseeing his sorrowful future. Leonardo and Clara knocked at the church's office door and the parish priest came out. Holding hands, they told him they wanted to get married in his church and wanted to book the date. He was very friendly and said it was always a pleasure to see two young people in love. They lingered a little to talk to him and then spent some time in the church's courtyard. It was exciting to try to imagine how that same place would look in the summer, with bright colors, warm air and the plants in bloom.

"You'll be the most beautiful bride and I'll be the happiest man," Leonardo told her.

"I love you," she answered.

Chapter 8
~ Families ~

Leonardo opened the apartment's front door gently pulling Clara by her hand; he hastened to close out the stairwell's cold air and loudly called his parents' names. He was bursting with joy. The apartment was silent and it seemed deserted.

"Are you really sure you want to tell them right now?" Clara whispered "I think it'd be better if you told them when I'm not here," she tried to suggest moving one step backward hoping to still have enough time to avoid what was about to happen.

Leonardo's father came out of the kitchen holding a knife he was using to slice some cheese and, seeing them, he smiled. The hallway that led to the bedrooms was dark and they could just barely see his mom's silhouette slowly approaching with heavy steps first on one leg then on the other. The light that came from the living room illuminated her and she stopped leaning all her weight on one foot and placing one hand on a perfectly ironed towel she was holding on her forearm.

"What a nice surprise! We were not expecting you here. Has anything happened?" Laura asked worried.

"Both of you, come sit on the couch," Leonardo said happily. "Before we go to dinner, we have some great news to tell you!" he added confidently.

Laura jumped and took the towel from her forearm and squeezed it crumpling it all up.

"Let me put down the knife and I'll be right there," Bruno hurried to say, intrigued.

"Since you are here, why don't you eat something with us? We were just about to have dinner. Don't be in a rush," Laura said almost imploring. "We can talk about your news later, when everybody's calmed down," she concluded hoping to defer, even just a little bit, the moment she had been foreseeing for a while. She looked at the two of them and raised a smile, but found herself grappling with the corners of her mouth that didn't want to rise.

"No, mom," Leonardo said with the tone of voice of one who understood what she was attempting to do. "We have to talk about it now because afterward, we have to go to dinner and we can't stay."

Bruno was already seated on the couch and he was waiting to hear the good news with the look of a child to whom a surprise has been promised and who doesn't have the slightest idea of what it could be. Laura sat down next to him with the facial expression of one who really tried hard to postpone the inevitable and miserably failed. Clara looked for Leonardo's eyes; there was still time to change idea, to make up an excuse, to tell a lie.

"Clara and I will get married in June!" Leonardo suddenly said with great enthusiasm. "We already booked the church," he concluded in a rush.

Ouch, he said it. Now it's out.

Bruno's face lighted up and the joy he felt exposed his teeth; Laura instead surrendered to sadness, stopped fighting her emotions and let her mouth's corners definitively drop down.

"I'm so happy for you!" exulted Bruno interrupting the moment of embarrassing silence that took possession of the room. "A good day can be told by its morning and the sincere love that unites you two is certainly an excellent start for a life together." He stood up and hugged Clara who, while witnessing the display of Leonardo's parents reactions, hid her own embarrassment behind a respectful silence.

"Mom, what's happening? You look troubled. Aren't you happy?" Leonardo asked getting close to his mother.

"On the contrary, I'm very happy," Laura answered reaching for his hands. "When you said you had news I thought Clara was pregnant or that the time to hear what I already knew had come."

"And?" Leonardo asked, not quite certain what his mother was saying or implying.

"Nothing. I'm only thinking aloud and I'm probably just gabbling," Laura said confused. "Clara, come here and let me hug you," she continued, pulling herself together and hugging Clara tightly — too tightly. "Did you already think of where you'll live and if your salary is enough for both of you since Clara doesn't have a job and she still needs to pay tuition? Maybe it'd be worth it to wait a little more," she suggested, trying, one more time, to delay the event.

"Mom, we'll live in my apartment in Rome and the money will be enough for everybody, don't worry. We'll make sacrifices if we need to."

"This is nonsense, Laura," Bruno intervened. "It's obvious that, in the beginning, they'll have to make sacrifices, *but* let me tell you, difficulties make the couple stronger if dealt with together. And don't forget, we'll always be here to help you. What's the point of being a parent if we don't help our children when they need it the most?" Bruno said looking straight into Leonardo's eyes.

"Thanks dad, but I'm sure we can do it."

"And if may say one more thing," Bruno added looking at his wife. "It's true that Clara is still a student and I know that nowadays girls want to have a degree and aspire to have a job or a career, but I'm old fashioned and I wouldn't find anything wrong if Clara decided to stay home and take care of the house and the kids, so try not to worry too much if she…" Leonardo felt Clara jumping at his father's words and decided to stop him before he could end the sentence.

"I think this is premature, dad," Leonardo said annoyed. "And Clara knows she'll be always free to do whatever she decides with absolutely no pressure from me or anybody else. Am I being clear?" Leonardo concluded hoping to never have to repeat himself.

"Ok, ok, I didn't mean to state that Clara must stay home, I wouldn't dare," Bruno reacted regretful and slightly resentful.

"Come on, dad, don't get upset now," Leonardo immediately said.

"Of course I'm not upset, I'm too happy to be," Bruno smiled sincerely.

"Ok guys, we need to go now," Leonardo said hugging his father and his mother goodbye, and heading toward the front door.

As soon as Clara saw the door opening, she squeezed in the slit tenderly saying goodbye to everybody and hoping to get out of there quickly. Laura grabbed Leonardo by a sleeve, and in the agitation of the farewells, she was able to recall his attention for a moment.

"Are you sure of what you are doing? Clara is still very young. Did you think it through?" she murmured extremely worried.

"She is the woman of my life," Leonardo answered peremptorily.

"I understand that, but you are a doctor, you'll have a weird schedule and a hard life at the hospital; will she be capable of understanding and helping you?" Laura insisted.

"She is the daughter of a surgeon, mom, I think she knows all too well what a strange schedule and a hard life at the hospital are. Why don't we talk about what really frets you, instead?" His look became softer and sweeter. "Don't worry, I love you and I'll keep doing that even when I am married," he said in a comforting voice.

Laura's face suddenly brightened up. Her fingers relaxed letting Leonardo's sleeve go. She hugged him vigorously, then, her eyes looked for Clara and, with the first easy and sincere smile of the evening, she said goodbye to her waving her hand.

Leonardo and Clara ran down the stairs. He was satisfied and proud.

"So, what do you think? It wasn't bad, right?"

"What did your mom say to you at the door?" Clara asked suspiciously.

"She just wanted to be reassured. I told her I love her and always will."

"Are you sure that's all? When you told them the news I thought she wanted to choke me. Instead, she began to torture that poor towel pretending it was my neck."

"I feared the same." Leonardo laughed. "She'll love you, just wait, she needs time to get used to the idea of me getting married."

"Your father instead took it very well, I can say. He already put me at home watching three or four grandkids…"

"Try not to be offended by what he said. He is old." Leonardo said closing the car door and hoping his father's words wouldn't start a fight.

"Offended? Are you kidding? I think he was very sweet. I'd just like it to be so easy also with my parents. I really don't know what to expect from them." Clara commented thoughtful.

"You are right, now it's your turn." Leonardo said getting close to her mouth, but the tension on her lips didn't give in.

~

"Are you really determined to tell them by yourself? My presence could be of help." Leonardo suggested.

"Yes, I think it is better this way," Clara answered worried with sweating palms. "I'll start with mother and then I'll see what happens," she continued even more nervous.

"Try to stay calm. I'm sure everything will be fine," Leonardo reassured her before hanging up the phone.

Maria was at her desk, an antique writing desk with little drawers and a secret compartment in which Clara would leave messages for her mother to find later. Clara stopped and looked at her mother from behind; she was checking some papers that looked like bills.

Maybe this is not the right moment, Clara thought retreating and returning to her room.

Pacing back and forth on the pink rug she looked for inspiration and courage in the convolute designs that decorated it.

"Mom, I have great news!" No, I sound like a fool; better if I start with the feelings we have for one another. "Mom, Leo and I love each other very much and ..."Simply pathetic! I have to stop thinking and just speak. What and how it'll come out won't make much of a difference anyway.

She mustered up the courage and went back to her mother, and this time she approached her. Maria noticed her.

"What's up, honey?" she asked cheerily, unaware of what was about to happen.

Clara tried to forget her heart was exploding and to stop the overlapping thoughts.

"Mom, I need to talk to you," was all she could find to say.

"Don't be so serious, you scare me. What is it?" Maria asked dropping her smile.

"Leonardo asked me to marry him and I said yes," she shot out.

"What!?!" Maria screamed jumping up from the chair. "Are you out of your mind!?! When!?!"

"Next June," Clara answered.

"Oh my God, Clara; are you pregnant? Because, you know, today you don't need to get married if you are," Maria said trying to calm down.

"No, mom, I'm not pregnant, I'm just in love," Clara answered feeling her legs collapsing beneath her.

"For God's sake, Clara, that's not enough! You are too young to know. Being in love is simply not enough! He is older, but you just turned twenty-three, you have too many things to do before becoming somebody's wife! Don't be childish and try to see reason!"

"I want to do everything I have to do mom, but by his side," Clara insisted.

Maria got more upset and raised her voice as the conversation went on.

"You don't know what you are saying, Clara. You have no idea what it means to be married!"

"I thought it meant to face life with the person you love."

"You are so naive, honey! You just met him, it's too soon to make plans of that sort," her mother whined.

"But that's not true; how long did you and dad know each other before getting married?" Clara asked laying her finger on one of her mother's weak spots.

"Don't you dare use my own life to justify your own mistakes, missy!" Maria yelled with her mind fogged by anger. "For us it was different; times were different! I went from my parents' supervision to my husband's. For you it doesn't have to be like that, you are just starting out."

"We are tired of being apart, mom. It's just unbearable for us," interrupted Clara raising her voice for the first time.

"I think Leonardo subjugated you. You are a victim of his arrogance!" Maria exploded.

"I know you think very highly of me, mom. What did you call me on Christmas Eve? 'Immature and insecure,' I believe; thank you! And you are the person I should trust?"

"He told you!!!" Maria screamed gasping and, outraged, rose from the chair. "I knew I couldn't trust him! He brainwashed you! He wants to turn you against me, don't you understand?"

"No, mom, he didn't say anything," Clara answered suddenly calm. "I heard you for myself. And he didn't brainwash me. It's you who's acting like a desperate person trying to control me through him. How did you dare plotting against me?"

Maria was confused and her rage went out of

control.

"You think I'm just a blabbing old woman, right? But if you won't listen to me, you *will* listen to your father. Let's go!" she said rushing to the family room. Clara could barely keep up with her mother's speed.

"Roberto!" Maria screamed standing in front of him. "Clara has something to tell you and if you thought you had already heard everything, just hold on."

Roberto raised his eyebrows, gave both women an inquisitive look and waited silently.

Maria shoved Clara making her take a step forward.

"Dad, Leonardo and I have decided to get married," she spit out keeping her eyes closed.

Her father stayed still, with his legs crossed and the book he was reading resting on his knees.

Clara saw his Adam's apple go quietly up and then suddenly down. His face didn't move and he didn't show any surprise.

"Well, don't sit there like a frozen fish!" urged Maria. "Say something!"

He waited a moment then, with a deep calm voice broke his silence.

"Are you pregnant?"

"No!" Clara replied firmly.

"You see!?! He is asking the same questions I asked!" exploded Maria.

"Maria, could you please shut the fuck up, for once?" said Roberto collectedly.

Then he looked at his daughter.

"Are you in love?" he asked fearing the answer.

"Yes, dad. I feel like I came to life the day I met him."

"Your life will be in Rome, are you aware of that?" her father continued with sad eyes.

"Yes."

"Do you already have a date?" he asked.

"June," she replied.

"Well, then," he sighed resigned.

"Well, then!?!" Maria shouted. "Have you all gone crazy!?!"

"Maria, they are adults," Roberto answered regaining control over his emotions. "If they have decided, there is nothing we can really do or say to change their minds. If I were you, I'd start to focus on the organization," Roberto calmly advised his wife.

"Thank you, dad," Clara smiled.

"Thank you for nothing!" said Maria refusing to surrender. Then, she turned to her daughter. "Now, you come upstairs with me to talk to your grandma. Lets hear if she still wants to kid around like last time."

She ran upstairs furious and opened the door so hard it banged loudly against the wall.

"Mom!" she called pushing Clara in front of her. "Come on, tell her!" Maria commanded.

"I'm getting married!" said Clara joyous.

"It's about time!" said Anna clapping her hands.

"About time!?! Has everybody gone mad today or what!?!" Maria yelled shocked.

Anna ignored her.

"It's great news, honey! Come here; give me a hug! He is a very nice man and you both are lucky to have met. I'm really happy for you,"

Then grandma turned toward Maria with a grave, but satisfied look.

"Release the grip, Maria. Your daughter has grown up."

Maria climbed quietly down the stairs; she hid for a few minutes in her bathroom and then went back to her desk. Clara closed her own bedroom door wondering if it was the right time to call Leonardo, taking advantage of the fact that her mother was refusing to talk to anybody.

She heard a soft and dense murmur coming from her mother's corner of the house; it sounded frenzied and stifled at the same time and Clara could clearly perceive her mother's effort to suppress her frantic emotions. It wasn't clear if she was talking to herself or somebody else, but soon Clara's doubts were cleared. She was about to call Leonardo when the phone rang. She waited for a few rings, but nobody answered, so she picked up the receiver.

"Hello?" she said annoyed that someone was delaying her conversation with Leonardo.

"Clara, is it you?" asked a familiar voice "It's aunt Gemma."

"Hi, Gemma! How are you?" Clara pretended to be happily surprised and dissimulated her true feelings.

Why didn't I think of it before? Of course she called aunt Gemma, I should have know better; where mom fails, aunt Gemma succeeds.

Clara felt naïve for not having anticipated her mother's next move. Every time there was a crisis in the family, Clara's mother would call her younger sister crying for help and asking her to say a few words to solve it quickly and painlessly. Over the years, being backed up by aunt Gemma had been a great resource for Maria; she was youthful, an intellectual, a little rebellious and, in her presence, Clara usually became very reasonable and malleable. Hearing Gemma's voice, Clara giggled, preparing herself to listen to one of her aunt's long monologues where she was just expected to be quiet, listen, agree and obey at the end.

"Allow me to cut the pleasantries, will you? You know why I'm calling; your mother told me the news and I must admit I was caught by surprise," she said sounding disappointed.

"Why?" Clara faked ingenuousness.

"Well, first of all, because it wasn't you telling me, but I had to hear it from your mom; and second, my dear, because in our family we have always cherished education and with this irrational behavior, you are risking jeopardizing your future," Gemma solemnly declared as if the truth was finally spoken.

While listening, Clara could imagine her aunt's hand passing through her long raven-black hair as she waited for her words to open up a new perspective in Clara's mind.

"But I have no intention of quitting my studies," Clara responded firmly.

"Since you decided you want to play adult, why don't you start behaving like one and begin to look at reality for what it is? The probability of you being married *and* finishing your studies is very low. You won't be just a student anymore, you'll be a wife and a housekeeper. Do you know what that means? It means that your husband's career and your kids will soon put your own life in the background," she pontificated.

"I don't think that will happen."

"Maybe not, but why do you want to risk it?" Gemma took the time to deeply inhale the smoke of her cigarette. "Do you really want to be one of those women whose only pride is knowing how to make homemade pasta?"

"I think your fears, and my mother's, are out of proportion. You don't know anything about Leo, about us, our plans or our dreams. I'm confident we can make it."

"We don't know anything about Leo, you are right, and honestly, I think this is part of the problem, but I know about life. You very well know that in my house there aren't any pictures of my wedding day, but only those of my graduation, and you know why, right? Because *that* is what I'm most proud of; and you would do well to do the same."

Clara heard a pause and another intense inhalation.

"I thank you for your advice; I appreciate it, really, but don't expect me to blindly follow your suggestion. Not this time; and you are more than welcome to tell this to my mom, also."

"Life is yours, just see that its best day is not your wedding day. Listen to me," she declared.

"It won't happen, rest assured," Clara answered a bit too quickly.

"Just promise you'll ponder on what I said," aunt Gemma concluded disappointed and, without giving Clara time for an answer, she said goodbye and hung up. Her duty of caring aunt was completed; she said what she was supposed to say but, for the first time, she couldn't reach the expected goal, finding a stronger Clara to confront.

This is done too. Claire sighed with relief. *Now I can finally call Leonardo.*

She was about to dial his number when suddenly Maria appeared at her door. She looked relaxed. She looked like a person who was beginning to accept her defeat.

"I heard what you said to aunt Gemma. Oh well, I tried. By the way, your father is right; there is nothing I can do to change your mind, but be careful, because, contrary to what they tell you in the fairy tales, the wedding day is not the final culmination of a beautiful love story, but it's just the beginning of a life full of obstacles. Do as you wish. If it doesn't work out, this Leonardo will be the first of your husbands."

Maria had found her own way to make peace with her daughter's stubbornness.

~

Clara was searching the house looking for her parents and overheard her mother shouting to her father. She stopped right outside the family room door.

"I already told you, but obviously I have to tell you again; I have no intention of cooking and opening my home to those people!" Maria was screaming.

"For God's sake, keep your voice down; Clara could hear you;" Roberto tried to calm her down.

"As if she pays any attention to what I think or say anymore; who cares, Roberto?!? These people are strangers and I don't owe them anything," she continued screaming.

"You can be more hardheaded than a mule, Maria. I'll tell Clara we think it's better to meet in a restaurant, but you have to behave yourself for your own daughter's good. You owe that to *her*. Have I been clear?"

Clara decided to show herself by stomping her feet on the marble floor and pretending she had just arrived and didn't hear anything of their conversation.

"There you are! I was looking for you. Leonardo's parents would like to meet you and invited all of us over for dinner as soon as you are available." Clara delivered the news as if it was the most joyful thing she could possibly say and kept smiling waiting for their answer. Roberto turned immediately toward Maria and she promptly said, "I was just talking to your father about inviting them here for dinner, but since they seem so eager to have us at their home, it's fine with me. It means I'll have to wait for another time."

Nice try mom, but you can't even fake being sorry.

A date was arranged, and watching Maria getting ready for the big encounter was captivating to Clara. Her mother took a long bath that started at four o'clock; she followed by spreading lotion all over her body and spraying an inspired unique mixture of fragrances around five. She began with the make-up at six and was dressed by seven. It was time to go and Clara's father imperatively called his wife like he used to do every time he was concerned she might deliberately be late. Maria didn't answer, but immediately showed up in the foyer wearing a red suit, red shoes, red purse, rubies around her neck and at her lobes, red lipstick, and red nails.

"Well, how do I look?" she asked not really caring for an answer.

"Red and ready to fight," said Roberto, chuckling and showing her the way to the door.

Clara's mother climbed the stairs to Leonardo's parents' apartment panting and complaining about the absence of an elevator 'that every respectable building was supposed to have' while her father followed her heartily reminding her to be patient and easy-going. Leonardo greeted them at the door; his parents joined him right after, a little thrilled and a little cautious. Clara nervously clutched Leonardo's hand and placed herself close to him so as to show which side she had chosen to be on and to warn everybody she was irremovable in her decision to marry him. Her father and Leonardo's father immediately hit it off finding many topics to discuss. They were close in age and soon became aware that they had a lot of memories to share; the blue couch in the living room became the imaginary stage where their old stories started to materialize. Most of those stories Clara had never heard, and she realized how little she really knew about her father's past. Every time she ever attempted to ask him about his childhood or youth, he'd turn melancholy soon after he began to talk and always found an excuse not to complete his tale.

"Clara told me you have a house in the Appennini Mountains," started Roberto with the intention of breaking the ice.

"For us it's not just a house, it's where Laura and I were born and raised. We consider it home, and now that we are retired, we spend most of the year up there," he answered conveying his devotion.

"You know, right after the war, I was transferred to the hospital closest to your town to help the local doctors. I was young and I was coming from the city; I remember I was disconcerted in knowing that there was no bridge to connect your town to our side of the valley," Roberto said still amazed.

"That's right; there was a Roman bridge that was bombarded at the end of the war and we had to wait until 1954 for it to be rebuilt," Bruno confirmed.

"We had only one doctor capable of reaching you by horse, doctor Santi; do you remember him?" Roberto asked.

"Of course I remember him!" Bruno laughed out loud as his memories came back to the surface "And one night he had to come to my house in the middle of a terrible rainstorm because I had hurt my hand with a handsaw while cutting trees in the woods. He arrived almost frozen to death; my mother offered him a cup of hot milk, which he never refused, and he used the time it took to sip it to the end to think hard on what to do with my hand. Eventually he decided to amputate my thumb right there on the kitchen table. My mom cried for the entire time while praying to all the saints in the sky and then, sent him home with two dead chickens and a few fresh eggs. Can you imagine the same thing nowadays?"

"The doctor would be sued and the patient would be rich!" Roberto joked. "Well, back then medicine was different and patients really trusted their doctors' decisions," he sighed and changed the subject. "But how did you manage to have provisions or to cross the river on a daily basis? It must have been hard," he asked Bruno, curious.

"We simply used horses, like doctor Santi. Laura was an incredible horsewoman; she rode without a saddle and often disappeared for hours in the woods."

"Do you remember the winter of '65 when there was that terrible snowfall?" Clara's father asked suddenly recalling a new episode.

"If I'm not mistaken, I think it wasn't '65, but '68," Bruno answered grasping immediately the episode to which Roberto was referring.

The two mothers, on the other hand, had a more difficult time interacting; this was not helped by the ten-year age gap that separated them and by their totally different personalities. Leonardo's mom, short and simply dressed, seemed insecure around the shrew in red that showed up in her home.

"Tonight everything is homemade!" she proudly informed Clara's mother.

"When I have events, I definitely prefer to cater and, for sure, I never learned how to make any kind of dough," Maria rebutted haughtily.

"I mastered how to feed crowds of hungry people when we were running our hotel; more than once the chef quit right at the peak of the season and I had to cover for him until we found an adequate replacement," Laura explained.

"I have never worked a single day in my life," Maria concluded not leaving too much room for the conversation to go on.

Laura straightened up her apron's knot and withdrew to the kitchen to check the food. Maria silently stood at the kitchen door unable to make the decision whether to go in and help her or leave her alone and join the others on the blue couch. The kitchen timer went off and solved her dilemma by loudly announcing to everybody that the food was ready and it was time to sit at the table.

"Doctor Maro, maybe this is not the right time to tell you," Bruno began to say looking at Leonardo who shivered knowing his father could be extremely ill-timed. "You can't possibly remember it, but many years ago you had to operate on Laura and you saved her life."

"Incredible!" answered Roberto surprised. "I'm very happy everything worked out for the best."

"Actually I don't find it incredible at all," Maria said, jumping into the conversation. "You operated on more than half of the city; I feel comfortable saying that I'd be more amazed if nobody in Leonardo's family had been under your knife," she concluded snottily.

"Maria, that's not the point," Roberto replied discouraged.

"I know what the point is. I get it," she interrupted him and turned toward Clara. "Aren't you lucky, honey? How many girls can say their father saved their mother-in-law's life? You must be very proud and this makes your love story even more special. Don't you think?"

Maria's strident voice finally stopped. Clara felt the impulse to bite her right in the neck, but used all her strength to ignore her. Leonardo noticed her effort to control her feelings and caressed her leg under the table to calm her down. Laura asked if anybody wanted more roast beef before she brought the dessert.

"I'll have another slice, if you don't mind," said Clara's father; "it's so tender and juicy."

"You had enough, Roberto. Please, Laura bring it back to the kitchen before he'd be sorry."

Roberto froze, his eyebrows frowned and his cheeks became red. Everybody feared he had had enough of his wife's unpleasant behavior and that he was ready to go off. Bruno intervened.

"Mrs. Maro is right, Laura. You always push people to eat too much, but he is a doctor and probably carefully watches his caloric intake," he tried with some irony.

Clara's stomach shrank to the size of a grape and she didn't notice how hard she was squeezing Leonardo's leg until he protested by emitting a soft moan.

"Stay calm, it'll end soon," he whispered leaning toward her.

"I know, but my mom is detestable," she sadly acknowledged.

"What do you care? Let them all be. They don't have to be best friends, they just have to manage to get through dinner without stabbing each other with the silverware," Leonardo laughed perfectly understanding Clara's feelings.

"And do you think they'll be able to make it?" she joked and relaxed a little hearing his calm voice.

Clara's father raised his glass and announced, "With dessert coming, I'd like to propose a toast to Clara and Leo; may their enthusiasm for each other and for life last forever!"

Maria rolled her eyes to the sky and grabbed her glass exposing a huge ruby surrounded by diamonds.

"I want to see if my mother drinks to that," Clara softly laughed.

"She is drinking, you see?" Leonardo teased her.

"She is sipping it with her lips tightened. I think she did it just to show off her ring," Clara bitterly replied.

Leonardo's mother reemerged from the kitchen holding a wide tray and proudly revealed the dessert.

"Homemade crème brûlée," she declared satisfied and encouraged by Clara's father's appreciation.

"It's my favorite!" exclaimed Roberto brightening up and grabbing a spoon.

"I'm so glad you like it," Laura said strutting like a peacock opening its tail.

"Now you know where to come when you want your favorite dessert," Clara's mother broke in resentful.

"You know I love it. I just wish you'd make it for me more often," he replied honestly.

"Is this enough for you?" asked Laura handing a portion to Maria.

"Sorry, but none for me. It's not my favorite and I have never had so much homemade food in my whole life; I wouldn't want to get sick."

Maria's shrill tone and harsh words pierced Clara deeply in her heart. She felt all the many things she wanted to say halting in her throat and choking her while she threw her napkin on the table and stared furiously at her mother and father. Roberto knew it was time to leave, so he graciously refused any coffee and disclosed that the time had come to say their goodbyes.

"We'd really like to stay, but tomorrow I have to be in the operating room very early. I guess you'll stay a little longer, Clara. I'll see you at home."

Before leaving, he lauded Leonardo's mother once more for her culinary skills, thanked Leonardo's father for his warm hospitality, and accomplished accompanying his wife out the door before she could say anything unpleasant again.

Clara and Leo retired to his room.

"I'm so tired, Leo," Clara sighed crumbling on Leonardo's bed. "It's been exhausting; everybody claiming to be worried about me being too young to behave like an adult, but in the meanwhile, they act like spoiled kids. And my mom has no regard for anybody else's feelings," she growled.

"Take it easy. I know it's simple to say, but," Leonardo started to say.

"Did you hear her tonight? I have so many things to tell her, but I don't know how," she concluded with frustration.

"Soon you'll find your voice," Leonardo reassured her.

"And what do I do in the meanwhile?" she asked with her brown eyes wide open.

"You go ahead with your own life."

"It seems to me they don't want me to grow up, they just want me to be who they planned for me to be," Clara complained.

"Give them time to adjust."

"Do you think they'll ever understand that I held back too long and now I don't give a shit anymore? I don't give a shit about what they think of me, of you, of us, and I simply made my decision."

"I think they know it very well and that they are scared," Leonardo answered looking for physical contact.

His delicate fingers around her waist placated her harsh mood.

"Let's go help your mom clean up," Clara said jumping off the bed.

"She doesn't expect you to," Leonardo responded hoping to convince her to stay in his bedroom.

"I know, but I don't want her to think I'm snobbish like my mother," she smiled.

"She already knows you are not," he insisted one more time.

Clara gave him a long soft kiss and pulled him off the bed "Let's go, you are helping, too."

Chapter 9
~ Friendship ~

Maria took charge and immediately switched to event coordinator mode; she took the situation into her own hands and started planning the wedding of her dreams. She couldn't change the church Clara had chosen, but she decided that the more appropriate location for the reception would be the Grand Hotel, a marvelous white liberty-style building right on the ocean that over the years had become one of the symbols of their town. It still treasured the original Venetian furniture and decor from the eighteenth century; master gardeners looked after the outside in every detail and the surrounding atmosphere catapulted one into the splendor of the past. Maria believed it would be the perfect place to entertain the guests and also to spend the wedding night. Clara had to admit it was a very elegant setting. It wasn't the first time she was there. She knew well the majestic foyer, some of the rooms where she had listened to concerts and lectures, and the pink velvet dining room where she celebrated her eighteenth birthday, the windows of which faced the garden. The hotel manager, a refined woman with bright red hair, welcomed them saying how well she knew their family and, showing a lot of enthusiasm in having them there, she had them take a seat in a nice little room that Clara had never seen before. A great harmony and understanding sparked between her mother and the hotel manager and they immediately agreed on both the menu and the decorations.

"Do you prefer a menu based on meat or seafood?" the manager asked as the first routine question.

"Absolutely both," Maria answered as if it was the most obvious thing to say. "We'll have people of all ages and I want to respect everybody's taste. For the same reason I'd like plenty of vegetables too, since some of the youngest are following this new trend of being vegetarian."

"Exactly what I'd have suggested if you'd asked," the manager commented proudly. "Clara, your mother must be a great hostess," she said satisfied looking at Clara.

Clara smiled nodding timidly.

"Later we'll choose in detail the dishes to serve, but for now I'd like you to concentrate on the decorations. First of all I need to know if you have your own trusted florist or if your prefer to put the matter in our expert hands, and then what kind of flowers do you wish and where do you want them," she continued ready to take notes in her notebook.

Clara silently observed her mother and the hotel manager talking about the tiniest details and debating about the smallest trivialities with great energy and passion, while she felt like the usual fish out of water.

It was decided that they would not use the dining room, but to set the dinner tables outside instead.

"It is a pity to close everybody inside when outside they can enjoy a beautiful warm June night," her mother said.

"I couldn't agree more, and if we put the tables next to the exotic garden the choreography will be outstanding," the manager answered. "The bride and groom can liberally stroll through the greenery entertaining the guests, and the pictures will have a lush background," she added.

Maria declined the idea of a buffet because she considered it unrefined and not comfortable enough for their older guests. She opted instead for a seated dinner served by waiters wearing livery, but with a fast pace so as not to bore the younger ones by forcing them to be seated for hours.

"Your band can stay here and you can dance there," the manager said showing them an outdoor platform placed in front of a wide paved floor and surrounded by plants. "Here in June everything will be in bloom, Clara. It'll be marvelous," she told the bride-to-be.

Clara's mother was ecstatic.

"And now it is time to talk about the 'spicier details'; we have to decide on the room for the first night," her mother said cheerfully.

"In strict confidence, I want to tell you that the rooms we reserve for the wedding nights are very nice, but they are not the best we have. Considering that I have known your family very

248

well for years, that your husband saved the lives of many of my relatives, and that I know what kind of guests you are inviting, I'd like to make a very good impression by offering you a different room," the manager said as if she were revealing a secret upon which the safety of all humankind depended. Joy lighted up Clara's mother. The hotel manager went close to Clara and began speaking to her with the tone of voice of a teacher who has to explain to a new student things, that, for her, are obvious.

"Let's see; each room is identified by a name and for your first night, I'd suggest the one called 'Fureur[9],'" she smiled maliciously and winked at Clara's mother.

That name made Clara blush like a schoolgirl and she detested herself for not being able to prevent her cheeks from betraying her emotions.

"It is one of my favorites. It is romantic, but with a zest. It overlooks the sea, and the morning after, breakfast will be served on the small balcony from which you'll be able to see as far as Croatia. It's marvelous!" the manager said taking them to the third floor. The elevators were old, small and narrow. The corridors had cozy antique furniture and a plush, nappy atmosphere thanks to a yellow carpet with red flowers that led to the door of the room. A little foyer opened onto a sitting room of green velvet furnished with a Luigi XIV sofa and chairs covered with gold leaf. They proceeded into the bedroom through a

[9] French for 'Passion'.

decorated arch. In the middle of it stood a huge chiseled wood canopy bed wrapped in a cloud of red silk. As the manager anticipated, a French door opened onto a charming little balcony overlooking the sea where there was just enough room for a small wrought iron table and two chairs. An antique inventive inlaid Italian writing desk, open next to the window, was waiting for someone to use its precious stationery and inkpot. The bathroom was ample with the sinks and tub made out of malachite green Carrara marble and brass faucets. The tub looked dug in the stone and inspired sumptuous and lavish relaxation.

"This room is perfect for your first night, right Clara?" her mother exclaimed radiant with joy. "The name 'Fureur' already says it all, but with a bed and a tub like those I bet you and Leonardo won't sleep much," she said chirpy.

A shiver of embarrassment ran up Clara's backbone. For her, the presence and the gaze of her mother in that room was an intrusion of her privacy and those last words violated her intimacy with Leonardo.

At the end of the day, when everything was decided and they went back home, Clara was thankful it was over.

~

After dinner, Maria and Roberto were in the family room. He was following a quiz show on television and simultaneously reading the newspaper while she was writing something down on her notepad. Unexpectedly Clara joined them after talking with Leonardo on the phone and when her mother saw her coming in she took a bunch of magazines from the coffee table and put them in front of her.

"Since you are not pleased with anything the shops have shown you, I took the liberty of selecting these bridal magazines. Maybe you'll find a dress that appeals to your taste," said Maria in a tone of voice that was close to irritation.

"Thanks, mom. This is great," Clara said enthusiastically ignoring the shades in her mother's voice. "I want to call grandma. She loves when I tell her how the organization is progressing and especially about the dress. I'm sure she'll have fun flipping through the pages with me," Clara said happily.

Grandma came down slowly and sat heavily on the couch.

"Here I am," grandma said breathing laboriously as if she had just finished climbing a mountain.

"Take these magazines, grandma. Start with these and let me know if you find something you like," Clara said putting some magazines on her knees.

Grandma shrunk in her seat and silently turned the pages without really pausing on any of them.

She found it difficult to participate in the conversation that was going on and she didn't comment on the dresses or the things Maria was saying. It was like she wasn't even noticing the pictures and hearing the voices. She was distracted, uninterested and distant.

Clara's father got up and announced that it was time for him to go to bed. He wished everybody a good night.

"I'll be there in a moment," said Maria sleepily.

"Take your time," he answered going toward the bedroom.

Clara was halfway through the magazines when a picture of a bride resting on a trellis covered with white roses caught her eye.

"This is it. I found it," she said satisfied.

It was her dress, romantic and simple.

"Let me see," said Maria snatching the magazine from her daughter's hand. "Are you sure?" she asked.

"Yes! You know me. This is it. I've made up my mind."

"It's a vintage Valentino, we'll never find it," her mother said pensive. "We'll have to go to a tailor's shop."

"Is that a problem?" Clara asked worriedly.

"Are you kidding? It's great!" her mother exclaimed with joy coming out of her eyes. "We'll have to choose the fabric, decide the details, you'll have several fittings; it'll be a lot of fun!"

"And you, grandma? What do you think? Do you like it?" Clara asked.

"It's beautiful," grandma answered distracted.

"Are you sure? You don't look convinced," Clara said.

"I like it a lot, honey. I'm just tired."

~

There were no reasons to keep the wedding a secret anymore. Clara's parents promised to have not revealed it to anyone, yet, but Clara knew them and found it hard to believe it. She was sure they had started to tell some of their closest friends and she knew it was time to tell Paola before she heard it from somebody else.

"Hi Paola, it's Clara," she said after Paola picked up the phone.

"Clara, how are you?" Paola answered surprised to hear from her after such a long time.

"I'm fine. If you are home, can I come by for a visit?"

"Sure. Has anything happened?" Paola asked.

"I just need to talk to you," Clara told her friend.

"In order to turn up so unexpectedly after such a long time, it must be a very important thing you have to tell me," Paola commented harshly before hanging up the phone without waiting for Clara's answer.

It was a cold February day. Paola's house was just a few hundred yards away and Clara was walking along the gates of the other houses trying not to stumble upon the roots of the trees that were protruding from the ground. She was excited and a little afraid of Paola's possible reaction, but also confident that their friendship would prevail.

It wasn't possible to remember how many times over the years she had walked along the same path to reach her friend and spend some time with her. During childhood it was to play, later it was for homework sessions, and during adolescence it was to talk about boys and dream about the future. Clara felt confused. She stopped in front of the intercom and wished she could just go back home. *There is no reason to be a chicken.* She rang the doorbell.

"What is it Clara?" asked Paola coldly after she took her into the living room.

"Leonardo and I are getting married," she abruptly said.

"So it's true!" Paola exclaimed shocked.

"Did you know already?" Clara asked surprised.

"Yesterday my mom was at the bakery in front of your house and overheard two ladies talking about you. I refused to believe it. And when will the blessed event take place?" Paola asked with sarcasm.

The electricity in the air was so thick Clara could touch it and she knew that the smallest spark would initiate pandemonium.

"June," she answered determined and pretending to ignore Paola's bad mood.

"Are you pregnant?" Paola asked confused and looking for explanations.

"This is getting really annoying," grumbled Clara. "Why does everybody think I'm pregnant!?"

"Why? You are asking me why? Why the fuck else would a right-minded twenty-three-year-old woman get married?!?! It's the fucking nineties, or didn't you notice?" screamed Paola losing her composure all of a sudden.

"No, I'm not pregnant," Clara answered hastily afraid of Paola's reaction. "Satisfied?"

"I feel like I don't know you anymore, Clara," Paola said disappointed. "Why didn't you tell me before?"

"It happened very fast. We decided to keep it to ourselves for a while and, since the beginning, you've been acting so antagonistic. You even came to my house and yelled your disbelief in my face. I didn't feel comfortable confiding in you," Clara told her.

"But I just tried to warn you," Paola said suddenly attentive. "You are getting yourself into big trouble, Clara. Whatever it is you two have, it won't last. He needs a different kind of woman at his side."

"Paola, listen; since last summer, anything you've said about Leo and me has been very offensive. I'll try to act as if you said nothing, but I'm sure you are not really worried about me. Something else is going on here. I admit I had my secrets for a while, but I think you are not telling me everything either. Are you in love with Leo? Is that why you are mad at me?" she asked really nervous.

"Don't be silly," Paola said trying to look indignant and trying to hide the blushing that made her cheeks red-hot. Suddenly, Clara understood.

"I see, so that's what this is all about. You are trashing our friendship over a crush on Leo I didn't even know anything about. May I ask if at least *he* knows?" Clara asked ready to fight.

"No. He doesn't know," answered Paola admitting her feelings.

"And why didn't you tell him?" Clara asked puzzled.

"Because he has always treated me like nothing more than a friend. I don't even know if he ever even noticed I'm a girl!" Paola said starting to cry.

"What I don't understand is why are you angry at me," Clara said trying to put order to her thoughts.

"Because you have always been the princess and now you've found your prince. Are you happy?" asked Paola bitterly.

"Princess? What does that even mean?" Clara was confused. She was disconcerted.

"It means that I'm tired of always being a step behind you!" Paola yelled bursting into tears. "Clara the skinny one, Clara the tallest, Clara the one with the parents who are always ready to grant any of her wishes. When it was time for college Clara couldn't go to Bologna like us common mortals; no, it wasn't good enough for 'your highness!'" she screamed enraged. "You had to go to Milan, of course, the big city! And then, one day, you decided to step down from your pedestal, to join us poor human beings for one night, you met Leonardo, and now you are marrying him. Couldn't you have stayed in Milan forever?" she erupted with no control.

Clara felt pain grip right at the center of her heart.

"If you only knew how I have really felt all these years; I'm very sorry, Paola. I don't know what to say right now. I just wish you could be happy for me."

"This time, dear Clara, I don't think I can," Paola said turning her back.

"Well, you will be receiving an invitation. If you can get over your anger, you are welcome to come."

Clara went back home crying. Her happiness was causing a lot of distress to the people she loved the most and that in the past she protected; but now things were different and she was determined to go on and fight.

"Grandma, what are you watching?"

"Fred Astaire and Ginger Rogers. Come on, sit down with me," Anna said patting the seat next to her on the couch.

Clara sat on the green sofa. It was dark and grandma didn't notice the tears that were wetting her face.

~

After several weeks Leonardo was finally able to leave Rome for a weekend. He picked Clara up and when he saw her he gave her an insecure hug, different from the hugs he had given her in the previous months. She felt he was a thousand miles away. He didn't suggest, as he usually did, that they run to his parents' apartment on the coast for a few hours, instead, he suggested they take a walk in downtown. It was Saturday. It was cold. It was difficult to imagine that in a few weeks winter would end. The streets were wet and even though it was the time for the strolls, only a few people were outside. Leonardo was silent. He embraced Clara, but he was absorbed in thoughts bigger than himself and he noticed neither the coldness nor the wetness. Clara wanted to go into a café to warm up.

"What are you having?" Leonardo asked agitated.

"Chicory coffee and this irresistible apple tart," Clara answered quickly.

"I'll have an espresso," Leonardo said concisely to the waiter. "Can you bring everything to the table?"

"Listen, what is it going on? You have been acting so strange these last few days," Clara said while getting comfortable at a table in the rear.

"You are right. I have very important news to tell you. It's been a few days since I knew, but I didn't want to talk about it over the phone," he said sounding excited and alarmed.

Clara was scared.

"Are you having second thoughts about the wedding?" Clara asked hesitant.

"No, what are you thinking? The wedding has nothing to do with this, but it is true that what I'm about to tell you could have repercussions," Leonardo told her.

"Come on, Leo, tell me. I'm exploding," Clara implored trying to smile.

"It's something big, Clara. It could be good or bad; it depends on us and it can have different kinds of consequences," he said worriedly.

"Now I'm even more agitated than before. Come on, shoot and lets get over with it."

"Ok. My boss asked me to go to the States for one year to learn a new technique," he stopped and remained silent to give Clara some time to think. Clara was still. Her eyes widened. She stared at him speechless.

"They don't ask just anybody. This means they are investing in me. It's a great honor, but," he hesitated.

"But?" was all she was able to ask.

"But I need to know what you think about it. I can't decide without you," Leonardo said with slight relief in his voice.

Clara suddenly woke up. Her thoughts started to spin once again.

"Are you asking me what I want you to do?"

"Well, I'm asking you what *we* should do. It's not just me anymore, it's us, and I need to know what you think. Do you wish to go? Because I don't think I'd go without you," he told her honestly.

"So, you are not asking me to postpone the wedding?" Clara asked surprised.

"Not at all!" Leonardo said. "But I'm afraid that now that I've told you, you'll *want* to postpone it."

Clara tried to clear her mind.

"Did they tell you where in US?"

"Portland, Oregon," he said trying to make it sound exciting.

Clara looked at him dismayed. "Never heard of it," she said trying to summon her knowledge of geography.

"Never heard of it, either," confessed Leonardo smiling. "I just know it's on the west coast."

"The west coast!" Clara cried out even more stunned. "No less than on the other side of the globe. And did they tell you when we should leave?"

"Next November," he told her.

"So soon? It's right at the beginning of the new academic year. Right when I'm supposed to begin my new path," she said in a soft voice almost speaking more to herself than to Leonardo.

"That's another reason why we need to think about it very carefully," Leonardo said. "Your future is at stake, too, not just mine."

"Leo, this is really big news. And I mean *big*. My family is still trying to digest the fact that I'm getting married and moving to Rome, and now I have to tell them we are going to the US, and on the west coast. For how long did you say?"

Each question helped her to order her thoughts.

"At least one year, but honestly, it could be longer; but you don't have to forget about your own plans, you know. You want to study psychology," he answered.

Clara took his hands in hers and signaled for him to let her speak. She started thinking out loud.

"Everyone thinks I'm crazy to marry you and now this; let me think. I'm sure my mother would tell me to cancel the wedding, let you go, and forget about you. I'm sure she'd be thrilled. My father would probably suggest that we still get married, but that you go alone so I can take my time to finish law school," she paused.

Leonardo was holding his breath not understanding where she was going to end up. "It would probably be the most cautious thing to do," he said trying to sound reasonable.

She raised her gaze, looked straight into Leonardo's eyes and squeezed his hand.

"Ok, my love. Let's go to Portland!" she said laughing.

"Are you sure?" he asked incredulous. "I mean, don't you need some time to think it over?"

Clara smiled "Don't you know me by now? I said let's do it!" she said hugging him.

"You have guts Clara, let me tell you. But what about your dreams? Psychology? Have you considered that?"

"Don't worry about me. I'll find a way. It's just another twist on the road from A to Z. You see? I'm learning your lessons, but don't tell me I'm getting better than the teacher. I can go to school there, I can go to school here or I can even wait. As you said, we are in this together and together we will make it."

~

It was another gray and rainy day — the ideal day to host an extended family Sunday lunch and linger at the table until late. Everybody was about to arrive exactly as they would for an out-of-season Christmas celebration. A festive setting gladdened the dining room and Clara was helping her mother to arrange the last few things on the table when the relatives started to show up at the door. The desire to see each other was thrilling the atmosphere and the air was filled by enthusiasm. Everybody was present, like in the old times, when Clara was a little girl. Grandma, seated in her usual spot, silently listened to Aldo and Flavio tell the adventures of their recent vacation together. Their wives kept an eye on the children making sure they didn't break any of Maria's precious glasses and dinnerware. The eccentric aunt Gemma, bound in a cloud of smoke, repulsively observed her husband while he shamelessly devoured everything that was placed in front of him. Then, all of a sudden, Clara's mother got up from her chair and, clapping her hands, sent the kids away.

"It's time you go play somewhere else and leave my silverware alone. We have some grown-up talking to do. But, be careful, this house is full of precious things that need to be preserved, so, don't break anything! Understood?" she finished yelling while they were happily rushing out of the dining room as if it was a prison from which they could finally escape.

"Everybody, make yourselves comfortable because now it's time to start," she said speaking to the adults that remained seated at the table and grabbing their attention.

"What is it time to start?" Clara asked caught totally unprepared.

Aunt Gemma began speaking for everybody. "Well, why do you think we are all here today?" she stopped and fiercely looked at Clara. "We are here to talk about your news. It's like you recently woke up from a slumber and got into more trouble than in all of the previous twenty years of your life."

"I'm sorry," intervened Flavio turning to his sister. "But did you really think we were all reunited here only for the pleasure of seeing each other one more time?"

"Well, yes," Clara answered stunned.

"It is you that brought us here today, silly! You and your recently found irrationality," Aldo commented mocking her.

"Are you talking about my wedding?" Clara asked hesitantly.

"Not only that, but also your trip to Portland," Flavio exclaimed.

"And how do you know about *that*?" she asked appalled.

"We know you didn't want us to know, but, by now, you should have learned that lies don't last long and that even the walls have hears," Flavio sneered.

"Ok, but I'm still confused," Clara answered.

"I'm not a bit surprised, you have always been so jejune. I bet you'd like us to tell you that we are proud of your courage to marry a complete stranger and to follow him to the end of the earth, right?" her mother retorted with venom in her voice.

The humiliating loud laughs that filled the room lacerated Clara's self-confidence leaving it in tatters. She raised her eyes and saw everybody transformed. The hard laughs deformed their faces and made them look somewhat non-human. The room became dark, but her father's eyes turned red and then the eyes of everybody else followed resembling those of hungry beasts consumed by rage. It wasn't possible to distinguish their single faces anymore and their voices started to growl in unison.

Clara got up from her chair. Scared.

"Where do you think you are going? You can't run away from us," a strident voice screamed while somebody else's hand tried to hold her.

"Let me go!" Clara screamed imploring. "Don't you understand that I have to go away from here?"

Clara saw their red eyes getting closer and, from the roaring of their mouths, her father's voice emerged.

"I'm very disappointed in you. I thought I taught you better than this," he disapprovingly said.

"We had so many hopes for you, and you willingly decided to just throw them away," her mother said, echoing her husband.

"We don't like you anymore. We want the old Clara back!" they all said in a chorus.

"I'm sure this is a mistake and you'll pay for disappointing us," her mother threatened.

Then a voice stood above the others. "Run Clara! Now!" grandma screamed tearing their communal threat.

Clara freed her hand with a strong pull and started running toward the door. It was closed, but she could open it. She tumbled down the stairs, but recomposed herself and ran faster. She lost her shoes and the friction of the asphalt abraded her bare feet like sandpaper on butter. The streets were dark and deserted. Clara was horrified. Never looking back, she arrived at the beach and stopped, breathless. Leonardo stood on the sand. He smiled and waited. She began running to him, but the more she tried, the further away he seemed to be. Reaching him was impossible. Her family had found her; she could hear the rumbling noise of their voices getting closer. She could feel them. She felt her energy abandoning her and she started crying. When the warm tears wetted her cheeks, she finally woke up.

~

America. Clara hadn't seen that one coming, for sure. Seated on her bathroom floor with her legs crossed and the atlas on her knees, she was deep in her thoughts while studying the geography of the world. Still and absorbed, with the big book wide open to the North America page and her index finger on Oregon, Clara realized that, like everybody else she knew, she always thought of the US as California or, at most, New York City; but, Oregon. She was able to collect a bit of information about what, to her, was an unknown state without arousing her mother's suspicion. The travel book she bought, now hidden under her mattress, said Portland was the main city, but not the capital. It was surprising to learn that the state capital was never the most important city; she had never really noticed that before. It was a message for the people. The guide said Portland was known as 'the city of roses' because its climate was ideal for growing them. *I have to tell Leo. He said I'm his rose and we have to go spend one year in the city of roses. I find it romantic and amusing.* Suddenly, many details she had never considered important when reading of a new place seemed fundamental. The fact that Portland was a rainy city became highly interesting when her prolonged reading revealed that it was a peculiar rain. She found herself wondering how rain could be 'peculiar.' Apparently, heavy showers were rare and, most of the time, the rain consisted of fine drops that came down slowly and penetrated the soil deeply, allowing the plants to thrive during the drier months. The travel book said the umbrella was rarely necessary. Her readings also disclosed that the residents, known as 'Portlanders,' were very attentive toward the environment, very outdoor-oriented and extremely proud to have the biggest city park in all of the United States. It wasn't totally clear to Clara what all of that really meant, but it sounded fun. The park had many trails on which to walk or bike, there was a peaceful Japanese garden in which to meditate and a lot of wildlife to observe or with which to interact. A small note at the end of the page, highlighted in pink, said it was possible to feed peanuts to the wild squirrels. Amazing. Expanding her research, Clara found out that Oregon had many forests with trees that are thousands of years old and that these wooded areas are the homeland for many animals she had never seen, like cougars, eagles, bears and sea lions. In January, from the coast, it was possible to rent a boat and go watch the whales migrating south. Startling. Clara spent entire evenings reading about those new places with award-winning roses, squirrels to feed, gardens in which to reflect and real whales to observe in the feral Pacific Ocean. She was as excited as she was frightened, and having to keep it for herself made it even more difficult. Sometimes she wanted to scream her joy to somebody. Sometimes she only wanted to express her doubts. Was following Leonardo to the other side of the world the right choice? Was it reasonable? Rational? She didn't know. She just knew it was the only possibility she had. Her heart and her mind wouldn't tolerate any other alternative. Nothing else made sense, but to be with him. She knew what others might say and sometimes she could clearly hear their voices: "Let him go; if it's really true love, one year won't make a difference; if it is true love, it'll be even stronger when he comes back; if it was true love he wouldn't leave you." But she wanted to be with him, by his side, to help him, to be helped by him, to grow together and to live together whatever life had to offer.

Chapter 10
~ In sickness ~

Spring was close. Winter still tried to resist, but the aromas of life that revive impregnated the warm wind; the pollens were now ready to germinate the air, and Clara felt an unusual euphoria. Her mother was in the garden giving orders to three gardeners, completely disregarding their ten-year competence, and was instructing them in detail on how to prepare the grounds for the warm weather about to arrive. They patiently listened while her bossy voice could be heard from upstairs. The wedding preparations were flawlessly moving forward and the first meeting with the woman who would be making Clara's dress was about to take place that afternoon. Her mother activated all her acquaintances and was able to find the best seamstress in town; her name was Noemi. She was a young woman with a tender voice, a sweet face and a big mole that made her upper lip interesting. She worked at home, in an apartment in the suburbs in which she assigned one room for cutting and sewing and another for the fittings furnished with a big mirror and a screen behind which to undress. She greeted Clara and her mother offering them some coffee. She took the picture of the dress from Clara and quietly pondered for a few minutes, carefully studying it. Thoughtful, she went to the window, came back, leaned against her desk, smiled with relief, and explained to Clara and her mother where to go to order the fabric they needed. They had to drive fifty miles to reach that store and during the drive they often wondered if it was really necessary to go so far away. Once there, however, they were both amazed by the ample assortment of different textiles and their accurate selection. The store was huge and had the walls fully covered with fabrics carefully rolled and laid on shelves, divided by type and organized by colors. At first, they browsed by themselves among the narrow aisles guided only by curiosity and instinct; soon however, they felt lost and decided to ask for help. They showed the picture of the dress to an old lady who looked like she had spent her entire life there; she was short and round with a flaccid and wrinkled double chin. Aware of the importance of the details, they reported exactly what Noemi told them to say and were very disappointed when the old lady said that, among that infinite amount of fabrics, they were missing just what they were looking for.

"It is a precious lace that needs to be ordered directly from France," she said trying to give meaning to their discouragement.

"How long will it take to have it delivered?" Maria asked worriedly.

"No more than a couple of weeks," the old lady answered with an optimistic tone of voice. The movements of her mouth produced soft waves on her double chin that mesmerized Clara. "You could buy another kind of lace, less refined, but that we have in stock; however, your seamstress is right and I assure you that the final result wouldn't be the same. I'm sure it is worth waiting for exactly what you want."

Therefore, everything slowed down for a few weeks and Maria had to restrain her expectations. Finally, one afternoon, Clara's dress was ready to be tried on and she and her mother were both excited.

Noemi opened the door smiling with a cigarette dangling from one corner of her mouth and led them into the fitting room that was secluded from the rest of the apartment.

"I hope Clara's dress won't smell like tobacco," said Maria tartly, looking at the seamstress with venomous eyes.

"No worries; I never smoke while I work and I always leave the cigarette outside the dressing room," she answered with a reassuring tone of voice typical of a person who regularly deals with demanding clients and who has learned how to calm them.

"Are you ready?" she asked with a smile that let excitement shine through.

With a theatrical motion she removed the light wooden screen and exposed the dummy that was wearing Clara's dress. There was no time for an answer. The dress waited imperious for their reaction; it wasn't finished, alterations and the addition of a few parts were expected, but it already reflected Clara's personality and her feelings for Leonardo.

Clara's mouth dropped. Maria, shaken by emotions, took a tissue out of her purse.

"You won't start crying, will you?" said Clara to her mother, trying to joke to defuse the atmosphere.

"I'm trying not to," said Maria drawing in a deep breath.

Dressed in white, Clara struggled to recognize herself in the big mirror. Her mother, standing behind her, stared, moved by her daughter's image in the mirror.

"You are beautiful, honey. To make it perfect it's missing only the veil," she whispered very touched.

"But I don't want any veil, mom," Clara made clear interrupting her mother's flow of sweet emotions.

"But that's absurd, honey. Now you are upset and can't think clearly. A bride must have a veil!" Maria sounded outraged.

"I don't care what a bride is supposed to have or not have, the dress is fine as it is and I have no intention of wearing a veil, mom," Clara said with a tone of voice that didn't allow any reply.

"It's all Leonardo's fault, he turned you into a stubborn girl," murmured Maria irritated, squeezing her fists so as not to make a scene in front of a stranger.

Clara was new to such strong determination and she was the first one to be surprised at her own words; without knowing it she began rebelling at her upbringing and at her years of strict education that had suffocated her ability to impose herself to the point that she couldn't discriminate her wishes from her parents' anymore. Her mother was not used to taking her opinions into consideration; she was never interested in knowing her wishes and interpreted that now as Clara expressing them as stubbornness. Clara's past behavior had made her a perfect daughter, easy to raise and always ready to surrender, but also a perfect candidate for depression and unhappiness. Maria was right, Clara was changing and she was not the docile and malleable girl she used to be. But it wasn't Leonardo's manipulation; he just gave her the freedom to be in touch with her own feelings and the confidence to trust them. The rest was happening by itself. Now, for Clara the veil was a symbol of submission and as far as Clara was concerned, those days were over not only for her mother, but also for God.

~

"Don't say anything to your father about the dress, you know men don't need to know the details and he can't keep a secret," warned Maria in the car. But Clara couldn't keep her enthusiasm to herself and called Leonardo as soon as they were back home.

"Leo, I love it! I'm sure you'll love it too."

"If you are in it, I'm sure I will. Have you told your parents about Portland?"

"No, not yet. I want to wait a little longer, but I won't change my mind. Be sure of that. When are you coming up? Isn't it time they give you a break from that hospital?"

"I was about to tell you; I'll be there tomorrow. I miss you."

"Great! Maybe we could choose the music to play during the ceremony! I miss you, too."

~

They were kissing holding hands in front of a half eaten pizza.

"The other day something very strange happened," started Clara.

"What happened?" Leonardo asked without unplugging his lips from her mouth.

"I was driving back home after the gym and the traffic light turned red. As soon as I stopped the car I started feeling terribly — hot and sweaty. Suddenly the car became a trap from which I had to escape. I opened the car windows to let in some fresh air hoping it would give me some relief, but it hadn't been enough and my temperature kept rising. I felt oppressed as if the air itself was choking me," Clara explained to her fiancé.

He wanted to say something, but she continued speaking in need of freeing every emotion she had.

"Oh, Leo it's been awful. Trying to stay calm had never been so hard. I felt oppressed and I started to think my time to die had come; rather, more than a thought it was a certainty. I had the urge to scream, 'Somebody help me, please, because I'm dying!' I had the compulsion to run away and find someone who could help me and save me from death. I kept repeating 'I have to get out of this car, now!' and I was actually about to open the door, when the light turned green and distracted me. The motion of the car calmed me down and the terror I felt dissolved leaving me in disbelief. It was so *weird*, Leo, I was so sure I'd die," she concluded still incredulous.

"It's not weird," said Leonardo "You had a little panic attack."

"Panic attack? What is that?"

"It is a chemical reaction in the brain that triggers important physical symptoms like the one you had."

"Is it dangerous?" Clara asked sounding nervous.

"No, it is just a frightening experience that happens when there is no real threat and possibly no known cause. It can definitely scare the person who experiences it, but it is nothing dangerous. Many people stop going out fearing it could happen again," he told her.

"Do you think it will happen again?"

"It's hard to say; right now you are in a delicate time of your life and a lot of things are up in the air — the wedding, your studies, now even a big move to the US and, don't forget, me." He attempted a joke. "But, seriously, uncertainty and stress can definitely be possible causes. Try not to worry too much; for now try to be patient and I'm sure everything will settle down."

Clara got close to him looking for his reassuring arms. A quick look into each other's eyes was enough to make them decide to leave the restaurant. They hid in Clara's bedroom.

"I want you so much, Clara. I'm going crazy without you," he said undressing her. His hands rested on her delicate hips and pulled her closer. "It's been ages Clara; come here, baby."

"Baby?! This is new," she laughed kissing him "Do you like my new underwear?" she asked mischievously.

"Yes, if I can take it off quickly," he answered keeping her close. "Your breasts drive me crazy, I think of them day and night."

Leonardo sunk his face into her softness and caressed her. Soon his touch changed. It slowed down. It went from being the brush of a passionate lover to the clinical touch of a doctor examining a patient.

"Lay down, for a moment Clara," he said, suddenly serious.

Thoughtful he kept handling her breasts for a while.

"This nodule wasn't here last time. I'm sure it's nothing, but please talk to your father and get it checked," he told her.

Clara rested, still trying to smile and to contain the tears that dampened her big eyes.

"Now I'll have another panic attack and this time it will be a big one," she attempted to joke around before taking comfort in Leonardo's warm body.

The cloud of doubts and uncertainty sharpened their senses. Fear transformed into a game of love. Despair chased away modesty. The contact of their moist bodies intensified the scent of their skin and inebriated the desire to live. Their sighs became music. His strokes reverberated into her chest dictating the rhythm of her breathing and making her feel alive.

~

Clara talked to her father the next day and he immediately called his colleagues in the oncology and radiology departments. The mammography revealed a mass right under the right nipple, and the shape of which was not perfectly round, raised concerns about malignancy, and the size suggested it was growing fast. The doctors decided it needed to be removed quickly and then analyzed. The procedure was booked for the end of the month.

Clara's father couldn't hide his concern and he became a shadow; at night he couldn't sleep and during the day he roamed around the house like a hungry wolf in search of prey, restless and sullen. Grandma Anna, a breast cancer survivor of more than twenty years, cursed herself and the hole that was left on her chest, consumed by guilt for passing the wrong genes to her granddaughter. Maria on the other hand, an expert in pretending everything was great, concealed her inauspicious doubts about Clara's health showing exaggerated and out-of-place good humor. Everybody became weak human beings, terrified by their own fears, petrified by their demons. Maria and Roberto swore Clara to secrecy as if having a nodule was a terrible fault to hide and as if being silent meant good luck. The nodule was a reminder that life was not perfect and this time, there was nothing Clara could say or do to protect them.

Clara was trying to stay serene finding comfort in Leonardo and taking things one day at a time.

"It crushes me to see them so worried. I feel helpless and I hate it," she said to Leonardo over the phone.

"In your family everything is upside down, Clara. It's not you who has to reassure them, they are the parents and you are the one who needs attention and reassurance right now. I wish I was there to hold you day and night," he sighed.

"But Leo, I can feel your arms around me even when we are apart and I thank you for it."

"You don't have to thank me; I love you. Everything will be fine," he told her.

"Everything will be fine," he reassured at the end of each phone call and his words continued to vibrate in her heart. Life was a tangled ball of yarn, but the way he looked at it was so pure that all the knots unraveled easily; a few, simple words and all the questions without answer, all the doubts that gripped her, and the fears that tormented her, disappeared.

"Everything will be fine."

~

At home the atmosphere was unbearably heavy, so Clara decided to go to Milan with the excuse of having a lot of things to still do in the apartment. Francesca and Ella knew Clara was coming and waited for her at home. When she arrived they were at the door ready to jump on her and hug her as soon as the elevator door opened. Clara could see happiness and also concern in their eyes. Seated on Francesca's bed, she told them everything they wanted to know about the last few months. Meeting Francesca again and being able to openly talk with her helped Clara to more calmly wait for the surgery, and having the unglued Ella around reminded her the beauty of life's hues. She decided to proceed with her plans for the future as if everything was fine and to go to end her enrollment in law school. While she was going to the university, the bus drove through the same route; it went to the front of the St. Vittore prison, turned, stopped in front of a shop that sold fruits and vegetables as perfect as if they were made of ceramic, and it passed by the Cathedral of St. Ambrogio. Clara suddenly remembered the first time she saw the school. She was eighteen, alone, scared and determined to pass the admission test. The university was in the center of the city, located inside a former Cistercian[10] monastery and, from the outside, it was austere and intimidating. She remembered the first time she got off the bus, how she felt, how the entrance seemed far away, and how the impressive iron gate restrained her. A few seniors prepared some wooden desks and helped the new students by answering questions and giving directions. Clara feigned interest in their brochures, but was actually only trying to postpone passing through that gate. When she finally decided to step through the main door, her heart beat fast. She walked on the uneven cobblestone being careful where she put her feet so as not to trip and stopped, amazed, in front of the beauty of the two exquisite inner courtyards that were the pulsating heart of the university. They were filled with a multitude of chatty and busy students. Groups of boys and girls were lingering under the old colonnades. Passing through, Clara could hear them talking about vacations, upcoming classes, exams, and heartaches. At that time she felt young and immature, but also impatient to start; she pictured herself soon participating in some of those conversations. Now, the same hopes, the same dreams and the same energy that brought her to Milan in the first place were taking her somewhere else and she needed to put an end to

---

[10] A member of a Christian order of monks and nuns founded in 1098, which follows an especially strict form of the Benedictine rule.

what was keeping her from moving forward.

She entered the administrative office.

"Hi Clara!" said the man who for the last three years had helped her keep track of all the college bureaucracy.

Clara greeted him in return, realizing that all she really knew about him was his name. She informed him of her intention and he tried to persuade her to change her mind.

"You have a few exams left, don't do anything drastic. Why don't you simply freeze your enrollment? It's possible to leave everything as it is for eight years without paying tuition. You won't be allowed to take exams, but you won't lose the ones you've already taken. So if you should change your mind ... " he didn't finish the sentence waiting for Clara's reaction.

Clara took a moment to think about that opportunity. A thought accompanied by a chill crossed quickly her mind. *Do I even have eight years?*

The possibility of not erasing everything was captivating, a dangerous temptation; keep what she had worked hard for and take time to verify the seriousness and reliability of her new intentions. Preserve a safe place to which she could return; a warm nest ready to receive her back at any moment. Comfort, however doesn't often agree with high inner drive and Clara knew it could distract her from going ahead. She didn't want to leave any room for second thoughts.

"Thank you, Mario," said Clara calmly. "But I'm sure; I want to end it once and for all."

Mario wished her good luck and she left the building with the blood pumping hard in her veins. Waiting for the bus to go home, this time she didn't turn back to look at the university. It was over; she wanted to, must, could look only forward.

~

The night before Clara went back home for the surgery was long, fogged and fun. Francesca brought home three pizzas, Clara supplied the wine, and Ella the cigarettes. The three of them sat in the living room and spent hours between the couch, the bed and the octagonal table eating, drinking and smoking like in the old days, never stopping chatting and never losing the opportunity for a loud laugh.

"I found the dress to wear at your wedding," Ella said. "But I wont tell you what it looks like; it must be a surprise," she concluded proud of her secret.

"A classy surprise, I hope," Francesca said staring at her.

"Of course, silly. It'll be my chance to put myself on the market for the affluent catches of the Adriatic Riviera. I want to make a good impression," Ella answered serious.

"Does that mean that this time you'll actually wear your panties?" asked Francesca roaring with laughter.

"And, please," Clara said laughing, "if you

won't, this time try not to show it to everybody!"

They made a toast laughing, but a shadow of concern clouded Clara's face and both her roommates noticed it.

"Clara, is everything ok?" Francesca asked worried.

"Come on, don't become so serious," Ella said. "I promise I'll behave."

"Actually, Ella, I was thinking about the surgery," Clara said pensive.

"Everything will be fine!" Ella said happily waving her cigarette. "Here, drink some more and have a cigarette. My grandfather always said, 'a little wine carries away all the whine.'"

Francesca, on the other hand, was less cheerful. She took a long sip from her glass, took Clara's hand in hers, and caressed it.

"Being worried is natural, but I'm sure you have nothing serious and everything will be fine. You know what? I promise that if you are fine I'll be the one coming to your wedding without panties!" Francesca said bursting into laughter.

Clara tried to imprint every moment of that night in her memory, the last one of a beautiful chapter of her young life.

The next morning, Francesca and Ella started the day as usual; a brief breakfast and off to class. Instead, for Clara it was time to take her things, say goodbye to her friends and make promises that probably none of them would keep. They would meet at the wedding; Francesca was excited to be the bridesmaid, but they knew nothing would ever be the same. An important part of their life and friendship was ending. Ella went out merrily; she said goodbye to Clara telling her she would see her at the wedding. Francesca couldn't break up their hug or hold back the tears.

"Hey! Are you rehearsing for the wedding day?" said Clara trying to cheer her up.

"I'm sorry, I don't want to be sad, but so much is happening so fast," Francesca answered wiping her nose with her jacket sleeve.

Clara looked into her friend's eyes and saw the tears she wanted to cry. She hugged her hard and wept softly.

~

The day of the surgery was a gorgeous day at the end of March; warm and sunny with soft white clouds that lacerated the serene sky. The surgeon, a friend of the family, came into the small private room where Clara was waiting. Her father, her mother and Leonardo stood up straight. Clara remained lying down in her hospital bed.

"Roberto, do you want to be in the operating room?" the surgeon asked kindly.

"Thank you, Giorgio, but, since it's my daughter, I think you'll work better if I'm not there."

The surgeon nodded in approval with Roberto's choice.

"Don't worry, young lady, this is a routine procedure. We'll cut just around the areola to minimize the scar; you'll be out in less than two hours, but probably you'll feel groggy until tomorrow," he said patting her on the shoulder reassuringly.

This was all he had to say to cheer her up and, knowing surgeons, Clara thought he did a pretty good job. Soon after, a nurse came to take her. Her parents were still standing; her father couldn't even blink, her mother was grabbing at Clara's bed and didn't let go. Leonardo's face was smiling, and Clara could hear their worried voices overlapping while they tried to reassure her. Then soon, it was just the noise of her bed's little wheels carrying her along narrow hallways. The cold and interminable journey to the operating room ended under an unpleasant surgical light. Clara was agitated, fearful, and couldn't stop her body from trembling on the mattress. A calm voice said, "Now you'll relax. Count to ten."

Clara started counting, the lights became blurry, and her eyes heavy. She fell asleep for a while then, suddenly and against any prediction, she opened her eyes for a brief instant, just in time to see the surgeon leaning over her and his eyeglasses reflecting, like a mirror, the image of her skin opening under the scalpel. There was a moment of general commotion and then everything went dark.

She woke up in her room from the noise of the

dinner cart that was passing in the corridor, a voice that was asking if anybody wanted coffee, and the light coming through the window that was bothering her eyes. Her mother ran to close the curtains and to hush the nurse. Leonardo was at her side with his head on her pillow.

"Leo," she said dizzily. "You didn't have to stay here all this time. Why didn't you go home?"

"I have to take care of you. You are my rose, remember?" he said caressing her softly.

With that, she closed her eyes and went back to sleep.

~

The wait for the results of the biopsy was even more nerve-wracking probably because they were already tired from the previous waiting. Her father reacted to the surgery by becoming even more discouraged and taciturn, and her mother even more hyper and talkative. For Clara it was very hard to control her emotions and stay positive.

"You are always so well-balanced," her mother said almost bothered by Clara's behavior. "I really don't understand how you can be so cool about this," she continually marveled making Clara's anxiety skyrocket and making her also feel guilty for her self-control.

"Well, someone has to hold it all together and, if it's not you or dad, it needs to be me," she answered showing disappointment, but her mother didn't catch her allusion and kept to expressing surprise.

One week of torturous waiting and the results came back. One morning her father called from the hospital screaming the wonderful news that the biopsy was negative. Everybody sighed with relief. Grandma, who had been acting composed the whole time waiting quietly for the surgery and the results, hugged her granddaughter and cried with relief.

"I was sure it was nothing," she had just enough time to say before the sobbing choked-off the rest of her words. Roberto and Maria wanted to celebrate by taking Clara and Leonardo out for dinner. During the flowing of the lavish courses, they proposed one toast after another deriding bad luck and congratulating Clara as if she could have done something to positively affect the results.

"You made it, honey!" her father said finding his smile again.

"Our girl is strong, she can't be easily defeated," her mother said.

Clara was embarrassed; she didn't know what to say or how to react. She smiled; for the first time in weeks she could breathe, dream and be happy, but she couldn't feel totally relieved and she didn't understand the sense of victory that her parents felt. She had been lucky; she didn't want to sound ungrateful, but the sense of immortality that usually accompanies youth had left her forever and, in its place was left the awareness that next time she might be less fortunate and that there was no time to waste.

286

Chapter 11
~ Goodbyes ~

After the surgery, Clara's mother immersed herself in the planning of the wedding; she spoke to the seamstress almost every day, she reprimanded the shoemaker who had to make the bride's shoes with the same fabric of the dress for his slowness, she called the florist to make sure the flowers to put on the two fathers' jackets would be delivered in time at the right addresses, and she designed the dresses for the two young nieces who were to be the flower girls. What took most of her time was deciding what she herself would wear. Everything she liked was made of white lace, very similar to Clara's and, since she couldn't realize by herself the inappropriateness of such a choice, Clara had to step in, get upset, and tell her that day the only person in white lace could be the bride. Therefore, Maria opted for an azure dress that gracefully followed her figure with a deep scalloped neckline and a big scarf to throw on the shoulders with nonchalance during the ceremony.

The last fitting of Clara's dress was planned for that afternoon and Clara wanted grandma to go with them.

"Grandma, come down at four so we can leave immediately," she sang joyfully.

"I decided not to go my dear. I don't feel like going out today," grandma answered apologetically.

"Are you ok?" Clara asked seriously.

"Yes, don't worry," grandma said with a fragile smile that struggled to stay on her lips.

"But, you always said you were looking forward to seeing me wearing the dress and now you don't want to go. I find it strange, that's all," Clara answered, sounding hurt.

"I'm sorry, but I'm very tired and today I don't feel strong enough to leave the house. Do you think you could wear it only for me when you bring it home?"

"Sure. I'll ask mom to take some pictures so you can have a preview anyway before we pick it up," Clara said forgetting her previous concerns about grandma. "But before I go, I have to tell you something very important, it's a secret and you have to promise to keep it for yourself at any cost. Mom and dad can't know about it until after the wedding."

"You know I love keeping things from your mother," grandma smiled intrigued.

Clara sat on the couch with her heart pounding in her chest. It was the first time she spoke about the upcoming trip to Portland with a person other than Leonardo and she feared grandma, who supported her until then, might disapprove this time, and try to change her mind.

"I hope you won't freak out, but, next November Leonardo and I are leaving for the US."

She said it. She felt relieved, but at the same

time she felt the burden of having to wait for a reaction; it didn't take long to come.

"For heaven's sake, Clara, this is great!" Grandma cheered clapping her weak hands.

"Really? You don't think it is crazy?"

"Of course I think it's crazy and that's why I love it."

"We'll stay at least one year and then," Clara started to say.

"And then you never know in life, my dear. Don't look too far ahead. One thing at a time, remember? I'm very happy for you. It'll be good to be far away from family dramas for a while and having to concentrate only on your relationship with Leonardo," grandma advised.

"I'm so glad you agree," Clara sighed with relief.

"You know, I might be old, but I was young long before you and I did the same thing with grandpa when we were young. It wasn't America for us, but to me it may as well have been."

"Tell me more about those days," Clara said getting comfortable on the couch as if grandma was about to tell her a fairy-tale.

Like her granddaughter, grandma Anna had been a determined, naïve and much in love young woman when, just married, with the innocence of her own twenty years of age, she left her beloved island and followed her husband Giovanni. People fall in love for the most peculiar reasons, and she was swept away by his height; he was the tallest man in their little town, and she was stunned by the way he looked in his Carabiniere[11] uniform. Their families were both landowners in the northwestern part of the Sardinian island, but after World War I, they wanted more than to just get by selling their ancestral land piece by piece and left with the hope in their heart that living on the 'continent' would provide a better future to their children. Their honeymoon was the trip they took to reach their new home in the city of Modena. They settled down quite easily in their new environment and spent the following fifty years of their lives fighting and bickering over just about anything and everything. In the beginning Anna was discreet, proud and money-savvy, while Giovanni was by nature outgoing, generous and stubborn. They were two young kids very much in love, but unable to show it, and they pushed each other to an extreme direction; she became hard-hearted, stingy and controlling, he became frivolous, a big spender and a "Don Giovanni."

After World War II, Giovanni decided to leave the military force. Happy to be alive and in search of a new future, he decided to move the family to the Adriatic coast. Anna and their two daughters reluctantly packed their belongings and followed him. Giovanni sold the house in Modena and used the money to buy a new one close to the beach. When Anna and the girls arrived, he proudly showed them the house he bought and they were ecstatic; it

---

[11] One of the national police forces of Italy.

was a charming little art-nouveau villa, painted in a light yellow color. The ground floor was hemmed in with an adorable arched colonnade, while the first floor had white decorated trims around each window. A gorgeous mature garden with grass, several fruit trees and a huge wisteria surrounded the whole property and, for a moment, dreams came true. But soon, they needed to reinvent themselves. Post war Italy was bursting with enthusiasm and it was time to rebuild the nation. Money was flowing. The Adriatic coastline was coming to life as a prestigious tourist destination, and they decided to take advantage of the situation. Half-heartedly they drained their savings to convert the villa to a family-operated hotel. **Since that day, Anna worked hard with just one goal in mind — to be able to set aside enough money to buy a new house. But life decided not to be very kind to her.** When her daughter Maria married Roberto, Clara's father, there was an empty apartment on the top floor of their **building** and, since Roberto was the owner, he asked Maria's parents to move closer to them. They did, but Anna always felt like a guest and kept dreaming of being able to move into a new house sooner rather than later.

"But why grandma! You are not a guest, this is your home," Clara had said, almost offended.

"I know honey, but I wanted more. I wanted my little art-nouveau villa back," grandma answered holding back her tears.

One day, Anna knocked on Maria's door and

complained about pieces of furniture that had disappeared from the apartment.

"That's crazy, mom," was Maria's first response to the news. "Are you sure you didn't move them or give them to charity?"

"Are you implying I'm losing my mind?" Anna replied.

Mother and daughter found out that Giovanni had bought a house. Not to surprise his dearly adored wife, but rather to punish her for the rigidity she had shown him during all those years. The house was full of animals — turkeys and chickens in the yard, cats on the first and second floors, and doves in the attic.

"I can't believe it, grandma! Nobody ever told me," Clara exclaimed in disbelief.

"Oh, yes! And I was furious, my dear. Giovanni had taken my life's dream of having a house of my own and crushed it like a bug. He had to pay."

"This is better than a movie; what did you do?" Clara asked excited.

Anna decided she couldn't be defeated, that she had to fight back. So the next day, she dressed in her favorite blue dress, attached a white collar that she crocheted herself to the neck line, put on a pretty blue hat with long white feathers, framed her tiny feet in high heels to disguise her 4'9" height, and went to the bank. Smiling to the bank manager, she removed her husband from all their bank accounts.

"Now, he was furious!" cackled grandma. "I

had crushed his pride like he did with my dream."

"Wow! That must have made him really angry."

"Oh yes, you are perfectly right."

As revenge to Anna's deed, Giovanni began spending all his pension money, the only money he could dispose of, on gifts for other women and also started to purposely leave around the house the love letters he received from them. They both drove each other crazy until the end, but they never stopped living in the same house and, Maria, whose bedroom was right under theirs, could hear them making love almost every night, unless Clara was there for some cuddling.

Clara's mother called from the staircase and grandma stopped the narration.

"Go now, I'll finish up later," Anna told her precious granddaughter.

"I don't want to go, this is too much fun. Why haven't you told me before?" Clara said as if she didn't want to wake up from an entertaining dream.

"You were too young," grandma said patting Clara's hand. "I promise tomorrow I'll tell you everything else there is to know. Now, go to try on your beautiful dress and have fun."

Clara gave her a big hug and, with light steps, disappeared down the stairs.

Anna remained alone. She looked at Clara hopping toward the door and vanishing. She envied her young age, her inexperience, and her ability to be still optimistic. Giovanni had died almost two years before; he was eighty-eight, and from that moment Anna hadn't been the same. She was alive, she felt relief in counting her savings, she loved Clara, and she liked to spend time with her watching old movies, but she lost interest in life more and more every day. Her granddaughter couldn't possibly know what it meant to be old, to be the last survivor of a family that didn't exist anymore. She couldn't know what it meant to watch your parents, your brother, you sisters, your husband die one at a time, waiting for your own turn, and in the meanwhile trying to stay fond of life and what was left of it. "I'm tired, it's not my world anymore," she wanted to say to her sweet Clara, but she knew that youth couldn't understand the grief of the old and that it was how it was supposed to be. Watching Clara that day, with the innocence of her twenty-two years of age, unaware of exactly how to confront her life, she felt a deep tenderness for her naiveté, sympathy for what was waiting for her, jealousy for the time she still had in front of her, and rage for the way her own had gone.

~

The next morning, Clara was in her bedroom and she heard a scream coming from upstairs.

"Clara! Clara! Come here now!" Grandma was yelling from the stairway.

Clara ran immediately upstairs; grandma sounded very excited. She went to her bedroom and heard she was speaking with someone.

"Look who's here, Clara!" grandma said ecstatic. "Aunt Caterina came to visit me from Sardinia!"

Aunt Caterina was Anna's older sister; she had never left Sardinia and had died fifteen years before. A cold chill ran up Clara's back; she hesitated for a moment then grabbed the phone and called her father at the hospital.

"Where is your mother?" asked Roberto when he saw Clara arriving. The white coat made him even more authoritative then ever.

"Out running errands, I guess. I left her a message on the kitchen table. But what's happening to grandma?" she asked very anxious.

"She is in kidney failure," he answered promptly. "Her kidneys don't filter the toxins that stay in her body, causing hallucinations."

"It'll pass, right?" Clara asked with the gaze of a person who wants to believe in a happy ending.

"We'll do our best, honey to make sure that it will," her father answered, but not very convincingly.

When Maria arrived at the hospital, Clara hugged her to find comfort, but her mother took her deed as an act of charity and she stiffened, dismissing it. Grandma was in a long, narrow and dark room with seven other people. In the hospital bed she looked even smaller and more frail. The symptoms had worsened, and when she saw Maria she didn't recognize her as her own daughter, and kept calling her "Lea," the name of her favorite childhood friend. The words she said were clear and limpid, and the language she spoke was a mix of Italian, Catalan and Latin. In the beginning, they were able to follow what she was saying; in her mind she was back in Sardinia as a young girl, surrounded by family and friends. But soon, the language she was speaking became more and more obscure, the Italian more archaic, the Catalan and the Latin more incoherent. As a result of Maria's protests, Anna was transferred to a private room. The treatments started to work and made her alternate between moments of total lucidity and moments of total confusion. Maria and Clara spent all the free time they had during the day with her, and their mood oscillated with Anna's mental and physical health. Leonardo, when he was in town for the weekend, never missed the opportunity to visit and he had a good influence on her; most of the time, the two were able to chitchat a little.

Anna had always valued her exterior appearance, so Clara often brushed her soft hair that framed her face in white; she refreshed her face with a wet towel and applied some lotion to soften her thin and delicate skin. Grandma appreciated her attention and the caresses.

"Thanks, honey," she said when she was able to recognize her. "Too often young people forget that the old ones like to be cuddled."

"Do you remember how many times you made me fall asleep by scratching my back?" Clara answered smiling. "Now it's my turn to cuddle you a little," Clara said sweetly.

Attempting to keep her mind alert, Clara updated her grandmother on the smallest details of the wedding, the latest news and gossip, the weather and, especially, Leonardo, who seemed to always have a good influence on her. Slowly, with the passing of the days, the hallucinations decreased leaving more and more room to lucidity. After three weeks, the worst had passed and the doctors said she was ready to go home provided that she follow a few simple recommendations; she had a special diet that didn't stress the kidneys, she had to have a full check-up in one week's time, and she had to wear a corset. During the routine exams the doctors found severe osteoporosis and they considered the use of an orthopedic corset appropriate to support her back and prevent possible fractures.

At home everything was ready for her return. Clara's mother had the apartment scrubbed from floor to ceiling and had the bed fixed with Anna's favorite sheets. She personally put fresh flowers in every room and opened the curtains to let in the sun. Clara's father recommended not going to pick up grandma before eleven o'clock to give the doctors time to complete all the discharge papers. Clara was very happy and for the first time in weeks she could see a speck of relief on her mother's face, as well.

"Did you have the car washed for grandma?" Clara asked pleasantly surprised while they were going to the hospital.

"Don't be silly, Clara. I had it washed because it

needed to be washed," Maria answered slightly annoyed by the fact that her daughter had noticed it.

"I don't recall you minding a filthy car," Clara continued trying to joke around.

"Stop it, please. Why do you have to be always so polemic?"

Clara was well aware that her mother was not ready to express her relief just the same way that she couldn't confront her pain and fears during the whole hospitalization. Clara understood and broached a generic and impersonal topic that didn't upset anybody's sensitivity and that didn't make her mother feel hunted.

That day, Clara found the hospital incredibly joyful and colorful. The patients seemed happy, the doctors kind, and the nurses relaxed. They found Anna seated on the bed arguing with the nurse who was trying to teach her how to wear the corset.

"Hi grandma, are you ready to go home?" Clara asked kissing her on the cheek.

"Finally you've arrived. Please help Natalia understand that I don't really need this infernal contraption on me," grandma growled.

"Good! Not only are you ready to come home, but you are more combative than ever," Clara said as she silently began collecting her grandma's belongings from the closet and nightstand.

"Mom, do you remember that we already talked about it?" Maria intervened with a calm voice. "The doctors believe the corset is necessary."

"It's very easy to put on, I'm sure you'll learn

fast," said the nurse.

Anna was still very dedicated to her looks and expressed her concern.

"Do I really have to wear this deforming thingy for the rest of my life?" grandma asked with a thin voice, resigned and disappointed.

"Don't worry, mom," said Maria smiling. "It'll barely be noticeable under your clothes. Trust me, it won't ruin your figure."

The nurse looked at Clara and Maria; they exchanged an understanding look and they all giggled a bit at an old lady's vanity, that at the age of eighty-two she still cared so much about her appearance. However, Anna didn't laugh along. She looked at the nurse and without saying anything simply reclined her head. The "rest of her life" was gone. Forever.

~

It was a Wednesday afternoon in May. Anna's funeral had been arranged in the Church of San Nicola, the same one where Clara had been baptized. A few people occupied the benches — some of Clara's parents' friends and some pious woman who was there to pray. The mass was about to start and Leonardo showed up. Clara wasn't expecting him to come. She knew he had asked for a family emergency permission, but the head physician had refused to grant his authorization believing that the death of the grandmother of a wife-to-be wasn't a good enough reason to leave the job. Clara didn't know that, at the last minute, a kind colleague offered to substitute for him and that Leonardo had been driving all morning to be there on time.

Until that moment, Clara had been staying calm and keeping a straight face as suited a mature person who doesn't want to show too much of her emotions, but the warmth of his hug crumbled her defenses at once, and with her head on his shoulder she started to cry.

"I'm so happy you are here, thanks," she said wiping her tears.

"Stop thanking me, Clara. I want to be here," Leonardo answered holding her tight.

Clara wanted to scream, cry, yell, and curse the world. It was supposed to be a joyful year; a true love was born and a wedding was about to happen, but first her family didn't share her joy, her mother took her happiness like a personal insult and started a fierce and silent conflict against Leonardo, Paola vented years of hidden rivalry and jealousy, the adenoma in her breast warned her not to let her guard down and, now, grandma was dead. In her young mind, Clara had always pictured life like a long, smooth straight line marked by moments of joy and moments of sadness, but the last few months had revealed that the line could be quite short; she realized it was twisted and filled with bumps, and that joy and sadness are not interchanging, but coexisted.

Returning home from the cemetery, Clara was about to close the front gate when Paola passed by on her bike. She saw the surprise in her friend's eyes and the regret of not taking another route; she saw her hesitation, her embarrassment and the moment she, resigned, realized that her only option was to stop and express her condolences.

"Hi, Clara. I heard about your grandma. I'm sorry I didn't come to the funeral, but you know I don't like them."

The pain that fogged Clara's mind became pure and sharp, and her thoughts clarified turning limpid and pitiless. Those words that had to comfort her brought to her memory the afternoons and the evenings her grandma took tender care of them both, preparing snacks, reading them books and sewing clothes for their dolls.

"You don't like funerals?!" Clara responded looking Paola straight into her eyes. "Fuck you! Who *likes* funerals, Paola!?! Do you know anybody who enjoys going? What would you like me to say? That I'm grateful you stopped by and are forgiven for not coming to the mass? The other day you talked about my pedestal, but I think it is time you get off *yours*."

She turned her back on her friend and began climbing the stairs. Her mother was waiting for her at the top.

"Don't you think you have been too harsh with poor Paola?" she asked Clara with a criticizing tone.

"No, I don't," Clara answered dryly, continuing up the steps.

"Each one of us reacts to death in a different way and I don't think Paola deserved such a strong reaction from you," her mother continued.

"Mom, you don't have the slightest idea of what Paola deserves or not."

"I just wish you'd stop being so intransigent with people because …"

"Mom," interrupted Clara. "I know this is a delicate moment, but for once, just once, could you take my side and not anyone else's? Or maybe, if you can't do that, could you at least gather all the information about what is happening before expressing your opinion or shut up?" she said as she stopped on the last step.

"It's better if we discuss this another time. We are all tired and worn out," Maria said irritated and taking the victim's attitude.

"You know what?" Clara said staring at her mother's black eyes. "I have no desire to talk about anything with you, and you know why? Because communicating with you is impossible. You constantly refuse to accept anything that could take your blinkers away. Are you happy in your little world? Good, stay there, but stop badgering me; I'm tired of feeling your breath on my neck. It's been difficult enough to grow up with you never on my side. Can you at least leave me alone?"

Maria was shocked, offended, and stood speechless. Her father was about to intervene, but Clara looked at Leonardo.

"Can you take me away? Anywhere," she said to him with a thin voice.

In the car neither of them spoke. Leonardo drove. Clara, void and empty, looked out the window lacking thoughts. She was not surprised when the car stopped in front of the Church of San Fortunato.

"I'll wait for you here," Leonardo said when in the courtyard. "Take your time, you need some time alone. I'll be outside."

The church was empty, the benches deserted. She was alone and chose a seat in a dark spot. On her left several red votive candles were burning under the statue of one of the "white monks," and somewhere, somebody was hoping for his or her own prayers to come true. Clara raised her eyes toward the altar and saw baby Jesus in Vasari's painting. He was just born, chubby and inquiring. He was a jubilant baby who was looking at the world from his mother's arms. Then she looked at the crucifix that was on the altar; Jesus was bleeding hanging from the cross with his head bent.

"Look what they did to you; you were a happy baby and then," she choked. "What do you want from me? What are you trying to tell me from up there? Because, you know, I don't understand."

Warm tears started to descend on her cheeks.

"In less than four weeks I'll get married right here, in this church, in front of you, and first you send me Paola's rage, then the tumor in the breast; ok, it was benign, thanks. And now you take away grandma? I don't understand. Is it about the veil? I hope not because I won't wear it, anyway. Or maybe this is your revenge because I'm not your obedient and submissive girl anymore? Tell me something! Answer me!" she screamed. "What the fuck is it you are trying to tell me? That life is all about suffering? That we'll all end up on a cross? Speak!"

She wept holding her head between her hands until she had no more tears.

The church was dark, but outside the light reverberated on the stones and was dazzling. As soon as her sight adapted to the glare, she saw Leonardo; he was walking on the other side of the courtyard with his head down keeping his hands in his pockets; he was thoughtful, but he raised his head, saw her at the top of the steps and smiled as he moved toward her. Clara remained still. She looked at the sky with its blue, striped by soft clouds, and interrupted by the flight path of the birds, it was infinite and mysterious. She looked at the verdant hills with their multiple hues of green, and stained by the colors of the flowering trees, they were a triumph of life. She looked at the sea with its waves that dotted it with white and a few boats that left their wake; it was fascinating and dangerous. Leonardo approached her and held her hand. Clara gasped and looked one more time back at the cross. *I think I'm beginning to understand, thank you.*

~

The wedding day got closer and closer. As the

precious presents began to arrive, Maria arranged them on the tables in the formal living room; she carefully opened them and left their cards next to them to be sure not to make any mistake with the thank you notes. Access to the formal living room was usually forbidden, but Clara's mother thought that it was now the right place to keep the presents. It was a huge room that Maria kept like a sanctuary and that she would illuminate only every Thursday night to host their closest friends for the weekly game of bridge. The women sat on the couches talking and gossiping, while the men played cards and drank cognac. For the rest of the week, the room was absolutely off-limits not only to family members, but also to the sun that Maria kept outside by closing the heavy velvet drapes so it wouldn't fade the Persian rugs' beautiful colors. Clara saw that her mother went into that room several times a day to silently contemplate the gifts.

The upcoming trip to the US was still a secret between Clara and Leonardo; after her grandma's death, Clara decided to wait until after the wedding to say anything about it. Her parents had already received enough bombshells and they'd have a few months after the wedding to get used to this further hit. Clara was in her bedroom and heard her father knocking on the open door making her aware of his presence.

He never went into her bedroom.

"Hi, dad."

"I need to talk to you," he said looking worried.

"Ok."

"I wanted to ask you," he started a little embarrassed. "Are you really sure you want to get married?"

A light smile appeared on Clara's lips. She couldn't understand if he was serious or if he was joking.

"The wedding is in less than one week, dad; the house is full of gifts, invitations are out and, yes, I'm sure," she answered not knowing if she was supposed to laugh or needed to stay serious.

"Well, then, I just wanted to tell you that from the moment you are married, I'll consider you and Leonardo to be a couple of adults and therefore you are on your own."

Clara nodded trying to smile and accepting her father's will. She thought there were a lot of things to say to a daughter who is getting married and she thought the one he chose to be awkward, but it was not the first awkward thing he had said to her anyway. She had always been afraid of him. He was an extremely reserved man, a man of few words, with deep feelings, but absolutely unable to show them. She had grown up trembling at the thought of his reactions. He was wise, proud and devoid of any presumption, and Clara had always feared his judgment. But, he was also extremely sensitive, and in order to not hurt him she had always tried to behave correctly. Right now, she just wished that this embarrassing moment could end soon, and as soon as she thought it, he left her room and returned to his newspaper.

~

The last week before the wedding was not an easy one. The more the big day approached the more emotional everybody became. Clara tried to avoid creating sparks in the electric atmosphere by confining herself as much as possible to her bedroom. She didn't always succeed. One day after lunch she was in her bedroom with the excuse of taking a nap and her mother showed up satisfied with a flashy piece of jewelry.

"Look what a stunning beauty!" she exclaimed handing the jewelry to Clara. "I had them custom-made just for you and your wedding dress."

It was a necklace with a two-inch cameo held straight by six strands of pearls along with matching earrings and bracelet.

"Thanks, mom, they are beautiful, but I want to wear grandma's pearl necklace," Clara told her.

"But I had them made just for you," Maria said appealing to her guilt feelings.

"It's too heavy for me, mom."

"But only a person with your long neck can wear it," Maria said, trying to convince her daughter.

"I want grandma's pearls, mom."

"But only a person with a neck like yours can *afford* to wear it," Maria persevered hoping that Clara would change her mind and would want to please her.

"I'll wear grandma's pearls," Clara answered once more, hoping not to have to repeat it again.

"They are so simple and predictable. You'll look like an ordinary bride," Maria commented in a whiny tone.

"I don't care. They are grandma's and they better reflect who I am," concluded Clara disappointing her mother's expectations once more.

Even Leonardo was tense and nervous because of his final exam. It wasn't easy to deal with him, either. Suddenly, things started to unwind and, two days before the wedding, Leonardo called triumphant. The final exam had been a success, he was officially a cardiologist; finally he could relax, go home, and get married.

~

According to superstition, bride and groom were not supposed to meet the day before the wedding, but they decided to ignore it; it had been too long since the last time they had seen each other. They had several fights due to tensions of the exam and the wedding and they both needed to talk and find comfort and reassurance in one another before meeting at the altar.

They spent the day at his parents' house, where things were somewhat more relaxed.

Laura and Bruno had the power to instill serenity and Clara felt at home with them. After lunch, Laura brought the espresso to the table and said, "Clara, I have to tell you that, even if the announcement of your wedding was no surprise, at first I had a hard time accepting it. Not because I think you are not right for Leo, but only because I was afraid to lose him. Now that I know you better, I feel like I'm not losing a son, but I'm acquiring a daughter."

"Thanks, Laura." Clara said deeply moved and touched by her future mother-in-law's words.

She hugged her tightly forgetting about her temperament and her acquired inhibitions.

The afternoon went by quickly in Leonardo's arms and soon it was time to go home. They were both exhausted. They hugged one last time.

"Are you sure about tomorrow?" asked Clara.

"Yes," he answered resolutely.

"There is still time to change your mind," she insisted.

"I don't want to change my mind. And you?"

"No; I'll be there," she told him.

Leonardo kissed her.

"I'll wait for you."

~

On the morning the wedding day Clara's father couldn't find any aria to sing and he let

Clara sleep until late. When she opened her eyes she saw it was a marvelous day, warm and sunny. She got out of bed, went into her mother's bathroom and filled the pink marble tub. The water was lukewarm and she was immersed, naked and content. So many things had changed during that year. On the outside she was still the same, but inside she was a different person. Her deepest desires were no longer buried in her subconscious. Her new path had just started; she didn't know where it would take her, but this time she was not alone. This time the sun that was shining outside was also illuminating her heart with hopes and aspirations. She passed a finger around her belly button and the micro air bubbles that were resting on her skin floated to the surface. It was nice to watch them being freed and she liked the mark of their absence on her white womb.

"Are you still in my tub, Clara?" yelled a tense Maria from outside the bathroom door. "It's time to eat something. We are in the kitchen. Move!"

Some things never change.

She wore a light dress and joined her parents in the kitchen to share with them her last meal as a single woman.

"I didn't want my hair to stink so I ordered in," said Maria dishing out food from aluminum containers. "Tortellini with cream or chicken tenders and fries?" she asked.

"Tortellini," answered Clara serenely.

"Not for me, thanks," said Roberto. "I'll just have a small piece of chicken and a full glass of wine."

He looked fragile.

Clara thought of all the times she had sat in that same spot eating with her parents, of how many times she wished not to be there, of how many times she found excuses to get up early or not join them at all, and of how many times she cried over her food while they were giving her a lecture. She looked at them; they were tense, emotional, sad, and proud. They looked like two old people, clutched to their own frustrations, unable to truly understand what was happening, and she felt sorry for them.

After lunch, the hairdresser came and Clara sat in front of the mirror. Her name was Lucia; she and Clara were a few years apart and they met when Lucia was a very young apprentice. She was a very determined young woman who learned everything she could from her boss and then opened her own shop. She was full of energy and new ideas. Lucia was talking while nestling a few small satin roses in Clara's hair, but Clara wasn't listening. She just looked in the mirror and thought about Leonardo's last words, "I'll wait for you." Her mother had offered to help Clara with her makeup or to hire a makeup artist, but Clara chose to do it by herself. Leaning against the sink to be closer to the mirror, she drew a dark brown line on her top eyelids, blended it softly and applied some mascara, a little blush on the cheeks and she was ready.

Maria barged into her room waving the bronzer brush.

"It's time to get dressed or we'll be late!" she yelled impatiently.

Clara didn't want anybody participating in the dressing, not even Francesca whom she asked to wait for her at the church. Her mother, growling and muttering of her obstinacy, arranged the wedding dress and all the accessories in her bedroom and Clara found everything ready. She started with the precious underwear. The bra and underpants were of fine lace, the garter belt, an old seduction tool, made her feel irresistible; the garter made her smirk. She lifted grandma's pearls from the dresser and fastened the necklace warily, ensuring the latch was closed. Now she felt she was close. The dress had an infinite number of delicate buttons covered in silk on the back and Clara did ask her mother to help her close them.

"Tonight, in your beautiful room made of red silk, Leonardo will take hours to undress you. Do you think he'll be able resist?" she said faking nonchalance and forcing a chuckle.

Clara didn't answer thinking that, until the end, her mother was trying be part of what didn't belong to her.

"Don't forget the tissues, in case you cry," warned Maria.

"It's my wedding, why should I cry?" asked Clara surprised.

"You never know; just let me put them in your bag," concluded Maria, seeming irritated.

Clara was ready. Now she had to face the rest of world, but before she left the room, her mother stood in front of her and stopped her.

"Before you go, I want to wish you to be happy at least half of what I have been with your father. That would be enough to have a wonderful marriage," she advised her daughter.

What does that even mean? My parents are really not the best at speeches.

She smiled pretending to appreciate her mother's heartfelt words; she thanked her and walked to the family room where all the relatives were waiting for her. She heard the applause that started when they saw her appear; she perceived a few words of encouragement and some compliments, but the only thing she could truly see were her father's eyes as he silently stared at her, amazed and emotional. He got closer and hugged her, seeming confused.

The car was waiting.

"Everybody out! It's time to go!" Maria shouted nervously.

"Mom did you close the windows?" Clara asked.

"Oh, no! I forgot!"

~

In the car, Clara was sitting in the back seat with her father. Her mother was in the front. The church was just few minutes away, but to Clara it seemed the ride took a lifetime.

She got out of the car in front of the church and waited for her father to go around it and then accompany her. The guests were waiting on the cobblestone in front of the entrance; they were talking cheerfully, enjoying the view and the beautiful weather. As promised, Leonardo was waiting for her. He was elegant in blue, but looked uncomfortable with the bouquet in his hands. Clara and her father started walking arm-in-arm. Together they reached Leonardo; Roberto slightly bowed in front of him as a sign of greeting and respect. Leonardo looked at Clara stunned and he felt relieved. He bent over her, kissed her on the cheek and handed her the flowers. The bouquet was round and simple, made of white roses that had a blush of pink at the top of the petals and a few green leaves that softened up the arrangement.

Their hands touched briefly. He winked. She smiled.

The priest appeared at the top of the church steps and invited the groom and the guests to follow him inside. Clara and her father were the only ones left outside. Arm-in-arm, they climbed the stairs and stopped at the church threshold. The church was full and the guests, neatly seated in the pews, were silently waiting for the bride to go in. Clara tried to recognize some familiar faces; her mother, Laura, and Bruno were in the front ready to cry. Francesca was right next to them waiting with the rings in her hands. Leonardo was smiling. The rest was all blurry. The organ intoned the Canon in D major of J. Pachelbel. It was mesmerizing. It was time. Clara tightly held her father's arm. He was tall, straight, and proud.

They looked at each other and, together, took the first step toward the altar. Clara saw the tip of her shoe appearing from under the gown, then, she raised her eyes and kept her gaze on Leonardo.

One last thought before facing her destiny. *Let's hope for the best.*

Acknowledgments

A big thanks goes to Paula McManus for her friendship and the good laughs we had at my expense. I hope we can do it again soon.

A special thanks goes to Lisa Daitch, my editor, for her competence, her insight, and for taking my project at heart.

I wish to thank my daughter, Bianca; she was only nine years old when I wrote this book, but her faith in me kept me focused when I wanted to give up and she encouraged me when I felt downcast.

Anto…need I tell you more?

About the Author

Maria Chiara Marsciani was born and raised in Rimini, Italy. She was trained as a clinical psychologist at "Universita' La Sapienza" in Rome and moved to the US in 1994. Now, she lives in Potomac, MD with her husband and their daughter in a home full of pets.

'Urbino, Unexpectedly' is her first novel.

For more information, please visit:
www.mariachiaramarsciani.com

www.ingramcontent.com/pod-product-compliance
Lightning Source LLC
Chambersburg PA
CBHW070914260626
47162CB00007B/2672